Longbow Girl

Longbow Girl

Linda Davies

CHICKEN HOUSE
SCHOLASTIC INC. / NEW YORK

Library of Congress Cataloging-in-Publication Data available

ISBN 978-0-545-85345-3

10 9 8 7 6 5 4 3 2 1   16 17 18 19 20

Printed in the U.S.A.   23
First edition, March 2016

Book design by Ellen Duda

To my father, the late Professor Glyn Davies, to my mother,
Grethe Davies, and to my brothers, Roy and Kenneth.

Diolch yn fawr,
Mange tak
Thank you.

Hywl!

"On the bank of the river he saw a tall tree: from roots to crown one half was aflame and the other green with leaves . . ." from the Mabinogion

Chapter One

Merry Owen saw a dark figure vault over the ancient boundary wall between her family's farm and the Black Castle. The old enemy, trespassing on her land again . . . coming her way.

She was alone but she had her longbow. An ancient weapon of war that had won battles and saved kings for a thousand years, and was still lethal today. In her hands, at least. Armed with this simple stave of wood, only just taller than her and primed by a decade of training, she always felt *more*: more powerful, alive, ready . . .

She nocked an arrow onto her string, drew back the bow to its quivering full extension, and eyed the approaching figure. Too far away to recognize, but close enough to hit. She imagined all her ancestors—the longbowmen of Nanteos—lining up like ghosts behind her, willing her on . . .

She loosed the arrow.

It scythed through the air, embedding itself in the straw target with a deep thud—dead center.

The approaching figure stopped, wary now. Merry smiled and shot another nine arrows into the colored rings of the target.

"What are *you* doing here?" she called.

Lord James de Courcy grinned, though his face was troubled. "Nice to see you too. Thanks for not shooting me."

"I thought about it. Might shoot your father if he gets on the wrong side of the wall."

James blew out a breath. "I heard about what happened, Merry. I am so sorry."

"Not *your* fault," Merry replied, gripping her bow tight, as the memories rushed back. It had happened just two weeks before, but she wondered if she'd ever forget it.

Her stallion, Zulu, galloping for his life across the open land of their farm, hurtling toward the old stone wall of the boundary, the Earl de Courcy's wolfhounds closing in. Zulu launching himself, hitting unyielding stone, twisting, spinning, and crashing to the ground. Thrashing hooves . . . the terrible baying of the pack . . .

"Your father's to blame," Merry continued grimly. "For not training his wolfhounds properly. They attacked the Joneses' sheep six months ago. Everyone knows they've gone feral, except him. Can't bear to have his pedigree dogs locked up or put down."

James shook his head, looked miserable and guilty, even though the guilt was not his. Merry didn't know if his father had offered any compensation, but her own da would have been too proud to accept it even if he had.

"So, why aren't you at boarding school, then?" Merry asked, after an awkward pause. "I didn't think your Easter holidays had started yet?"

"It hasn't. I've been suspended."

"*Suspended?*" Merry could only imagine the reaction of James's parents.

"Don't ask," said James, voice clipped. "I just want to forget about it for a bit. Why aren't you bent over a book?"

"Homeschooling's much more efficient than normal school," replied Merry. "You can get a lot done in the mornings if you start early enough. I always have Friday afternoons free."

"Lucky you," replied James sourly. He glanced at her bow.

"No way," said Merry, reading his mind. "My father'd skin me if I let you have a go. And don't think you'd get off lightly either."

"Yeah, on second thought . . ."

Merry's father, Caradoc Owen, was a skilled soldier who'd done eight years in the special forces, the SAS no less. No one with any sense got on the wrong side of him.

"I've got a better idea," said Merry. "There's a load of your soccer balls festering in the barn. Everyone's out," she added.

James nodded, relieved. He got on all right with Merry's parents, but he was still a de Courcy and the latest outrage didn't exactly help.

Merry watched him jog to the old stone barn. There was something different about him, she thought. He looked older, taller, but there was a new edge to him. They were both fifteen and their lives were changing, but he was still her best friend, her oldest friend, even though their families had been enemies for nearly seven hundred years.

Their friendship had survived their parents' enmity, his sister Lady Alicia's jealousy, survived too the accident she'd had at the age of twelve when her longbow had snapped at full draw, shearing back into her left eye. The air ambulance had come for her, but too late to save the eye. So she wore a patch to cover it, which gave her something of a piratical air. She'd been impossible in those early days when she'd thought the loss of her eye meant the end of her

3

dreams. She'd shouted and yelled and tried to push everyone away, but James had stuck with her. He'd told her she looked like a true warrior princess. He'd encouraged her to take up the new longbow her father had made for her, reminded her that she was still the longbow girl, and he'd kept her company in the long cold hours when she trained like fury till she was better with one eye than she'd ever been with two.

She and James had always shared a love of the wild terrain that was their home. On foot, bike, and horseback they'd explored the five hundred acres of the Owens' farm, the ten thousand acres of the de Courcy estates, and the encircling, ice-carved mountains beyond—the Beacons. They'd played games of skill and strength and aim. Always competing, always egging each other on. The motto of their childhood: *Anything is possible.*

Merry went to the target now, hauled the arrows out of the straw as James returned with his soccer balls in a net bag. Sparrows chirped in the greening trees, and high above, against the backdrop of the mountains, a peregrine falcon circled, eyeing up prey. James helped her to forget the stallion, but he also reminded her. He was a de Courcy: How could he not?

James dropped five soccer balls at her feet, and played keepie-uppie with the sixth. He made it look effortless, bouncing the ball off his feet, his knee, his head. He was still able to glance at her and smile.

"Now what?"

"You aim them at my target. Shoot for the bull's-eye—the gold. From fifty yards."

He laughed. "Nice one."

4

Merry indicated the start point. James lined up a ball and sent it bulleting forward. With a bang, it thudded into the edge of the target. He grimaced, tried again. Got the other edge. He muttered under his breath, and just missed the gold with the third. But nailed it with the fourth, fifth, and sixth balls.

Merry kept her face deadpan. "Not bad."

"Your turn," he said, grinning.

Merry picked up her longbow, walked back another twenty yards. Aiming from instinct rather than by sighting, she loosed twelve arrows. The bow thrummed softly, singing its song of death.

"Six bull's-eyes," called James. "That makes us equal, according to my math . . ."

"Double or quits?" responded Merry, wrenching the arrows from the target once more and dropping them into the forest-green leather quiver, the length of a baguette and twice as thick, that hung from an attachment to her belt.

"Okay. I'm on for that. What's the bet?"

"I bet," said Merry, head to one side, grinning evilly, "that you can't hit the target from a hundred yards."

"Oh, come on!" James exclaimed. "Most pro soccer players wouldn't be able to do that."

"All the more reason for you to go for it, seeing as you want to be one."

James blew out a breath. "All right then. I'll do that and you can try and shoot the ball midair with an arrow. From a safe distance," he added hurriedly. "Like fifty yards!" Merry opened her mouth, then closed it again. A static target was one thing. A moving one was something altogether harder. A ridiculous challenge. She'd never do it. *She had to do it.* She took her bow and arrows and counted off fifty yards forward and fifty yards to the side as James walked back to the hundred-yard point.

"One ball, one arrow," Merry shouted out.

James sprinted forward, and with his right foot propelled the ball skyward—just as Merry drew back her bow, tracked the ball, and released her arrow. She heard James shout as it thudded into the ball, punching it from the sky.

"Happy, longbow girl?" he asked with a clear mixture of admiration and irritation as he jogged back to her.

Merry shook her head. "Not until you tell me why you got suspended."

James gave her a pained look. "It's a long story."

Merry smiled. "I'm not going anywhere. C'mon, let's go and sit down."

They walked to the bench Merry's father had positioned perfectly to take in the hillside view and sat side by side. Merry could feel the turmoil inside James, so she waited. This view always soothed her, and she knew it had the same effect on him.

Just over a mile to their left on the valley floor was the village of Nanteos. A hundred yards to their right was the Owens' cluster of stone buildings: the barn, the stables, and the two-story farmhouse where Merry lived with her parents and baby brother. Way off to the right and higher up the hill was the little whitewashed cottage of Seren Morgan, where Merry spent two hours a week in the cozy kitchen studying botany. Seren was the latest in a long line of herbalist healers who were also said to have the gift of *sight*, the ability to see into the past and the future, and, worryingly, into people's minds. From odd incidents throughout her childhood, Merry felt sure this was true.

Below them, emerald-green fields dotted with oak trees and squared off by hawthorn hedges rolled down to the valley floor, where the Nanteos River emerged from the thick forest and meandered lazily through her family's lands and on through the village. Beyond that was the boundary wall of the de Courcy estates, then the manicured parklands, which rose up to the Black Castle, James's ancestral home. With its huge castellated walls, arrow slits, and moat, it dominated the hillside opposite, glowering down on the valley and across to their farm, a reminder of the bloody past of this part of Wales.

"It was soccer, of course," said James at last. He turned to face Merry. "There's this Russian guy, Alexei, his father's some oligarch, and he goes round saying things like, *'If you upset me, my father'll have you taken care of.'"* James's eyes blazed with quiet anger. "So anyway, we were playing this match and competing for the same ball. I got it, ran on toward goal, and then he comes in again with this slide tackle, cleats up—"

"What?" yelled Merry. "He could have broken your legs!"

"Exactly!" continued James. "So I told him what I thought of him, he punched me, and I punched him back."

"Good on you!" exclaimed Merry. "I hope you punched him harder!"

James gave a rueful smile. "I did, actually." The smile faded. "The oligarch heard about it, made a complaint, so the school suspended me. To be fair, they suspended Alexei too."

Merry blew out a breath. "For how long?"

7

"Till the start of the summer term in five weeks. They let me play in the National Schools Final—I scored the winning goal, by the way," he added, with a broad grin. "Then they sent me packing."

"And what do they say back home?"

James frowned at the dark mass of the Black Castle; then his eyes skimmed over the parkland, across to the flanking forests, and up to the bleak mountains where he'd roam to escape his family. "They say that if this is what happens when I play soccer, they're going to stop me playing. And coming over here too."

Merry gasped. "They can't do that!"

"No," said James quietly, turning back to Merry. "They can't."

There was a look on his face Merry hadn't seen before. It was hard, a look of sheer determination, of someone who would go his own way, whatever the cost.

Merry eyed him full on. "What are you planning, James?"

"I'll tell you when there's something to tell," he replied evasively.

Merry was about to say something else when she saw her mother, Elinor, striding across their land, a Wellington-booted stranger following her.

"Who's that?" asked James.

Merry swore under her breath. "A buyer, come to sniff around our best broodmare. We have to sell her to buy a new stallion."

"You know how I feel about this," said James.

Merry knew he desperately wanted to help but she also knew he had no funds of his own. As a means of trying to persuade him to knuckle down at school and follow the path they'd set out for him, his parents gave him hardly any cash, but even if he did have money, they both knew Merry would never have accepted it.

"Like I said, not your fault." Merry looked away. "But I can't stand around and watch this. I'm off for a ride." She got up from the bench. "See you, James."

"See you, Merry."

"Stay out of trouble," she called over her shoulder.

"You too."

Merry gave a wry laugh. "I'll do my best!"

Chapter Two

>>>>———————————————▶

James got up from the bench and walked slowly down the hillside. He watched from a distance as Merry rode Jacintha, her Welsh Mountain pony, through the stream at the bottom of the valley. It was swollen after weeks of winter rain and she lifted her boots high. He heard her laugh as the pony shook herself vigorously on the other side.

Merry didn't use a saddle or bridle unless riding in a show. Bareback felt more real, she said, and she had trained Jacintha—and all the farm's Welsh Mountain ponies, which had been the Owens' livelihood for centuries—to respond only to gentle pressure on the halter. She didn't call herself a horse whisperer, said it was just kindness, patience, understanding, and a good-hearted pony. But to James it always seemed like magic.

With Merry, Jacintha had become a major prizewinning show pony in the jumping and hunter classes. With her fine conformation, her jet-black coat, the white sock on her rear off leg, and the white star on her dished head, she was like a fairy-tale image of a pony. She was fast and high-spirited. Merry loved her fiercely. At least it wasn't that horse who'd died, James thought now.

Jacintha cantered across the valley, picking up pace now. Merry was lining up her pony, aiming at the boundary wall. Too high, surely, to jump . . . But Merry gathered in her pony, let her measure the distance, then threw herself flat over Jacintha's neck so it seemed there was just one animal galloping away from him. The black pony leaped into the air. It looked for a second as if girl and animal were flying; then Jacintha cleared the wall and landed safely on the other side.

James rolled his eyes. Typical Merry: having fun, pushing it, and making a point. He knew it was an act of defiance, her trespass. Not that he would ever see it as such. When his parents and sister were off the estate, Merry would often come around. But the de Courcys were all in residence. And this was Merry's not-so-subtle message to them.

With her straight-backed poise and waist-length blond hair streaming behind her, he thought that Merry looked more than ever like a marauding warrior princess.

The Owens had been given Nanteos Farm in the fourteenth century, so long as each heir swore to protect the Crown by the skill of the longbow. For seven hundred years, the Owen family had stood ready to do just that, and Merry was the first female heir. Now it had become an honorary concept—James couldn't imagine how the current queen would need a bodyguard archer—but without the longbow, Merry didn't know who she was. Maybe that was why she understood what soccer was to him—so much more than a sport or a game. But unlike Merry, he did not have the support of his parents. A career as a professional soccer player was simply not an acceptable occupation for the lord of the Black Castle. On one side was talent, yearning, and ambition. On the other was snobbery, convention, and the weight of history. He sometimes wondered if he'd ever break free.

Just before the boundary wall, James found the stallion's grave, marked by a simple headstone. He felt a slow burn of fury and shame as he tried to imagine the scene, if only to punish himself. Merry had witnessed the wolfhounds' attack, had been the only one at home. She'd then had to shoot her own stallion, put a bullet in his head to end his agony. He couldn't begin to imagine how she'd felt, wondered if their families would always hate each other.

He jumped over the wall and accelerated up the hill at a sprint, trying to burn off his feelings. His father's Black Welsh sheep, grazing decoratively, took fright at his approach and trotted away. The de Courcy flock had to be black to match the castle, his mother often joked, but they were in fact an ancient breed. The castle records that his father obsessed over showed that the de Courcys had kept these sheep for over five hundred years.

Above him loomed the Black Castle, Castell Du, built by his ancestors back in the 1200s. It looked like the fortress it was: dark, forbidding, a statement of power, money, and intent. But it was also a home, *his* home. He loved it, always had. He'd be sad to leave it.

He glanced across the elegant parkland to check on Merry, hoping she'd jumped back onto the safety of her own lands. But she was still cantering along on the wrong side of the wall, putting on her show of defiance. Picking a fight, looking for trouble, almost as if she were summoning it from the cold spring air.

He slowed down as he saw the slight but ferocious figure of his mother appear on the drawbridge that spanned the castle moat. She was scowling.

"Can you believe it, that feral Owen girl trespassing on our land?" she said.

"Seeing is believing and all that, Ma."

"I honestly don't know why you bother with her," the countess continued. "Why don't you bring home some of your friends from school instead?"

"There's a lot you don't know," James answered, refusing to engage in the fight his mother so clearly wanted.

He walked under the portcullis, across the cobbled courtyard, up to the pair of phoenixes, the de Courcy emblem, that guarded the great front door. He hauled open the oak, slammed it shut behind him. The boom echoed through the castle and down to the dungeons like a roll of thunder.

Chapter Three

>>>>———————————————————————>

Merry crossed the de Courcy land. She knew she was barred, could almost feel the Black Castle glowering down at her from its hilltop perch, and imagined the Earl de Courcy, binoculars pinned to his disapproving eyes, spying. Maybe he'd set the wolfhounds on them both.

"He'd love that, wouldn't he?" she said into Jacintha's ear, and cantered on for another few hundred yards, making her point. She could see James crossing over the moat, disappearing under the teeth of the portcullis. And his mother.

"Better go back, girl," she said to Jacintha at last. "Don't want you killed too."

Safely over the wall and back on her own land, Merry hacked on toward the Black Wood. It was an ancient forest, said to be thousands of years old. She wasn't sure if it had taken its name from the thickness of the trees, which on all but the sunniest of days seemed to turn day into night, or because of its proximity to the Black Castle. The forest spread across both the Owens' land and the de Courcy estate. The trees respected no boundaries and there was no dividing wall within the forest itself.

Merry spotted a narrow break and entered the trees, following a natural pathway, perhaps made by deer and her own ponies seeking

14

shelter. The sun was warm on her face and she could smell the sweet, earthy scent of her pony's sweat.

Birdsong rang out: thrushes, robins, finches. Merry was sure she heard a nightingale, after which the valley of Nanteos was named, but the notes of its song grew fainter, as if the bird were moving away, leading them deeper into the forest. With a light squeeze of her legs, Merry guided Jacintha to follow it. Jacintha was nervous. Ponies were prey animals, and the forest was anything but silent. The trees spoke to one another in surprisingly high-pitched squeaks as wood rubbed against wood in the gentle breeze.

Pony and rider meandered off the path, onto a smaller track. Merry ducked under low-hanging branches, gazing around her. She knew almost all her family's lands intimately, but this part she had never explored closely. Legend had it that the forest was haunted. Looking around, Merry could almost believe it. Moss climbed up the tree trunks, shrouded the branches, fell in tendrils toward the earth, velvet green, pervasive, almost prehistoric.

The nightingale fell silent. Jacintha stopped abruptly.

"What is it?" asked Merry, looking around. Not the wolfhounds, she prayed, fear flickering through her. She slid off Jacintha's back, grabbed a solid branch and, heaving on it, broke it off the tree with a loud crack that echoed around the forest.

But Jacintha was still standing to attention, so Merry felt sure the wolfhounds were not there. She would have heard them by now, and Jacintha would be more frightened. So what was it? She led her pony forward, under an especially low-hanging branch.

"Ah! So that's it."

Ahead of them was a huge, uprooted oak tree, its roots tilted skyward. Merry felt a pang. The oak was a healthy one, probably at least four hundred years old.

"What have you seen, old tree?" she asked softly. "Did the spring gales bring you down?"

She hooked Jacintha's reins over a branch and went closer. The tree had fallen at a strange angle, over an oddly symmetrical mound of earth over twenty feet long and about ten feet high. It looked man-made. Like the burial mounds she'd studied in her history lessons. The tree must have grown over the top of it.

She skirted back to the roots. There was a huge, gaping hole where the roots had been. Merry paused, tilted her head. Something was down there, a rectangular shape. Intrigued, she scrambled down, muddying her hands as she slipped. Then she reached down, worked on the earth, and pulled the object free.

It was a small chest, the size of a large shoe box. She brushed off more dirt, revealing ornately worked metal. It looked very old. She felt a sudden wariness. Was this how Howard Carter and Lord Carnarvon felt when they stood on the threshold of Tutankhamen's tomb, when they first caught the gleam of gold within? Before the supposed curse of Tutankhamen took Carnarvon's life six weeks later?

Don't be ridiculous, she chided herself. *It's just an old chest. In Wales.*

Yes, said a competing voice, *but it might be from a tomb just the same.*

There was a clasp, rusty, rough-edged. Merry tried to pry it open but it wouldn't yield. She fiddled, pulled, pried, cut herself, swore.

Then with something between a hiss and a sigh, the chest opened. Inside was an oblong bundle covered in tatty cloth the color of old leaves. Biting her lip, Merry unwound the cloth. It spooled at her feet like the wrappings of a mummy.

Inside was a book.

It was ancient looking, written in an elaborate, cursive script on pale parchment. She thought it looked like old Welsh. Some pages were illustrated with beautiful and detailed colored drawings.

"Wow! What have we got here?" Merry whispered, shivering slightly. Whatever it was, it must have been a treasured possession of whichever Welsh chieftain had been buried in the mound. She quickly wrapped up the book again and replaced it in the metal chest, then stood still, thinking. After a few minutes, she carried it back to Jacintha. The pony snorted and tossed her head.

"Hey, it's all right, Jac," murmured Merry. "Nothing in here to hurt you. "

She stroked Jacintha's warm muscled neck, soothing her, then, unusually awkward as she clasped the chest under her arm, she stood on a branch of the fallen tree, mounted her pony, and rode from the forest.

Jacintha was skittish all the way, shied at every sound. Bareback, encumbered by the chest, Merry nearly tumbled a few times.

"Calm down, Jac," she crooned. "Everything's fine."

Except that it wasn't.

Chapter Four

Merry was a storyteller. Since she'd been a little girl she'd come home from her adventures on the farm or in the hills and woods with ever more outlandish tales to tell her parents.

"I met a knight walking through the forest. In armor he was, polished silver, sword and all."

Or: *"Guess what, Jacintha jumped so high today she soared through the air. A gust of wind took us, half a mile we went, right up the Beacons."*

This story would be used to justify her being home half an hour late. The better it was, the more her parents excused her.

Merry didn't know where she got it from. Certainly not her father. He believed in what he could see, nothing more. Longbowman. But her mother, a talented artist, liked to tell stories in her paintings—vivid oils of dragons and harps and knights.

Both her parents were sitting at the kitchen table going over the farm accounts when she walked in. Her baby brother, Gawain, lay in his playpen gurgling away under a baby gym.

She hid the chest behind her back. "Guess what I found today?"

Her father looked up. His face was somber but when he locked eyes with her, it broke into a smile. He closed the file in front of him, pushed it away. "Now, let me see." He leaned back in his chair, hands behind his head. "You fell down a well and before you managed to haul yourself out you discovered a hoard of Roman coins?"

Merry shook her head, grinning. "Not this time, Da."

Her mother tucked her long dark hair behind her ears and studied her quizzically. "A stranger wandering in the hills. You could have sworn you saw the outline of wings beneath his coat. You spoke to him for a while, then turned away for just a second, and when you looked back he'd gone. Disappeared into thin air. You spent hours hunting for him and that's why you missed lunch, isn't it, Spinner?"

Merry laughed. *Spinner* was her mother's nickname for her: spinner of tales. "Nice one, Mam. But no."

She brought the chest from behind her back, set it on the table.

"I found this," she said, opening the chest and unwrapping the book with a flourish.

Her parents eyed the book. Her father leaned forward as her mother slowly turned the pages, her long white fingers delicate on the ancient parchment.

They looked up, silenced by a real story this time.

"Where on earth did you find this, *cariad*?" asked her father. *Cariad* meant "sweetheart" in Welsh. Merry loved her parents' various names for her, made her feel that she was lots of different things.

"Get your boots on," said Merry. "I'll show you."

Her father carried Gawain in a sling across his chest. Six foot four, he always walked at military yomp pace, eating up the ground. Merry and her mother were used to it, reckoned a walk with him equaled a workout.

When they got to the burial mound they were glowing with a sheen of sweat. They paused. Around them the forest was silent now. No birds sang. Probably frightened away, thought Merry.

"Down there," she said, pointing to the hole in the ground. "You can see the shape behind it, now that the tree's blown over. It's got to be a burial mound."

Her father cast his eyes over it. "I think you're right, *cariad*," he said. "You know, in all the years I've never noticed it."

"It's as if the tree was guarding it," said Elinor. "Or hiding it." She paused and murmured, "Maybe this is why they say the forest is haunted."

Caradoc Owen gave her a brisk look. "Who's buried here? That's what I'd like to know."

"Someone important," said Merry. "Some chieftain or prince. Must be to have had a book like that."

"We need to find out," Elinor said. "And we need to decide what to do with the book. We can't keep it hidden away in a cupboard."

"Something like that belongs in a museum," said Caradoc.

Merry looked down at the burial mound, wondered if whoever lay there minded that she had taken their book. She shivered with a sudden sense that they did. Maybe digging around in tombs was not such a good idea. She thought again of the Valley of the Kings and the curse of Tutankhamen.

"Maybe we should just forget about it and put it back," she said hurriedly.

Her parents gave her a strange look. *"Why?"* they asked in unison.

"Well, it belongs to whoever's down there."

"He or she is long gone," said Caradoc. "They shouldn't trouble you."

But they did. "Come on, let's go home," she said. She didn't want to be near their skeletal remains any longer.

Back at the farmhouse, her mother took her aside.

"You found the book. What do you think we should do with it?" she asked.

Merry shook her head. "I'm not sure. Half of me really does want to bury it again but the other half is curious. I want to know more."

"Look," Elinor said, putting her hand on her daughter's arm. "It's Friday. No need to do anything for a few days. Just sleep on it."

Merry did just that. When she went to bed that night she pushed the chest containing the book deep under her bed. But she kept thinking back to the hole under the tree. When had the chest been buried? And who had owned the land then—the de Courcys, or the Owens?

She stood in her cozy yellow-painted room with its two windows, one looking up the hill toward Seren's cottage, the other across the valley to the Black Castle, reliving the events of the day. So much had happened. James arriving home in turmoil, the buyer coming to look at their mare, her discovery in the Black Wood. It had started off like any other day and turned into something different. *Life has a way of surprising us, cariad*, her father was fond of saying. *Best be ready.*

But what did that mean? All she was ready for was a war she'd never have to fight. A war of longbows and knights in armor.

She opened the window facing the Black Castle for some fresh air. For a while she just stood there, breathing in the night, gazing across the black void to the castle, where distant lights glimmered. *What was James doing?* she wondered. *More arguments with his parents, or was he holed up in his room, avoiding them?*

She heaved out a sigh, closed her primrose-sprigged curtains, changed into her nightdress, and walked barefoot across the white-painted floorboards. There was a small rug in the middle of her room, but she liked the feel of the wood beneath her feet. She removed her eye patch, slipped into bed, and pulled the duvet and quilt up to her chin.

Half asleep, half transported by her own imagination and by memories of the tale her father had told and retold many times, her mind went back to the fateful battle nearly seven hundred years ago when the ownership of land changed, when her family's fortunes were made and the Owens' longbow tradition began.

A battlefield in Northern France, Crécy, 1346: the muscled archers hauling back their massive bows, sending up a hail of arrows that blackened the sky and brought death to the French and victory to the English. Against all odds. And sixteen-year-old Edward, the Black Prince, heir to the English throne, embroiled in close-quarter combat and fighting for his life, saved not by the noblemen who were his close guard, nor the fourth Earl de Courcy, who commanded that guard, but by Merry's own ancestor—a longbowman who, with a well-aimed arrow, felled the man who was swinging an ax to the prince's head . . .

And on that one arrow, the fortunes of the Owen family turned. The Black Prince rewarded Longbowman Owen with five hundred acres of land and enough gold to build a modest cottage. Five hundred acres taken from the ancestral estates of the Earl de Courcy, a royal punishment that cut deep.

The enmity between the two families started that day. Everyone knew the de Courcys still wanted back what they would always regard as *their land*. Its loss was an open wound, picked over by the generations so that it would never heal.

In her dreams, Merry saw the chieftain rising from the burial mound, saw the flesh recladding his skeletal frame, saw the rich robes of his rank once again swathing his body as he marched from the dark forest across the open fields, to reclaim his book. But more than that, to take back the Owens' land, their home, and return it to the de Courcys.

Chapter Five

————➤

It was a Saturday. Her father was up, feeding Gawain spoonfuls of freshly mashed banana and avocado, giving Elinor a much-needed lie-in.

"Morning, *cariad*," he said, as Merry appeared in her dressing gown and Uggs. "You all right?"

"Nope," said Merry. "Headache." Her dreams had segued into nightmares, and left her head throbbing.

"Here, finish feeding this little monster and I'll make us some banana pancakes. How about that?"

"Mmmm. Yes, please," said Merry, sitting down with a grateful sigh. Sweet comfort food was the best cure, and her father, despite being traditional in many ways, was a very good cook. "I like to eat so I'd be stupid if I didn't know how to cook" was his response to anyone who expressed surprise.

Ten minutes later, he handed Merry a full plate and a cup of hot chocolate.

"Eat up. Feel better. I'll see you outside in half an hour."

Mouth full, Merry nodded. Saturday mornings meant longbow practice with her father. Nothing got in the way except bad weather, and only then because it damaged the arrows' fletches and messed up the straw target.

This was a very different exercise from the arrows she shot with

James, hanging out with him, larking around while he honed his soccer skills. Saturday practice with her father was where the long-bowman handed down all his skills, where he pushed her always to get better, stronger, and more accurate, not for a war that would no longer be fought, but because it was part of who the Owens were, as essential to their identity as the land they lived on. Every year, he was required to demonstrate his prowess at the Royal Welsh Show, in front of the Prince of Wales. In a year it would be Merry's turn.

The longbowmen of the past were legendary, the most fearsome killing machine the Western world had ever seen. Their bows had draw weights of around one hundred and forty pounds. They could shoot their steel-tipped arrows from two hundred paces with suffi-cient force to pierce armor, and could shoot so fast that they could send three arrows scything through the air at any one time. They won unwinnable battles, gained untold lands, struck terror into the hearts of their enemies. Songs had been written about them, stories woven around them; they were the game changers of their age.

It was these ghostly giants of history that Merry and her father honored.

She had started training at five years old. Her muscles and tech-nique had been honed for over a decade. That was about as long as the archers of old took to develop the massive strength and skill needed to go to war with a longbow. Even though Gawain had come along, a wonderful surprise baby, his birth changed nothing. Merry was the longbow girl. Her parents wouldn't have dreamed of taking that away from her.

Merry finished her breakfast, already feeling better. She washed up, then pulled on her boots, grabbed her bow, her leather arm brace and quiver, and walked out to their practice field. She removed the tarpaulin cover from the straw target and strapped the brace to her left arm. She'd gone without a few times and the bowstring had given her some wicked bruises. Most longbow archers wore a finger tab to protect their skin when drawing the bow, but she and her father often forgot their tabs and went without. She'd grown large calluses on the pads of her two forefingers as a result, but she didn't mind. Calluses were better than gloves or tabs. You didn't lose them and besides, she liked to feel the bow cord and the arrow, to guide it with that extra bit of sensitivity.

Her father approached from the house, holding two bows.

"You can unstring that one," he said, nodding to the bow that lay on the tarpaulin and handing her another, longer bow. "You've grown again, *cariad*. Time for a new one."

"Oh, Da." Merry stood on tiptoe, kissed her father's cheek. The bow, her eleventh, was beautiful. She'd had a new one every year, from the age of five, and her father had made them all. Each bow was a surprise—she never knew when she'd get it—and seemed to have marked a watershed in her life, as if her father knew what was coming, or perhaps as if having the new bow *made* something happen.

He had also made the bow that had harbored the invisible, undetectable flaw. The bow that broke and took Merry's eye.

He had never forgiven himself for that, and the smile he gave her as he handed her the new bow was tinged with a sorrow that never went away no matter how many times Merry told him that it wasn't his fault, that he couldn't have known, that it was just bad luck. It was archers' lore that every bow when fully drawn was nine-tenths

26

broken, that all it took to cause a fatal rupture was one small weakness deep within the wood; a weakness that could lie dormant and invisible and undetected until it was too late. Like people. You never quite knew where the breaking point was.

Merry weighed the new bow in her hand. She held it, one end hovering just off the ground, the other reaching a few inches above her head. She prayed it was sound.

"Just right," said her father. "Here's the cord. Let's see if you can string the bow. Fifty-pound draw, mind you."

He would already have tested it, making the cord just the right length to give the bow the perfect draw length. Her perfectionist father.

Merry slipped the knotted string over the lower nock, pulling it tight. She found a soft piece of ground to rest the lower nock on, then, placing her knee on the handle of the bow, she pulled with her left hand until the upper limb bent toward her while with her right hand she worked the loop of the string toward the groove of the upper nock. With a final surge of strength, she slid it in.

She'd done it at the first attempt. No fumbling.

Her father gave a slight nod. Merry smiled.

She went through the routine that had become almost as familiar and as automatic as breathing. The longbowman's mantra, her father's mantra: *Ready your bows, nock, mark, draw, loose.* The same words that would have echoed across the battlefields of the Middle Ages.

She held the stave of her bow in her left hand, turned sideways onto the target.

Ready your bows . . .

She braced her feet, hip-width apart, left foot forward in the archer's stance. She reached back her arm and pulled an arrow from her quiver, holding it by the nock at the end, the slit that kept it in place on the bowstring. With its shaft of cedar and its metal tip, the arrow was twenty-seven inches long. It was fletched with goose feathers, like the arrows used at Crécy.

Nock . . .

She clicked the arrow on the string, making it thrum softly.

Mark . . .

She looked up, eyed the target, visualized the arrow slicing through the air, coming home to rest in the gold.

Draw . . .

She bent over from the waist, then in a fluid motion, using the strength in her legs, stomach, back, and arms, she straightened up, and with the forefinger and second and third fingers of her right hand on the string, she pulled her arm back and up till the bow was at full stretch, until her hand was just under her ear with her forearm parallel to the ground. Her back muscles bunched and strained, but she did it.

Loose.

The arrow was pulled back too far to aim by looking down its shaft. Instead Merry just looked at the target, released her grip on the string, and let the arrow fly.

The arrow thudded into the target. Dead center of the gold.

She glanced across the fields to the forest, where the chieftain lay, as if by her arrows, by her marksmanship, she could keep him at bay.

Chapter Six

>>>———————————→

Merry spent the rest of the weekend with her family. Weekdays on a farm were always so busy that they all valued whatever quiet time they could get on Saturday and Sunday. There were still chores to be done, but Elinor always made sure they went out on a family outing on both days, even if it was just a trip to Brecon.

Monday morning came and Merry spent the morning on the PC doing her distance-learning courses. Today she focused on math and science. By lunchtime she was done. Her father had gone out—stormed out, more like. She'd heard his raised voice as he took a call on his mobile, then the slamming of a door and the acceleration of their ancient Land Rover as he drove off somewhere in a hurry.

Her mother had taken Gawain to visit her sister in Brecon, so Merry got her own lunch. Canned tomato soup with grated cheddar and two slices of Seren's homemade bread.

She still hadn't decided what to do about the book. It made her feel restless, sitting up there under her bed. It was as if it were giving off vibes.

A text pinged in as she spooned up soup. James.

What you doing?
Lunch. You?

Meant to be studying. Can't face it.

Parentals aren't forcing you?

Parentals have gone off to Cardiff. Want to come round?

I'll still use the tunnel.

What is it with you and the tunnel?

Don't know. Just love it.

Used to frighten you.

That's the point!

Weirdo.

See you in the dungeons.

Love the dungeons.

Who's weird now?

She'd show her book to James, Merry thought. That'd distract him from his woes.

She cleared up lunch, then set off, the chest and a headlamp hidden in a large plastic shopping bag swinging at her side. She climbed the boundary wall, checking there was no sign of the wolf-hounds, then headed toward the wilderness below the castle, where the gorse grew thick, concealing the entrance to the tunnel.

The de Courcys' escape tunnels were still a closely guarded secret, eight hundred years after their construction. Merry strapped on her headlamp, switched it on, and pushed through the thorny bushes, ducking under the low entrance. Inside, it was cold and damp. The beam of her headlamp bounced off the walls of glistening black rock. As she went deeper into the tunnel, her footsteps echoed so it sounded like she was being followed. She glanced around a few times, just to check, even though she knew nobody'd be there. The tunnels always did that, spooking her. Maybe it was the unquiet spirits of all those who'd walked this way before . . .

As always, Merry was relieved when she got to the door that led into the castle dungeons. She tapped it lightly and it opened immediately. James stood there eyeing her plastic bag quizzically.

"What you got in there?"

"Wait and see."

"Come on, then. You can show me in my room."

Merry pulled off her muddy shoes and socks and left them with her headlamp beside the door. Barefoot, she walked behind James, through the dungeons, past the cells now used to store wood and coal and odds and ends. She saw lamp stands, an old upright stroller, a grill, and two ladders. The iron bars were still there, though. She paused, reached out, took hold of one. Was there a flutter in the air, an echo of movement long ago, or was she spinning again? Something ran through her. She shivered and let go.

They filed up the narrow spiral staircase, came out into the cavernous Great Hall. In the dim lighting, Merry thought she saw someone on her blind side, turned sharply.

James laughed. "Just Sir Lancelot."

Merry blew out a breath and studied the life-size figure of the knight in full chain mail, complete with helmet and sword. "God! He always gets me!"

"Gets the dogs too," remarked James. "They still growl at him."

They walked across the age-darkened slate floor, buffed smooth over the centuries, and headed up the broad staircase.

From the dark wood paneling, generations of de Courcys glowered down from their massed portraits. At the bottom, most prominent, was the current countess, the twenty-first, James's mother. Anne de Courcy was a girl from Swansea, the daughter of a steelworker, blessed with the looks that had turned the head and, to everyone's surprise—including, it was said, his own—won the heart of the young earl, Auberon de Courcy. Dark-haired, with blue eyes and creamy skin, she was stunningly beautiful in that *mirror, mirror on the wall* way.

Looking at the portraits, Merry could see how strongly Anne de Courcy had passed on her spectacular physical genes to her son. James had the same thick, dark hair, strong eyebrows like two strokes of black, and quick blue eyes. His nose, however, was pure de Courcy, long and straight, the mirror of his father's and most of the de Courcys on the wall. Sadly for James's sister, Lady Alicia had only her father's genes.

Alongside James, Merry hurried up the multiple flights of stairs, along the hallway. They passed the priest hole and Merry felt again the shiver that different parts of the castle gave her. This tiny, airless space, just big enough to conceal a standing man, wasn't for ancient games of hide-and-seek. It had been built during the reign of Queen Elizabeth I, when the penalty for being a Catholic priest was death. What nameless priests had hidden here, wondered Merry, with the shadow of death hanging over them?

"Are you coming? Or d'you want me to shut you in there?" James called from ahead, cocking his head as if contemplating it.

"You and whose army?" Merry replied.

James laughed. "You haven't got your bow, Merry Owen. You're defenseless!"

Merry spluttered at that. James knew her father gave her lessons in self-defense.

Together, they walked on to the end of the hallway, to James's corner room. Merry always blinked at the sheer scale of it. Windows facing west across the valley to her own house, and north to the Beacons. There were a double bed, a large desk, and a giant beanbag, and still what felt like acres of space.

"So, what's in the bag?" James said, nodding to it. "You're hanging on to it like you've got the crown jewels in there."

"Not far off," replied Merry.

She took out the chest, opened it, carefully began to unravel the swaddling.

"Please don't tell me there's a baby in there," said James.

"Ha ha. Not quite." Merry removed the last bit of wrapping, set the book on the desk in front of James.

He stared at it, then looked up at her, his mouth open to speak when another voice cut in.

"What's all this?"

Merry spun around.

The Earl de Courcy stood in the open door. Tall, slim, straight-backed, immaculate in his handmade suit.

Merry hissed in a breath, struggling to contain the anger bubbling up. This man was responsible for her stallion's death. For the problems her family was now facing.

The earl's angular face showed no emotion. Only his eyes moved, sharp, cold like stone. That's how he always seemed to Merry: the Stone Man.

"God, Pa! I thought you were in Cardiff!" exclaimed James, looking awkward and annoyed.

"I came back," retorted the earl.

He nodded to Merry. She managed to nod back.

The earl walked up to the desk. "What *is* this?" he asked, his eyebrows rising. He bent down to scrutinize the book, then looked from James to Merry, waiting for an answer.

Merry had no choice but to speak to him. "I'm not exactly sure," she replied in a clipped voice.

"It's yours, I assume," said the earl.

Merry nodded. "I found it on Friday, in the forest. On our land," she added.

The earl eyed her, got her meaning perfectly. "Really."

"Yes," replied Merry. "I did."

"May I?" the earl was asking, his hand already on the book.

Merry felt like shouting: *No! You may not!* But what could she do? She was in his castle. Reluctantly, she nodded.

The earl turned the pages. "Exquisite," he murmured. "What do you think it is?"

She blew out a breath. "Something precious," she said at last. "And very old."

"You haven't shown it to any experts?" asked the earl, straightening, looking at Merry with cool speculation.

"No, I haven't! I only just found it. I've hardly had time to figure out what to do with it." That was a lie, but she had no intention of sharing her superstitious fears with the earl.

"I was in Cardiff," replied the earl puzzlingly. "At the train station. Collecting some guests. You've met one already," he said to James. "Dr. Philipps."

"Your pet historian," replied James. "The one who discovered that Henry VIII had stayed here."

"Don't be facetious, James," reprimanded his father. "We have an important history. It needs documenting." The earl turned back to Merry. "As it happens, Dr. Philipps is also an expert on old manuscripts."

He picked up her book.

"Would you like to come downstairs and meet him?"

Merry felt another flare of anger. She exchanged a pained glance with James, who gave a helpless shrug. Only for his sake did Merry hold on to her temper.

What I would like to do, thought Merry, *is to yank my book out of your hands, fall through the floor into the dungeons, and head back through the tunnel as fast as possible.*

But the earl was already walking through the door, carrying Merry's book, so she had little choice but to follow.

Chapter Seven

The earl led them through another series of twists and turns to a part of the castle Merry had never visited before. He finally paused before a dark wooden door.

"The castle's muniments room," he said. Merry looked blank. "It contains important family documents. Going back to the eleventh century," he added. "When we started building the Black Castle."

Merry almost felt dizzy as she thought of all those years, rolling by. She noted the *we*. The old family and the new were still so closely entwined, even after nearly a thousand years. *Just like her own family.*

The earl opened the door. "Please," he said, gesturing Merry inside.

Two men were sitting at a large green leather desk surrounded by scrolls and laptops. They got up when the earl entered.

"Gentlemen, I have something rather extraordinary to show you," the earl was saying, putting down Merry's book on the huge desk. "Anthony Parks, Idris Philipps, meet Merry Owen."

Parks looked to be in his mid-thirties, with brutally short black hair. He had the blazing eyes, wiry body, and taut face of a marathon runner, and was dressed head to toe in black: jeans and a tight, long-sleeve thermal top.

"Good afternoon, Miss Owen," he said crisply.

"Afternoon, Mr. Parks," she replied.

"Actually, it's *Professor* Parks."

Merry resisted the urge to scrunch up her face. Pomposity was her pet loathing.

"Oh, so sorry," the earl said. "And this is my son, James."

"Hello, James," said Professor Parks, with a great deal more enthusiasm, reaching out to shake James's hand.

"Lord James," replied James stiffly.

Merry nearly burst out laughing. She felt some of the tension leave her. James *never* used his title. He was, she knew, doing it solely to amuse her.

Parks reddened slightly and something in his eyes hardened a fraction, but then he recovered quickly, shaking James's hand with what looked like an extra-firm grip.

"And this is Dr. Philipps," the earl went on.

Merry shook hands, said hello. Dr. Philipps had a thatch of unruly dark hair, extravagant eyebrows, and smiling eyes. Donning a pair of white cotton gloves and squinting to keep a monocle in place, he bent over the book.

He just stared at the cover for a while, saying nothing, not even seeming to breathe; then, very slowly, he opened the book and turned the pages.

Finally he looked up. "Well," he said. "You know what you've got here, then, do you?"

"Not really," replied Merry, her heart beginning to beat faster. "I mean, I know it's something special and very old, but that's about it."

"I'd like to show my colleagues, I would, at the Museum of Wales. We'll have to carry out carbon dating too, if you were to allow me, but my gut feeling"—he rubbed his large stomach—"my *gut* feeling is that what we are looking at here might be, just might be, mind, one of the lost tales of the *Mabinogion!*"

Merry heard Professor Parks swear and the earl took a step closer to the book, looked from it to Merry, eyes flickering.

"The *Mabinogion* itself, as I'm sure you know," Dr. Philipps was saying, "is a collection of eleven stories taken from medieval Welsh manuscripts from around 1060 to 1200. Some say it's myth. Others truth. Some tales feature King Arthur."

Merry nodded. She'd been taught about it at the school in Brecon she'd attended before her accident, before she had begun to be homeschooled.

"But there are suggestions, references in some manuscripts that other stories exist," Dr. Philipps continued. "They are referred to as the lost tales. And this," he concluded, giving Merry a profoundly serious look, "is, I hazard, one of them."

"Goodness," Merry managed to say.

"Bit of a miracle it survived in such pristine condition. Bit of a miracle you found it after all these years."

"Where did you find it?" asked Professor Parks.

"In a burial mound," replied Merry. "On my land."

"Whereabouts, exactly?" asked the earl.

"In the Black Wood."

"Ah, the forest that borders our land."

"This was some way from the border," replied Merry. She felt a sudden surge of panic. Hoped she was right. It was hard to tell in the forest, dense as it was, and she had taken a meandering path.

"I am sure this is very precious to you," the earl went on smoothly, "and I can see you feel very protective of it, but may I just keep it for a few days? I could photocopy it, then have it translated for you."

"I could make a start on the translation," cut in Dr. Philipps. "I'm familiar with Middle Welsh."

Merry hadn't and wouldn't forgive the earl for their stallion's death and the strains it had put on her family. She didn't want to hand over the book. But she did want it translated. Very much.

"Forgive me being presumptuous here," interjected Professor Parks, "but I would counsel you most strongly to allow us to retain the book here at the castle for safekeeping. Rather valuable. Might attract unwanted attention."

"Oh, don't worry," Merry replied airily. "This part of Wales is incredibly safe. No one even locks their doors around here."

"Maybe they should," Dr. Philipps replied, looking concerned.

Stung into decisiveness by the rebuke, and feeling trapped, Merry stared at him, then turned to the earl.

"Actually, I'd prefer to keep the book with me. It is mine, after all," she added.

She saw a mix of emotions race over the earl's face: surprise, annoyance . . . He wasn't used to being denied.

"Of course," he replied with cool civility. "That is very much your prerogative."

"May I at least take some pictures with my phone?" Dr. Philipps asked.

Merry nodded. "Okay. That's fine."

She watched him carefully turning the pages again. He paused at the same one that had caught her attention: a still, dark pool reflecting clouds scudding overhead; a ray of sunlight arrowing down through the water; a thicket of thornbushes; a nightingale atop an oak, like a witness to some scene occurring off the page . . . it was beautiful and sinister.

Yet it drew her in . . .

"I'm dying to know what it says on this page," she found herself murmuring.

Dr. Philipps met her gaze, his own eyes glowing with a kind of sharp intelligence and fascination. "All right, young lady. Give me a little while."

Mrs. Baskerville, the de Courcys' housekeeper, arrived, struggling under a gigantic tray of teapot and cups. She glanced at Merry in amazement. She was well used to seeing Merry in the castle hanging out with James when the family was out, but not here mingling with the earl and his guests.

When she left, Dr. Philipps took a sip of tea, put down his cup, and said, slowly, his eyes on the page: *"There is a cave where the green turns blue, where the earth beside does shimmer. A veil of water guards it well, of its secrets not a glimmer. There is a hole in the stone of sand at the back in the gushing flow; follow it through to another land and all treasures will you know. Twenty strokes have many tried, turning them to blue, of those venturers many have died, only the strong pass through . . ."*

His words echoed around the room. For a while, no one spoke. Merry felt almost dazed, as if she were under some kind of spell. Everyone in the library seemed to feel the same. They all had a distant look in their eyes.

Merry jumped up. "Right!" she said, her voice coming out unnaturally loud. "I need to get back." She picked up her book, re-swaddled it, and enclosed it safely in the chest, which she slid into the plastic bag.

She seemed to have broken the spell, because everyone started moving and talking at once. James walked out with her and she felt the eyes on her back, and in the air the burn of covetousness.

Chapter Eight

"That was intense," remarked James.

Merry blew out a breath. "I still feel a bit dazed," she replied.

"I'll bet." They walked in silence until they emerged into the Great Hall. "Apart from everything else, you and my father actually speaking was remarkable."

"Call it the power of the book," said Merry.

"There's a lot of power in that thing. Wait here and I'll run down and get your shoes and headlamp," he added. "No point in sneaking out in the tunnel now you're in such favor."

While Merry was waiting for James, Professor Parks appeared, materializing on silent feet.

"I was wondering if you'd be kind enough to show me where you found the book?" He spoke crisply, in an emotionless, academic tone, but his eyes shone, betraying his interest.

Merry wanted to say no but couldn't think of a polite way to do so.

"What, *now*?" she asked.

"That would be most convenient. Thank you so much," he added as if her question had been an offer.

Merry scowled at the floor. She was going to have to learn to be a lot ruder and more forceful if she was going to deal successfully with the earl and his crew. It had been a lot easier treating him as an enemy than as a pseudo friend.

James came back with Merry's shoes and headlamp.

"Ah, Lord James, Miss Owen has most kindly offered to show me the burial mound."

"Has she?" asked James, flicking Merry a look of surprise. "I'll come along too," he added.

"Oh dear," replied Parks. "I do think I heard your father saying he was most anxious that you join him. I got the impression it was somewhat *urgent*."

James, also trapped by manners, found himself nodding, then marching back to the muniments room.

Merry, followed by Professor Parks, went out into the huge courtyard, surrounded by the high walls of the castle. She walked across the ancient cobbles, under the iron-toothed portcullis, across the drawbridge. She was used to it, but she could see Parks's head swiveling, taking it all in with a hungry, avid gaze.

"Living history," he enunciated. "A thousand years of it. What it must be like to own this place." He gave a half laugh. "I'm a historian. Sometimes I love history too much."

"Give me the twenty-first century any day," replied Merry. "Antibiotics and equality."

"Hrmph," trumpeted Parks in disapproval. "That's a somewhat narrow view, if I may say so. The past had many and subtle compensations."

"Well, we'll never know, will we?" countered Merry. "Look," she went on, "I really can't show you the burial mound without my father's permission." That was a lie, but one that she was happy to hide behind as she mounted her belated fight-back.

Parks widened his eyes as if seeing straight through her. "Well, perhaps you could ask him?" he replied smoothly. "You see, I'm more than just a historian. I'm an archaeologist. I could undertake an official dig."

"A dig?" asked Merry.

"Well, it would be the courteous thing to do. You see, with a find of this nature, the authorities could get a license to dig on your land, a *compulsory* license, that is. I just thought you'd like to do it in a rather less officious, let's say, rather friendlier way." He gave one of his tooth-baring smiles. "You see, I like to work alone. I'm sure you would prefer that to a large team traipsing across your land."

Merry said nothing as she tried to take in all he was saying and implying.

"The other thing," continued Parks silkily, "is I know how to sift through the area very carefully, with infinite patience, taking care not to destroy anything. There could be other valuable items. I can ensure they are properly and safely excavated so you would get the maximum for them."

"What do you mean?" asked Merry.

"Well, according to the Treasure Laws, the landowner is entitled to share the proceeds of any finds, should you sell them, fifty-fifty with the finder. Could amount to a substantial sum of money, Miss Owen."

And money, Merry knew all too well, was in short supply at home. Parks had unwittingly hit on her weak point.

"And lastly," he said with an almost conspiratorial smile, "in order to fully authenticate the book, we need to know much more about where it was found and attempt to find the other items that were almost undoubtedly buried with it. If we manage to authenticate the book, its value will be far higher."

"I thought that Dr. Philipps would be working on authenticating it," argued Merry.

Parks gave her a sharp look. "He will. Indeed. But he's not an archaeologist. He doesn't get his hands dirty," he added with relish. "He works with documents and archives. I work in the ground, with living history. History you can touch. We each have our own skills. We're complementary. That's why the earl employs us both."

That made up Merry's mind. The earl would only employ the best people money could buy.

"Okay. You can discuss it with my father tomorrow," she said. "If you come at eleven, he'll be taking a break from his farmwork. He'll be at the house then."

She hurried away across the parkland, keen to escape what she felt were becoming dangerous waters. Dealing with the book, with the attention it was already generating, with the earl and his experts skillfully maneuvering her, was making her feel way out of her depth. But it was too late to go back now. She'd found the book, and now not just the earl but two different experts knew about it. She felt like fate had forced her hand. All she could try to do now was what was best for her family.

Chapter Nine

➤➤➤━━━━━━━━━━━━━━━━━➤

Merry returned home to a strangely tense house. Her father sat at the small table in the hallway, bent over the farm accounts, his face taut. Her mother was closed away in the kitchen with Gawain for company. It sounded like she was cooking up a storm, banging pots and pans and muttering.

Merry hurried up to her room, hid the chest back under her bed, then headed out to see to her chores—checking ponies and foals and troughs. She didn't want to talk to anyone human for a while. The company of ponies was far less taxing. She took Jacintha out for a ride, deliberately avoiding the Black Wood and instead heading up to the Beacons, making the most of the late sunshine.

Finally, as the sun was setting, she headed home and arrived back in time for a late dinner.

Gawain was already in bed, so it was just the three of them tucking into a roast leg of lamb, green beans, and goose-fat-browned potatoes.

They didn't talk much. The food was good and they were all hungry but the silence was odd. They were usually a talkative household. When they'd finished, Merry's father got up and poured himself a glass of whisky. He downed it in one gulp, then sat down again.

"There's no easy way to put this, so I'm going to cut to the chase. We're in trouble. I kept it from you both while I tried to find a way out . . ." He rubbed his hands over his face.

Merry stared at her father: the farmer, the fighter, the longbowman, the soldier, decorated several times over for conspicuous bravery. Now he looked as if he faced an enemy he could not fight. The expression in his eyes made Merry feel a quiver of fear. She glanced at her mother. Elinor was twisting a strand of her long black hair around her finger. Her eyes were grave.

"We owe the bank sixty thousand pounds," Caradoc went on. "I borrowed money to build the extension, to rebuild the barn. We'd have been fine if things had gone well." He gave a bitter laugh. "But things often don't, do they, especially when you need them to. We simply haven't made enough to meet the mortgage payments for the past six months. I was relying on the stallion's stud fees to pay the mortgage." He paused, fisted his hands on the table. "He had eight bookings over the next six weeks."

"What about the insurance money?" Elinor asked, voice high. "The company'll have to pay out for his death . . . won't they?" she asked her husband. Her skin had turned ghostly white.

Caradoc's face became even more grim. He took in a deep breath. "I forgot to renew the insurance."

Merry looked at him in confusion. "No, you didn't. I heard you on the phone about a month ago. You complained about the size of the premium to me. I remember."

Her father turned to her, shaking his head with a kind of horrible regret that made Merry feel sick to her stomach. "Trust you to remember, *cariad*."

"I do remember!" she said hotly. "So why did you lie?"

"All right, the truth of it is this," he replied, his voice heavier than Merry had ever heard it. "Because you shot the horse yourself rather than letting him suffer in agony for the hour or so it would have taken the vet to get here and put him out of his misery, the insurance is invalid."

Elinor opened her mouth to say something, then closed it again.

Merry covered her face with her hands, trembling in shock. She felt a huge hand, warm on her shoulder.

"What you did was brave," her father said, urgently. "Humane. You must not blame yourself, *cariad*. You must *not*."

Merry uncovered her face, looked into his eyes, saw so many things there, most of all a horrible, unspoken pain.

"So this is where we are," he said, going back to his seat. "Selling the mare only buys us time. The bank manager phoned this morning. He was short and not so sweet: *Pay off the arrears and meet the new payments or else we'll have no choice but to foreclose.* He's given us six weeks."

Elinor gasped. "Six weeks? *Six weeks?* To come up with how much exactly?"

"Six thousand pounds," Caradoc replied, voice hollow.

Elinor reached across the table and grabbed her husband's hand.

"How on earth are we going to find that kind of money?"

"Sell the mare. And the little silver we have. These old dining chairs must be antique. They'll be worth something," he said, glancing around.

"And if we don't find the money," said Elinor slowly, each word like a hammer blow, "we lose the farm? We just hand it over to the bank?"

"Either that, or sell. Bits of it. Or all of it."

"And we all know who'd buy it, quicker than you can say *knife*," shouted Elinor in a rush of emotion. She pushed herself to her feet and strode to the window, gazing out toward the Black Castle. "Makes me wonder if the earl didn't let out his hounds deliberately."

"We'll never know, will we," Caradoc said, the muscles clenching in his cheek.

"Merry and Gawain's inheritance," said Elinor in a whisper. "And the longbow tradition . . ."

She sat down heavily, propped her arms on the table, stared at the aged wood.

"I know. Don't you think I know?" snapped her father.

Merry felt dazed. She gazed from one parent to another, appalled by the news, distressed by their misery, horrified by the part she had played in adding to their trouble . . . but then an idea came together in her head. "There might be a way out," she said, fists clenched, digging her nails into her palms, hoping, praying . . .

Her parents turned to her, faces edged with grief. They didn't really think she had a solution. They didn't know what she knew.

"It seems the book I found might be quite valuable." She paused, sucked in a breath, let it out in one smooth go. Maybe fate was helping her family, just when they needed it most. "I showed it to an expert. He reckons it might, just might, be one of the lost tales of the *Mabinogion*."

Her parents looked stunned.

"What on earth have you been up to, Merry Owen?" Elinor asked at last.

So Merry told them about taking the book to show James, about the earl walking in on them, and everything that followed.

Her parents sat leaning forward, eyes wide, listening in amazed silence.

"So it comes down to this," Merry finished. "Dr. Philipps will discuss the book with his colleagues and show them pictures he took with his phone. And *Professor* Parks, who is an archaeologist and a historian, says to help authenticate the book he needs to excavate the burial mound, get more information."

Her father stared into the distance for a while, processing it all; then he turned his gaze back to Merry. There was a new hope in his eyes and a kind of steely calculation.

"Presumably if this Professor Parks authenticates the book, then it will be worth much more?" he asked.

"He implied as much," replied Merry. "He also said that according to the Treasure Laws the proceeds of anything found there is split fifty-fifty between the landowner and the finder."

"Well, that means we get one hundred percent of the book anyway," said Elinor. "It was Merry who found it." She paused. "It *was* on our land, wasn't it?" she said urgently to her husband. "It's hard to tell in the forest and we went quite far in."

The look in Caradoc's eyes became distant again, and Merry knew he was going over the geography in his head.

"I'm sure it's on our side," he said. "Not by much, though. Maybe as little as a hundred yards or so." He turned to Merry. "We'll set out at first light tomorrow to check. Set your alarm for five."

She nodded. She couldn't speak. It *had* to be on their side . . .

"Parks thinks there might be other things there too, that were buried with the book," Merry managed to say. "Things that will help authenticate the book but that might be valuable in themselves."

"Whoever this Professor Parks is, we need his help," declared Caradoc. "We need to get him to start work on the burial mound immediately and authenticate the book. Then we can sell it and go fifty-fifty with him on anything else he finds."

"He's coming here tomorrow at eleven o'clock to discuss it with you," said Merry.

"Thank God for the burial mound and whoever's buried there," said Caradoc, exhaling slowly. "And thank God for his book."

"Thank God," echoed Elinor, slumping back in her chair.

Merry sat straight-backed, looking ahead, seeing not the walls of her kitchen but the upturned oak, the chest, and the book hidden inside. As if the earth had offered it up like a gift.

But she had the feeling even then that some gifts come at a price.

Chapter Ten

➤

News of the book spread quickly. Elinor told their nearest neighbors the Joneses. Mrs. Jones told her sister Christine, who told her best friend, Jemima, who told Mrs. Ivy, the barmaid at the Nightingale, Nanteos's pub, who told a selection of the regulars. From his guest room in the Black Castle, Dr. Philipps called his colleagues at the Museum of Wales and other experts at the British Museum and discussed the book with them, emailed them pictures he'd taken with his phone, created a veritable frisson in museums and universities around the country and beyond. Meanwhile, the Countess de Courcy, eager to discover how much such a book might fetch on the open market, telephoned two of London's leading auction houses, and told them all about it. They in turn made inquiries consulting experts and collectors around the world.

As darkness fell, the lost tale of the *Mabinogion* was anything but a secret.

Merry was in her bedroom, oblivious to all this. She was standing on the tapestry carpet in the middle of her room, holding on to her new bow as if it might give her strength, get her through the next weeks and months in which the future of the Owens' farm, *her* future, would be decided.

The Owens normally stored their bows and arrows, the ancient deeds to their land with the fourth Earl de Courcy's signature on them, and the little of value they owned in the tallboy, a massive old piece of furniture seven feet tall, that sat in the downstairs hall, but Merry had a habit of keeping every new bow in her room for a good few weeks. She'd done this since she'd been given her first bow.

Finally, she propped her bow in the corner and changed into her flannel pajamas. It was still cold at night in these parts of Wales and she always liked to sleep with the window open, letting in fresh air. But, even in her thick pj's, she shivered suddenly. Something more than cold air, a sort of sudden chill of apprehension, hit her.

Maybe she felt something of the reverberations, the ripples her book was causing, because she suddenly called to mind the warning of Dr. Philipps.

She had been keeping the book wrapped in its chest, pushed under her bed, but now she thought maybe that wasn't good enough. She lay down on the floor, pulled out the chest.

There was a loose board beneath where the chest had sat. She hadn't used it for years. When she was younger she used to hide things underneath it: a secret stash of chocolate, smooth stones she found in the river swimming with James, all the little treasures that pleased her childish mind. She remembered that and smiled and then coughed as a wave of dust tickled her nose.

The space wasn't big enough to fit the chest but it would fit the swaddled book in its plastic bag perfectly.

She hid the book, replaced the floorboard, and then put the empty chest on top of it. She felt better immediately.

She turned off her lamp, slid into bed, pulled the duvet up high, tucking it under her chin, and quickly fell asleep.

The light from a full moon slipped through a gap in the curtains, silvering the stave of Merry's new bow, which cast a shadow so long it disappeared under the bed. It was as if it crawled up to the chest, lifted the floorboard, took out the book, and leafed through it, because Merry's dreams were a mad mix of book and bow. It was as if each were a talisman, powerful in its own right, but infinitely more so together. Halfway between sleep and wakefulness, the words Dr. Philipps had translated ran through Merry's head:

"There is a cave where the green turns blue . . . only the strong pass through . . ."

The Merry of her dreams rode out, bow in her right hand, book in her left, hunting for the riddle cave. There was nothing to suggest it was the single biggest decision she would ever make, that her own life, and the lives of those she loved, would be marked by it forever.

Chapter Eleven

At five fifteen the next morning, Merry and her father set off across the dew-drenched fields, heading for the Black Wood. Neither of them spoke. Caradoc carried an Ordnance Survey map and a compass. Merry carried the tape measure they used for positioning their start point when they practiced on their longbows. Sometimes they would play with the distances, fifty yards, seventy, a hundred, the maximum range of the tape. They never thought it would be used to measure their future.

They entered the darkness of the Black Wood. The sun hadn't yet risen high enough to penetrate the forest, and father and daughter had to make their way carefully along the narrow track, avoiding the overhanging branches reaching down from the moss-covered trees.

The awakening birds sang but Merry stayed silent. Her father paused from time to time, consulted the map, then counted out his footsteps, paused again and consulted the map. He took a pen from his pocket and made notations on the map. As the light grew stronger, Merry could make out the swath of a yellow highlighter pen that marked the boundary between their land and the de Courcys'.

She could see from her father's annotations that they were getting perilously close to it.

Then at last, there was the dark mass of the burial mound and the stranded roots of the old oak. Caradoc Owen took one end of the tape measure from Merry. He checked his map again, checked his compass, marched forward thirty paces till he came to the mound, marked the map again. Merry paused, watched his back, felt the breath catch inside her.

He walked back to her, spooling the tape in, his face impassive, then he broke into a huge beaming smile. Merry threw herself into his open arms, felt them come around her tight, holding her close. She just stood there for a while and breathed.

"Ninety yards, by my reckoning," Caradoc said, releasing her and holding her at arm's length. "I could be out by twenty or so. Maybe as much as forty or fifty, but it's ours, *cariad*. It's definitely ours."

And Merry felt a lightening in her chest, and a warm wash of relief flood through her. Their problems weren't over yet, but at least now they knew they had a chance.

At eleven o'clock sharp, there was an officious knock at the front door. Merry and her parents, who'd been sitting in silence at the table, all got to their feet and exchanged a quick look, of hope, worry, and wariness. Gawain was lying in his playpen, kicking his heels in the air while attempting to eat his fingers, happily oblivious to the tension in his sister and parents.

Caradoc opened the door, studied the man standing there.

Merry walked up behind her father.

"You must be Caradoc Owen. I'm Professor Parks," said the man.

Her father nodded, gripped the man's hand. "Please come in."

Merry noticed Parks wincing. Her father's handshakes were notorious. He simply did not know his own strength. Or maybe he did.

"Miss Owen," said Parks with a nod as he walked into their house.

"Professor Parks," replied Merry.

The three of them sat at the breakfast table. Elinor had disappeared upstairs to put Gawain to bed for his morning nap.

"So," began Caradoc, "you'd like to excavate our burial mound?"

Parks nodded. He kept his face impassive this time, no sign of yesterday's gleam.

"I would," he replied briskly. "It's logical that there are more artifacts buried there. Those artifacts will be doubly valuable, first of all in and of themselves, and secondly in helping to authenticate the book itself. They will tell the book's backstory, they will help us date it and identify who is buried there. Researching that in turn will help with the authentication process."

Caradoc nodded. "That makes sense."

"I'm glad you think so," replied Professor Parks. "You see, there's a chain of events here, and your daughter, if I may say so, was spectacularly lucky to make her find in the seemingly effortless way that she did, but now we need to follow it up with weeks of painstaking work."

"Wouldn't it be faster if you worked in a team?" asked Elinor, appearing at the doorway. "I'm Mrs. Owen," she added. Professor Parks turned his gaze onto Merry's mother. Merry could see him taking in her beauty and the casual way she wore it, even in her paint-spattered overalls.

"It would if I could find a team of the highest caliber," he replied. "I've found through bitter experience it's often better in the long run, albeit more time-consuming, to work alone." He turned back to Caradoc. "So, Mr. Owen, would you be amenable to my conducting a dig on your land? Did your daughter explain that we would split the proceeds of anything new I find fifty-fifty?"

"She did. She also said that your excavations would help increase the value of the book."

Parks nodded. "That is correct."

"Any idea what the book might be worth?" asked Elinor.

Parks paused, and his eyes took on that distant gleam again. "There are private collectors who would sell their mother for such an artifact," he replied.

Elinor gave a snort. "I hope not."

"We wouldn't want to see it go to a private collector anyway," observed Caradoc. "This book belongs in a Welsh museum."

"You'd get much less for it, then. Still a substantial sum, though, especially if they had time to raise the necessary funds."

"Over sixty thousand pounds?" asked Caradoc.

"Quite possibly."

"Very good," replied Caradoc. "How long might that take?"

Parks gave him a sharp look. "Are you in a hurry? Digs take time. The whole authentication process takes time."

"In that case, you'd better get started," cut in Elinor.

"I take it, then, that you are happy for me to proceed with the excavation on the terms I suggested?" continued Parks.

Elinor, her husband, and Merry all exchanged a quick glance. Twenty-one generations of Owens had lived at Nanteos Farm for nearly seven hundred years. Losing it was unthinkable. If doing a deal with Professor Parks was the price to pay, they all had no doubt it was a price worth paying.

"Yes," replied Caradoc. "We are. Merry, would you be kind enough to show Professor Parks to the burial mound?"

Chapter Twelve

Merry and Parks walked out to his car. Parks opened the trunk and took out a huge backpack. He shouldered it, tightened the straps, looked expectantly at Merry.

"Shall we?"

She eyed his backpack as they set off down the valley toward the forest. Merry's second visit of the morning. "What's in there?" she asked.

"Tools for digging. Sterile containers for finds. A bodysuit so I don't contaminate the site."

Merry got the clear impression that this was some kind of reprimand to her. What was she supposed to have done? Left the chest where it was and called him in like Ghostbusters?

"How long d'you think the dig will last?" she asked, wondering how long she could stand this man—even though his presence was crucial—and how long it would take before they could sell the book.

"May I assess it all first, thoroughly, before I give you an ill-considered answer?" Parks replied.

Merry shrugged, veiled her irritation, increased her pace.

Parks didn't even break a sweat, despite the weight of his pack. "Where would you recommend I stay in the area?" he asked, oblivious to her annoyance. "I was meant to leave the Black Castle yesterday, but with all the drama, I stayed on another night. I'll need to move on today, though," he added.

"The Nightingale Arms in Nanteos," replied Merry. "They've got a few rooms over the pub and the food's good."

"Marvelous. I'll ring them later," replied Parks. "Thanks, Merry," he added, flashing her what was clearly meant to be a charming smile.

Merry was unmoved. "Hm," she replied.

They walked the rest of the way in silence.

Merry slowed as they neared the mound. The huge tree looked like the fallen on a battlefield.

Merry stopped beside it, looked down into the hole in the earth where she had found the chest. A breeze grazed her cheek, cold and sharp. *Hello, chieftain*, she said in her mind. *Forgive me.*

"I found it down there," she told Parks. "The rest you know."

"I do indeed," he replied, eyes never leaving the site. "Thank you, Miss Owen."

"One thing," said Merry.

"What's that?"

"What about whoever's buried there?"

"What about them?" Parks glanced at her with barely concealed impatience.

"What will you do with them?"

"Well, excavate them, of course!"

"And re-bury them?"

Parks narrowed his eyes. "What, d'you think it's an ancestor of yours, lying down here? Are you worried he'll come after you in retribution for disturbing his grave, taking his treasure?"

"Who knows," replied Merry.

"Let me put your mind at rest," replied Parks, all friendly condescension now. "Whoever is buried there is, how shall I put this delicately, a man of importance, a lord, a chieftain. Your family, as I understand it, were peasant farmers, skilled with a bow admittedly, but peasants nonetheless, who parlayed their skill into a smallholding. Whoever is down here is *not* from your past."

"Thank you for that," replied Merry, her sarcasm sliding off Parks's thick skin.

"My pleasure. Happy to put your mind at rest." Parks shrugged off his pack. "Now, Miss Owen, if you don't mind, I'd like to be left alone. I don't work well with an audience."

Reluctantly, Merry walked away. Parks was wrong. He had not put her mind at rest. He had spoken aloud her fears, brought them from the shadowy realm of half-realized nighttime worries into the full glare of day. She could not shake the feeling that there would be a price to pay for disturbing the chieftain's grave.

She broke into a jog, wondering with a rush of emotions just what she had set into motion. It was good, she told herself. Anything that meant saving the farm had to be.

Chapter Thirteen

When Merry got home she took the book out from its secret hiding place under her bed to reassure herself that they were doing the right thing. She opened it to the page with the picture that had so caught her attention and studied it. Something about it made her blood hum. From the second Dr. Philipps had translated the words, Merry had wondered about the riddle pool, its secrets and treasures. Now, with her family's desperate need for money, there was even more reason to go seeking those treasures. She didn't think about *the many who had died.* Instead she thought about *the strong who had passed through.* She was strong, she was fit, she was young. She wasn't naive enough to think that bad things could never happen to her. She knew too well that they could, but competing with that awareness was the strain of boldness that ran through her. Merry loved risk-taking, thrived on adrenaline, yearned for adventure.

That side won out over caution every time.

She put away her book again. Safely hidden. Out of sight but in no way out of mind.

She had to wait until late afternoon to go searching for the pool. She had a less-than-cheery family lunch, then her parents and Gawain set off for the antiques shop in Brecon, hoping to sell some family heirlooms to pay that month's mortgage.

Merry watched them drive off. Desperate to get away from the farm and all its worries, she set off into the fields to find Jacintha.

She looked up at the summits of the Beacons. The limestone of which the mountains and valleys were made had fissured and cracked over the millennia into hundreds of sinkholes and caves. There were some large waterfalls on the mountains, tumbling off the cliff faces. She could head up on the Roman road, Sarn Helen, and explore there, but there were far more waterfalls on the lower slopes, hidden by the thick forests that stretched over the common lands. It was even known as waterfall country. If she were to find the riddle pool, she felt sure it would be here.

She found Jacintha in one of the far fields, gave her a handful of oats, scratched her behind her ears for a bit, then hooked a rope onto her halter, fashioning it into reins.

"Time for an outing," she whispered; then, with a hand on her pony's withers, she vaulted on. Bareback, she guided Jacintha through the gate.

As she hacked across the fields, it began to rain, horribly and heavily. Trying to ignore it, Merry rode along the narrow paths, regularly dismounting where the gnarly roots from ancient trees made trips and barriers and traps. Under the onslaught of the rain, it was slow. Jacintha managed to pick her way along safely enough, but Merry slipped a few times and ended up muddied and sore. It almost felt as if nature were trying to keep her out.

She found lots of waterfalls and many pools, but no green turning blue, no shimmering earth, no cave that lay veiled behind the falls. Nothing that matched the riddle pool.

She'd just go out again tomorrow, widen her search. She'd go alone again, she decided. For some reason, this was something she didn't want to share with James, and besides, she was sure he had secrets of his own.

She wondered what he was doing. She pulled out her phone, protected in its waterproof cover, and tapped out a text to him.

What you up to? Everyone's out, want to come round?

She sent the text but there was no answering ping.

Ten minutes later, the rain turned to snow, as it so often did in the mountains, even in spring, and Merry forgot about her phone. By the time she got home an hour later, she was chilled to the bone, her fingers and face numb.

She didn't want to turn her pony out into the fields when Jacintha was still warm from exercise. So she rubbed her down, dried her with a towel, and left her with food and water in one of the old stables. The rest of the herd were fine to stay out. Welsh Mountain ponies were tough and hardy, well used to extreme conditions.

She ran to the house. No sign of the Land Rover. Her parents and brother were out there somewhere in the snow . . . they'd have to cross the high pass to get back from Brecon, that remote, barren road between the peaks where the winds howled with a peculiar savagery, where the snow drifted deep, where a breakdown or a skid could be fatal.

Fingers still numb, struggling against the wind, Merry battled to pull open the door to the boot room. She blew inside with a gust of wind and snow. She turned and leaned her whole body against

64

the door, heaving it closed again. Inside, she quickly made herself a hot chocolate to warm up, then, curling her fingers around the mug, she picked up the phone and called her mother. It rang and rang. No reply. She bit her lip and tried not to worry. Then her own phone rang. It was James.

"Hi."

"Hi. What's up? Where are you?" asked Merry.

"In Manchester."

"What the heck are you doing in Manchester?"

There was a pause and when James next spoke, he couldn't hide the excitement in his voice.

"You know I told you I played in the National Schools Final . . ."

"And scored the winning goal," declared Merry.

"Well, apparently, there was a Manchester United scout there. He rang my school yesterday, asked the coach if I'd be interested in having a tryout. The coach rang me straight away. I set off early this morning, leaving a note for my parents. They'd never have let me go if I'd asked them. So here I am!"

"Manchester United?" spluttered Merry.

"Yes!" declared James. "Anything is possible! Remember?"

"I remember, all right! God, James. Have you had the tryout?" She couldn't begin to imagine how he must have felt: excited, terrified, stunned . . .

"Just come out of it."

"And? Tell me, the suspense is killing me!"

James laughed in delight. "They've asked me if I can train with them for a couple of weeks and after that we'd have a discussion. About signing with the junior academy!"

"But that's amazing, James!" Merry yelled. She danced around the kitchen, phone in her hand. She felt a massive swell of pride, of joy for her friend bubbling up inside her. There was just one dampener. "What about your parents?"

"Yeah. Officially not happy. Try 'livid, let down, and deceived,' in their words."

"Try congratulations!" protested Merry.

"'Hmm, yeah, well, the only saving grace is the snow!" James sounded delirious. "I'm stuck here. Snowed in! There's this other guy who's sixteen, Huw, he's on the team. He said I can stay with him. Don't have much choice. All the buses and trains are canceled. Roads blocked too."

The house phone rang. Merry glanced at the number.

"Gotta go. It's my mother. Stay safe, have fun. And well done, James! That really is beyond brilliant. And you deserve it. You really do."

She hung up and grabbed the house phone. The moment to share her secret about searching for the riddle pool had come and gone, and besides, it seemed so small in comparison to James's revelation. Hers was just a vague quest.

"Mam! I was getting worried."

"Don't be. We're fine. But I think we'll have to stay in Brecon with your aunt Jenni."

"Okay . . ."

"I don't like leaving you alone."

"Mam, I'm nearly sixteen. I'll be fine!"

"You could go and stay with Seren."

Merry was fond of Seren and her adult son, Nat, but she'd enjoy having the house to herself for a change, peace and quiet and no one to account to. Plus, Seren and Nat could both read her far too well. They'd have heard about the book like everyone else in the valley, and they'd want to quiz her. It was hard to keep secrets from those two.

"I'm nice and comfy here. I'll be fine, Mam, honestly."

"Well, make yourself something nice for dinner, then. And lock the doors!"

"I'll lock the doors. I promise."

But distracted by thoughts of James and Manchester United, making dinner, obsessing about the riddle pool's location, and worrying about the chieftain's possible reaction to Parks's digging around in his grave, Merry forgot all about her promise.

She snuggled down in her bed, snow scything through the blackness, the wind rocking the cottage, oblivious to the fact that she'd left the doors unlocked.

Chapter Fourteen

Merry awoke with the sure sense that *something* had awoken her. Not the sound of the wind screaming or the windows creaking, but a deliberate, unnatural sound. Her skin tingled with a kind of charge, like the electricity of another person, the nearness of them, or their glance, sliding over you. She opened her eye, blinked in the darkness, heart pounding.

She reached out, making sure she didn't knock over her glass of water, and grabbed her Maglite flashlight. She always kept it handy, as blackouts were common. It was heavy and powerful and a good weapon. With a quick pulse of terror at what she might see, she switched it on.

No one. Nothing out of place. Her bedroom looked normal. Her door wasn't closed, but ajar, with an inch or two of space, just as she'd left it. But something was different. A disturbance in the air. An echo that lingered in the memory banks of her mind: a sound like a drawer opening and closing, slowly, softly, covertly.

Brandishing her flashlight, she got out of bed. She thought later that she should have just pulled the covers up over her head, but that wasn't her way. *Never turn from a challenge*, said her father's voice in her head. Maybe it had been her parents and Gawain, she thought, returning home after all. She glanced at her clock. Four thirty. Not a chance.

Holding her breath, heart pounding, she crossed her bedroom, feet soft on the wooden floor. Then one of the floorboards creaked as she put her weight on it, and, from downstairs, she thought she heard another creak above the roar of the wind.

She pushed open her door, sidled into the hallway, scanning the darkness with the beam of her flashlight. Everything looked normal. Down the stairs, step by step, down to the phone she had left on the kitchen table. *Call for help*, said the voice in her head. But downstairs was where whoever it was lurked . . .

Another step, and another, breath trapped in her throat with a lump of fear that grew with each second. And then a waft of pure cold and a click. The bottom step . . . the open hallway was before her, but there was no one. Not a hint of anyone, not there or in any of the rooms. Merry hurried through each one, checking wardrobes, the pantry, the broom cupboard.

There was no sign of any disturbance, just that buzz in the air.

But Merry, with her limited vision, didn't see the tiny patches of damp on the hall rug that stood by the front door, the melted flakes of snow that had blown through in that quick second while the door had opened and closed again.

Last, she checked the boot room. Clear. She bit her lip, glanced around, peered through the window into the snow-strewn darkness outside. She thought she saw something moving, a large shape. She pulled on her boots, her hat, her long down coat. She pushed open the door, aimed the flashlight.

It was Jacintha, sheltering under a tree in the garden, shaking snow from her mane. How the heck had she gotten out of her stable? wondered Merry. Hadn't she secured the bolt properly? Or had the wind worked it free? Was that what she had heard? The banging of the stable door?

Concern for her pony trumped her earlier fears. She shut the house door behind her and hurried over to her pony.

"Hey, Jac. You little escape artist. Let's get you back inside again."

She took hold of her pony's halter and, leaning in against the pummeling wind, she led her from the garden, across the concrete forecourt and toward the stables. A great bang sounded and Merry saw the stable door thud shut. She walked Jacintha up to it, pulled it open, sheltered her pony inside.

Her fingers stuck to the icy metal as she pushed home the bolt. She made sure it was all the way in. She'd been so cold when she stabled Jacintha hours earlier, maybe she just hadn't secured the bolt properly?

She shivered again, cold despite her layers, but chilled too by leftover fear. She turned and hurried back toward the farmhouse. But she was moving too fast and suddenly her feet shot from under her as she skidded on the ice-covered concrete. She fell awkwardly, putting out her hands to brace her fall, let go of the flashlight, which clattered to the ground. And went out.

Darkness closed around her. Merry felt a pulse of fear. She pushed herself up, blinked, wiped the snow from her face. She should have waited until her eye adjusted to the night, but she was scared and cold and desperate to get back inside, so she hurried on, hardly seeing where she was going. And then she hit something, or something hit her, slicing through the air, and she was falling again, too hard, too fast. With a thud, she fell backward against the ground.

Her head hit first. The blow knocked her unconscious. The snow spiraled down, covering her.

Merry awoke with a blaze of pain. Cold pain burning her. She let out a low moan, pushed herself to sitting. Had to get inside, in the warm. She got up, walked very slowly, on shaking legs. The snow still fell and the wind still howled. She walked, hands before her, checking for obstacles. The house was fifty yards away, but this was a route she should have known blindfolded. She blundered through the snow, and then there was the dark bulk of her house, looming through the blizzard.

Almost sobbing with relief, she yanked open the back door, got inside, pushed the door shut.

This time she locked it.

Still wearing her boots and her sodden clothes, turning on lights as she went, she hurried to the front door, locked that too. She climbed the stairs, went into the bathroom, ran the bath, hot tap only.

Shivering violently while it filled, she ran through her home, turning on every light. How could she have been so stupid? she chided herself. No one was there. No one in their right mind would be out on a night like this. Nor could they be. All the roads were impassable. Nothing had been disturbed. Money lay in plain sight on the hall desk where her father had left it. Silver photo frames stood untouched. *The book!* she thought then, panic gripping her. She fell to the floor in her bedroom, pulled out the chest, hauled up the floorboard, dragged out the plastic bag. And there was her book, safe and wholly undisturbed. Fingers shaking, she replaced it, hauled back the chest.

It had all been her imagination, that and her failure to secure the stable door properly. Nothing but her own fault. It must have been a gust of wind that pummeled into her, or maybe a broken branch, flying through the air, knocking her over. She could have died of hypothermia out there in the blizzard. Her parents would have returned to find her frozen body. Stiff and blue and dead. She let out another sob, then, leaving all the lights blazing, as if that way she could keep the darkness at bay, she lay down in the scalding bath.

A trick of her body made the water feel cold against her freezing skin. Only when she swirled it around her could she feel its warmth. She lay there, letting out water as the bath cooled, refilling it with hot water again until, finally, she had stopped shaking. She got out, quickly toweled herself dry, put on her warmest pajamas, turned on her heated blanket, and got into her bed. Through the haze of exhaustion and relief, her mind turned in on itself, posing the same questions over and over. Was it the chieftain's ghostly spirit, a living, breathing thief, or just a figment of her imagination?

Chapter Fifteen

>>>————————————→

The next morning there was an odd, sinister silence. No birdsong, no wind, just a kind of muffled, dense quiet. No Gawain, chortling or yelling. It was like the world was dead and she was the only survivor. Merry pushed off her duvet, pulled on her eye patch, and hurried across the wooden floor of her bedroom. Everything ached.

She drew back her thin cotton curtains and gazed out. White, everywhere. She squinted. The blizzard had stopped, but light snow still drifted down. In the distance, the Beacons loomed, snow-shrouded, with horizontal striations of rock drawn like gray pencil lines down the white. Spindrifts of snow blew off the summits like smoke from a frozen fire. The mountains looked bigger than usual, beautiful but menacing. This was their cold face. And it often brought death. To unwary climbers caught on the summits, to newborn lambs and their old mothers. So nearly to her if she hadn't come around in time.

Merry shivered, pulled on thick socks and her fleece dressing gown, and headed downstairs. She went through into the boot room and opened the back door. A good two feet of snow was piled up behind it and she had to put her shoulder against the door and push.

The cold stung her nose. Snowflakes blew in and coated her eyelashes. She blinked them away, gazed out at the fields. It looked like a foot of snow had fallen. Huge drifts lay banked against the hedgerows. She felt like she'd been transported to a different place. It even smelled different. The damp bracken scent of the Beacons, the grassy, muddy whiff of the fields had gone, replaced by the crisp, metallic tang of snow. She saw no sign of footprints. Told herself that she wouldn't have even if there had been any. The snow would have covered them.

She closed the door, hurried back to the warmth of the kitchen, busied herself at the Aga stove, pouring milk into the saucepan, whisking in generous helpings of chocolate powder, melting it in, getting the cream, adding a swirl. It was a snowstorm, just a snowstorm and a poorly secured barn door.

The phone rang, making her jump. Her mother.

She took a deep breath, blew it out, rubbed her face, pasted on a smile even though her mother could not see her.

"Hi, Mam!"

"Hi, Spinner. You okay? Everything all right last night?"

"I'm fine, thanks, Ma. Just woke up. Making myself some hot chocolate. How're you guys?"

"Oh, we're fine. I was just a bit worried about you is all."

"Well, don't be." She wouldn't tell her mother about what had happened. She wasn't even sure herself. No point worrying her parents unnecessarily.

"Listen, the snowplows're out but it'll take them a good day to clear the snow and it's still falling. We're going to be stuck here till tomorrow at the earliest. You're going to be on your own for another night."

Merry felt a stab of fear. She looked at the boot room door. *Lock it!*

"I'm really sorry, love," her mother added, into the silence.

"Ma, really, I'm fine!" Merry belted out too forcefully, overcompensating. "I'll go to Seren's if I feel in need of company or better food than I can concoct," she said, voice softer, trying to make up for it.

"Please do," said her mother, slightly stiffly.

"Promise. Now, I've gotta go, Ma. Got to break the ice on the troughs and take out hay."

The warmth came back into her mother's voice. "Merry, you're an angel. Don't know what we'd do without you."

Her words, rather than comforting Merry, sent a tremor through her.

"Love you. Bye."

Merry hung up. And froze. She stared at the tallboy. They kept it locked. *Always.* They kept the key in a blue glass vase. *Always.*

But there it was, in the lock.

A current of pure terror washed through Merry. She ran to the door, locked it, stood with her back against it breathing hard. It wasn't her imagination. Somebody *had* been in here last night.

Navigated his or her way through the darkness and the cold and the snow, pushed in through an unlocked door, entered the house while she slept. She rushed across to the tallboy, checked through it, hands shaking. Nothing had been taken. They'd fled empty-handed.

She knew without any doubt what they'd been looking for: her book. The fact that they'd ignored anything else of value proved that.

A thief had come, someone who wasn't put off by blizzards and subzero temperatures. Who wasn't put off by the fact that Caradoc

Owen, a trained, seasoned killer from his years in the special forces, should have been at home. Unless, of course, they'd been watching the farmhouse, seen that Caradoc had left but had not returned.

Merry sat down at the kitchen table, drank her now cold chocolate. She stared at the stove. She knew she should cook something but she had no appetite. She got up, sat down again. Paralyzed by indecision.

She was in danger. The thief could still be watching, might come back. But she had to go out and tend to the ponies. As she so often did when she was frightened or lost or challenged, she conjured her father's voice.

If you can, run. If you can't run, then fight. But fight clever. Fight dirty.

She'd think, she'd plan, she'd fight dirty. She'd neutralize that danger. But first of all, she had to go out. She would not call her parents back, tell them about the invasion of their home, steal her mother's peace of mind, trip the safety on her father's hair-trigger readiness for a fight. She would not ring James, secretly confide in him, ask for his help. She'd face this alone. She would *not* be trapped in her house by fear.

She pulled on her warmest boots, down coat, hat, and gloves, and she took from the chest of drawers in the boot room the present her father had given her for her thirteenth birthday. A flick knife. It was a typical Caradoc Owen gift: unique, useful, and, to gentler minds, wholly inappropriate. But not on a farm, where there were always a hundred uses for a knife: twine on bales of hay to cut, snagged ropes to free, feed bags to slice open. And now there was another use.

Merry slipped the knife into her pocket. Would she ever be able to stab someone? she wondered, as she unlocked the door, stepped out into the dazzling whiteness, locked the door behind her. She hoped it would never come to that. Another voice slipped into her mind: *Survival has rules of its own.* She jolted. Where had *that* come from?

She headed out into the falling snow. Wondering if there were eyes watching her even now, she looked over her shoulder, turned in circles, scanned the bushes in the garden, peered behind corners, checking. Rechecking. But there was no one around. No footprints, just the smooth untrampled snow, and her.

She released Jacintha from her stable. The pony'd be bored alone, would welcome the company of the herd, and was well able to handle the cold and the snow. But, more than that, Merry didn't want Jacintha penned up, vulnerable. When she cast her mind back, she felt pretty sure she *had* secured the stable bolt properly. She had the strongest sense that the thief had freed Jacintha to lure her outside. It hadn't been the wind that slammed the branch into her, knocking her over. It had been the thief, taking their chance, buying time to rush back into the farmhouse and finish their search for the book while she lay unconscious in the snow.

Jacintha shadowed Merry as she went to the barn, grabbed a bale of hay, and heaved it onto her back. It was as if she gauged Merry's mood, her jumpiness, and wanted to comfort her. The pony snuffled at Merry, then walked by her side as she trekked across the snow to the field where the herd huddled together.

She stopped every so often, turning circles. Saw no one. She dumped the bale of hay, pulled out her knife, and released the safety, and with a satisfying click, the blade sprang open. She cut the twine and pulled free armfuls of hay, scattering it on the rick for the grateful ponies. She closed the blade, grasped the hilt firmly, and used it to break the ice on the frozen troughs.

She headed back to the farmhouse. Still no sign of anyone, no movement in her peripheral vision. But she took no comfort from that.

Inside, she drank coffee, warmed up, then set to cleaning the cottage, top to bottom. She broke for lunch, forced down a bowl of soup and three pieces of toast covered with peanut butter; then she finished cleaning. Still the time crawled. She felt sick. She decided to bake. She made cupcakes, forty-eight of them. She put them in the oven. She paced. She listened. Swore. She felt like a caged animal. She peered out. It had stopped snowing at last.

If anyone was still out there, waiting, she'd give them something to watch.

She layered up with loose, flexible fleeces, unlocked the tallboy, took her bow, grabbed her quiver, and headed out.

She removed the tarpaulin from the straw target, strode back seventy paces. She didn't turn circles this time, not wanting to appear a victim, as if she were scared. But she still checked. She just made it look natural, as if she were merely walking back and forth to mark a line from which she would shoot.

She had her knife in her pocket, would always carry it with her now, but the longbow was her *real* weapon.

Whoever had come into her home last night had changed something in her. Bubbling up through the fear, through the sense of vulnerability and violation, was a growing fury. Whoever had broken in, whoever had slammed her with the branch and left her lying unconscious in the snow, had declared war on her, her home, and her family.

She strung her bow, nocked an arrow, eyed the target. She took in the rings of color: white, black, red, blue, and, dead center, the golden bull's-eye. For the first time in her life, she conjured another image, replacing the straw target. She visualized a man. The faceless thief.

Then she hauled back the string and let her arrow fly. In quick succession she shot ten arrows. Every single one hit the gold. Every single one was a kill shot. In her quiver, she had kept two spare arrows. Just in case . . .

Now she turned a full circle. Not a circle of fear. Not an invitation. But a declaration of her own. She was not a helpless victim. She was a trained archer with lethal skills.

Another of her father's favorite sayings slipped into her head. He'd told her how he and his army comrades used this one when they were lost and frightened. It was their own version of the Twenty-Third Psalm: *Yea, though I walk through the valley of the shadow of death, I will fear no evil, because I am the meanest son of a gun in the valley.* Merry amended it further: *I will fear no evil, because I am the Longbow Girl.*

She headed back into the farmhouse, locked the doors behind her, pulled shut all the curtains against the darkening sky, spent the evening deep in thought. The threat was still out there, she knew that. She could and she would defend herself, but what she really needed to do was make the threat go away. Neutralize it completely. And that meant getting rid of the book as quickly as possible.

Chapter Sixteen

The next day, a thaw finished off what the snowplows had started, allowing James to head home from Manchester.

He knew it was time to face his parents. He couldn't stay in Manchester forever—at least, not yet.

He walked to the station, took a train, then a bus, and walked again from the center of Nanteos, up the road, across the de Courcy parkland, into the Black Castle. It would have been so much easier to have driven, he thought to himself. Illegal, but easier.

Like many children who lived on farms, James had learned to drive way below the legal age. He considered himself a good driver. It was just the law that prevented him driving on public roads. He couldn't wait for his sixteenth birthday in a few weeks, let alone his seventeenth. To be able to get a job, *the* job . . . fund himself, drive, be independent. But in the meantime, he had to deal with his parents as best he could. He arrived home and headed straight for his father's muniments room, where he felt sure his father would be locked away with Parks and Philipps, deep in documents.

He paused outside when he heard the raised voices.

"Heard that the Owens are in some kind of financial difficulty. Falling behind with mortgage payments," his father was saying.

James froze.

"How d'you know that?" his mother asked.

"Bank manager tipped me off," replied his father. "Said if something doesn't come up, they might have to sell."

James recoiled in horror. The Owens losing their farm? It was unthinkable. Did Merry know? And was this because of the stallion?

"I imagine in that case," came Dr. Philipps's voice, "that they would want to sell the book. I'd heard the farm has been in their hands for over seven hundred years," he said gently, his voice laced with sympathy.

"Yes," replied his mother. "But interestingly, *not long enough!*" she declared, sounding oddly triumphant.

"What's your point, darling?" asked his father. "You're up to something, aren't you?"

His mother gave a little chuckle. "Well, how long they've had the land is rather crucial, when you think about it. You reckon the book comes from the twelve hundreds, Dr. Philipps?"

"That is my estimate, Lady de Courcy, but I would like to do some more testing back in the laboratory," replied the historian.

"Professor Parks, do you have a view?" continued his mother.

"I'll have more of a view after I've carried out a full excavation of the site, Lady de Courcy," said Parks. "It's still covered with snow. I cannot resume until it is fully thawed."

"Hmm," replied his mother. That wasn't the answer she was seeking.

James clenched his fists. He could hardly believe what he was hearing.

"Let's just go with Dr. Philipps's view for the time being, shall we?" his mother went on. "That the book dates from the twelve hundreds. That means that when it was placed in the burial mound that land belonged to *us*, to the de Courcys, *not* to the Owens. They did not get their mitts on the land until Crécy in 1346. So, legally, the book is ours. In which case they cannot sell it to save their farm . . . in which case *we* can buy the farm when they are forced to sell and *we* can get back our lands!" she declared triumphantly.

"It's an interesting idea," mused his father.

James's disbelief turned to outrage.

"I don't think it's that simple," came Professor Parks's voice. "Although the book likely dates from the twelve hundreds, it could have been placed within the burial mound at any time thereafter."

"Could doesn't mean *would*," his mother was saying. "That book belongs to—"

James had heard enough. He flung open the door and stormed in. "Why can't you leave the Owens alone, Ma?" he demanded. "They have little enough, but what they do have you can't help wanting to take. Their book. Their *home*?"

His mother opened her mouth to say something, then seemed to think better of it and closed it again.

"The prodigal son returns," remarked his father drily, eyeing James up and down. His father was immaculate in one of his tailored tweed suits. James wore sweatpants and a Manchester United hoodie.

His mother stepped toward James, but then stopped at a look from her husband.

Professor Parks and Dr. Philipps exchanged a look of their own.

"If you'll excuse us," said Dr. Philipps. "Time to pack."

The two men diplomatically excused themselves, closing the door softly behind them, leaving James alone with his parents.

"Manchester United. The soccer club, *really*?" continued his father, voice laced with scorn.

"Is that all you want to talk about when Merry and her family are facing ruin?" James demanded, emotions raging inside him.

"You are my primary concern," replied his father. "So I ask you again. *Manchester United?*"

"Yes," said James, struggling for calm. "Manchester United. The Premier League club. Most people's dream. My dream."

"Consorting with that feral, one-eyed girl, leaping to her defense," spluttered the countess. "It's not appropriate, James. She's a bad influence on you. She's encouraging you in this soccer madness, I'm sure!"

"My friendship with Merry is none of your business," replied James through clenched teeth. He glowered at his mother. Much as he loved her, the way she behaved toward the Owens and spoke of Merry filled him with shame, and rage.

"If I were you, I'd concern yourself less with Merry and her family and the book and more with behaving in a manner befitting the lord and heir of the Black Castle," declared his father.

"That's the point, isn't it?" James said. "You're *not* me."

He turned and made for the door.

"We'll have a full and frank discussion about this on holiday in Bali," called his father. "Don't think for a second this is over."

James walked out before he could say anything he'd regret, hurrying through the hallways, climbing the stairs two at a time, barely glancing at where he was going, as he rushed through the home he felt sure he was going to lose. The threat had hung in the air, underneath his father's words: the estate or soccer. He felt an odd lightness steal over him as he made his choice. It was easy for him, he realized with a savage pang. But across the valley, Merry had no choice.

Upstairs in his room, he called her.

She picked up almost immediately.

"Hi, what you up to?" he asked, trying to push down all his emotions.

"Not a lot. Waiting for the snow to melt. You back home?"

He wondered if she knew about her family's predicament or was just covering it up.

"Yep," he said slowly, blowing out a breath. "I am. And deep in it."

"I'll bet," said Merry darkly. "Listen," she said, her voice brightening. "I need to hear about Man U, about your tryout, about everything!"

"I can't wait to tell you, but that's not why I'm calling." He wouldn't tell her about what he'd heard about her home, but he had to warn her about his mother's attempts to get the book and stake another claim on the Owens' land. Selling it quickly to someone else looked like the Owens' only way out of trouble.

He paused, trying to think of the best way to say it. Merry, ever impatient, jumped in.

"Look. I was going to call you anyway," she said. "Are Dr. Philipps and Professor Parks still there?"

"Yes," replied James. "They are, but they've just gone to pack."

"Keep them there," said Merry urgently. "Tell them to stay put. I want to discuss my book with them." She paused. "Will I be allowed in?"

"Oh, you will be. Flavor of the month now, aren't you, with your book," he managed to say. "Look, Merry. Er, I think you should sell Dr. Philipps your book."

"Why?" she asked, the edge of suspicion in her voice.

"Oh. Just because then everyone could see it, if it's in a museum," he said, hoping he'd sounded casual enough.

There was a silence, then Merry laughed. "Funnily enough, I agree with you."

James felt a flood of relief wash over him, but he couldn't help wondering: What had made her change her mind?

Chapter Seventeen

→

Merry dug out the book from its hiding place. She sat cross-legged on the floor, holding it gently in her lap. She turned the beautiful pages carefully, gazing at the lavish images, then turning back to the riddle pool.

The dark pool reflecting clouds overhead, the sunlight arrowing through the water, the thicket of bushes, the nightingale watching from the oak . . . She didn't need the book to find the riddle pool. The image was seared into her mind. When she went to sleep at night, she saw it there . . .

She shut the book, wrapped it away safely in its swaddling, placed it inside its chest.

"Good-bye, beautiful book," she whispered. "I can't help thinking I was meant to find you, that there's something in you just for me, but I can't keep you."

She thought of her mother, of her baby brother. They weren't safe. And, despite her exhibition with her longbow, she wasn't either. Her father would obliterate anyone who threatened any of them, but he couldn't be around 24-7.

She thought of the chieftain, hoped he'd be at peace with her decision. But really, she thought as she squeezed the chest into a plastic bag and let herself out, locking the door behind her, what choice did she have?

She set off through the thawing fields. No tunnel this time. She climbed the boundary wall, walked straight across the parkland, up to the massive stone face of the Black Castle.

James was waiting for her on the drawbridge. He looked pale, thought Merry, and she could feel a current of emotion running through him like electricity. Soccer, she guessed, and his parents' threats.

They smiled at each other.

"Hi."

"Hi." She punched his arm. "Congrats, superstar."

"I'm not there yet."

"My money's on you."

"Thanks," he said softly. "But first things first. They're all waiting for you. It's a tad tense. Just had a bit of an argument, to put it mildly, but I interrupted Parks and Dr. Philipps in their packing. They'll help keep it civilized."

"Don't leave me alone in there," Merry whispered, feeling suddenly nervous. She had to pull this off, and cleverly.

James gave a grim smile that puzzled her. "Don't worry. I'll be there."

"What did they say about you, about Manchester United?" Merry asked him as they walked across the cobbled courtyard.

"They said we'll talk about it in Bali. Annual family holiday in the sun," he said with unconcealed misery. He didn't mention what they'd said about Merry. That was the last thing she needed to hear, and what she hadn't heard wouldn't hurt her.

Merry could imagine the scene. Sunscreen, coconuts, harsh words.

"When are you off?" she asked.

James glanced away. "Tomorrow," he mumbled. "As soon as Alicia's school holiday starts. We'll pick her up from boarding school on the way to Heathrow. But I might not go," he said, turning back to Merry.

"What d'you mean? You'll just refuse?"

"Pretty much. I mean, I don't actually want to go. I don't want to have those endless discussions."

"What do you want, then?"

"I want to move to Manchester. Carry on training. Try and get a contract."

Merry blew out a breath. "Wow! When will you decide?"

"Tonight. I'll make up my mind, one way or another."

"Call me when you do."

James nodded. "I will. Keep your phone on you, then. You're always off somewhere forgetting it."

"Promise," replied Merry.

In the muniments room, the earl and the countess, Merry and James, Professor Parks and Dr. Philipps stood in a circle, peering down at her book. Merry wasn't sure what the countess was doing there. She didn't think James's mother was remotely interested in books.

Merry turned to Dr. Philipps. "I've been thinking, about what you said about my keeping the book, about it not being safe."

He eyed her speculatively.

"How about if I sell it to you?" she asked. "Now."

He blinked. "Well . . . goodness! The Museum of Wales would absolutely love to have it. A Welsh museum is where this book belongs, if I may say so."

Merry beamed. "Yes," she only half fibbed. "That's what I think too."

"But there's a problem."

"What?"

"Funds. Or rather, lack of funds. You see, if you can wait, say, six months, we can launch a campaign, raise money for it, give you a fair price, but at the moment we've got very little in the kitty, I'm afraid."

"Are you certain it's yours to sell?" the countess asked Merry.

"Ma!" exclaimed James, glaring at his mother.

"It's all right," Merry said to him. She needed to fight this battle on her own. She turned to the countess, stood straight and tall. The countess wore high heels, but Merry could still look down on her. "Yes, actually, I am certain," she said, her voice level but vibrating with quiet fury inside. "My father and I checked and made sure that the land where we found it is on our side of the boundary."

"And is it?" continued the countess. "I mean, you two would say that, wouldn't you?"

"Mother, you are just—" started James.

"And even if that were the case," the countess continued, voice rising high. "What if the book were placed there while *we* owned that land? Then it would be ours, *wouldn't it*?"

"Well, you cannot prove that! Can you?" countered Merry. "And we *can* prove the land is on our side. Any independent surveyor would confirm that!"

"Miss Owen is correct, I'm afraid, Lady de Courcy," said Professor Parks smoothly. "The date of the book need not by any means tally with the date it was buried. What you are suggesting is hypothesis. Not fact."

Merry felt a surge of approval for Professor Parks, an unexpected ally.

"Well, in that case," replied the countess archly, "perhaps the Black Castle can buy the book."

Merry gazed at the countess in amazement. The woman was determined not to let this go. This had turned into a battle, and one she clearly intended to win.

"Sorry," said Merry with as insincere a smile as she could muster. "It really *does* belong in a museum."

The de Courcys buying the book was the last thing she wanted. First, because she felt there was something about it; it wasn't cursed, exactly, but freighted with bad luck. She'd felt that straight off, from the time she first unwrapped it as she sat on the chieftain's grave. She didn't want it anywhere near James. And second, her father would detest the idea of the de Courcys bailing them out. He would never allow it.

"A museum really would be the most appropriate home for a treasure such as this," said Professor Parks.

"Hmph!" declared the countess, sending Merry a poisonous look before pretending to examine her red-painted nails.

"Well, that seems to have settled that," Merry managed to say. She waited a few long, agonizing moments to see if there would be another challenge. But the countess, face tight with anger, said nothing, and the earl, the Stone Man, just stood there, unreadable but mercifully silent.

Merry turned back to Dr. Philipps. "So how much do you have in the kitty?"

"Well, I'd have to talk to the bursar, but from memory, we have only a matter of seven thousand pounds in our acquisitions budget. Like I said, we could raise more, but it would take time."

"I don't have time," Merry said aloud, earning a quizzical look from James.

She needed the mortgage paid off, but even more importantly, she needed to get rid of this book and keep her family safe.

"How about this?" she said. "You're leaving later today, aren't you?"

"I am."

Merry picked up the book, thrust it at him. "Take it. Take it with you. Sign a piece of paper saying that I am selling it to the National Museum of Wales for a down payment of seven thousand pounds. As soon as you get into your office, your bursar can write out a check, and then another payment of"—Merry thought wildly, wondered what it would be worth—"sixty thousand pounds." That would pay off their mortgage with a small margin to spare, and she didn't want to be greedy. "Which is to be paid over the next twelve months," she finished.

Dr. Philipps spluttered, but held on to the book. "It's a bit unorthodox."

"Bonkers!" was the countess's verdict. "What would your parents say? You can't simply go and decide this for them. You're just a schoolgirl!"

"I can promise you," lied Merry, "that my parents will have no problem with this. In fact, they agree with me! We've discussed it."

"That is quite true," cut in Professor Parks. "We did have that exact discussion a few days ago. Caradoc Owen was quite clear. The family wants the book to go to a museum."

The countess gave a huffy little shrug.

"Sounds like a pretty good plan to me," said James. He leaned over his father's desk and picked up a fountain pen. "I can write out a contract now," he said, glancing between Dr. Philipps and Merry. "You, Professor Parks, can witness it, and Dr. Philipps and Merry can sign it."

"That," declared Merry, beaming in approval at James, "is the most wonderful idea!"

James smiled back at her. His parents said nothing, but Merry could feel the annoyance radiating from them. They'd been outmaneuvered, in public.

"Well," declared Professor Parks, "it seems that this way we keep everyone happy."

Merry nodded. Apart from James's parents. And the thief, who would find it considerably more difficult breaking into the Museum of Wales than into Nanteos Farm.

"One more condition," she said. Everyone looked at her expectantly. Merry the hard-driving businesswoman was not a side of her that anyone had ever seen. Least of all Merry herself.

"And?" queried Dr. Philipps.

"You put out a press announcement. *Now*. I don't want to be named. It needs to say this: '*The Lost Tale of the* Mabinogion,'" began Merry as Dr. Philipps pulled out his phone and began to tap, "'has been sold today, to the National Museum of Wales, with immediate effect. The museum is delighted to be in possession of this beautiful and historically important book. As from—'"

"Hold on a minute, would you please, Merry? I'm not a trained stenographer."

"'As from today's date,'" Merry continued after a suitable pause, "'the book shall reside safely at the Museum of Wales.'"

Merry waited for Dr. Philipps to finish inputting her words.

"Any more?" he asked with a smile.

"No, thank you. That covers it."

"Not very press-release-type language, if you'll forgive me for observing," murmured the earl, exchanging a look with his wife, who clearly agreed.

"Well, I'm terribly sorry," replied Merry, "but I'm just a farm girl, not a PR supremo."

She caught James's eye. He was struggling not to laugh. At least she had improved his mood.

"That's the way the language has to be," said Merry, serious now. "Word for word."

Dr. Philipps nodded. "Word for word," he agreed.

James wrote out the rest of the contract at his father's desk, conferring with Merry as he did so. "That do?" he asked at last.

She nodded. "Mhm. Very much so."

Dr. Philipps and Professor Parks read it and signed it, Parks as witness. James walked over to a large machine and made a photocopy of it.

"Keep this safe," he said, handing it to Merry. She wanted to hug him, to thank him for so coolly and smoothly helping her plan along, but she felt his parents' eyes boring into her the whole time. She'd only get him into trouble. All she could do was take the piece of paper and smile.

The deal was done. Dr. Philipps got up to leave with the book in its chest, tucked under his arm.

"Could you email me with the translation as you go through it, please?" Merry asked. "I'm still interested in the book, in what it says."

He beamed at Merry, clearly delighted to be in possession of the book.

"Of course," he said. "Happy to."

"Thanks," she replied. "Oh, and one more thing," she added, putting her hand on his arm. He looked up at her in surprise. "Don't, for any reason, be tempted to take it home. Go straight to the museum."

The man looked at her for a while, deep brown eyes shifting as he seemed to be trying to figure her out.

"That's a little melodramatic, isn't it?" intoned Professor Parks.

"A little rude, I thought," murmured the countess just loud enough to be heard.

"I am happy to oblige," replied Dr. Philipps, eyes still locked on Merry. "It was I, after all, who warned you against keeping it at your home."

Merry's whole body flushed. Could it have been him? Had she entrusted the book to the one person who had tried to steal it? She felt a sense of horror, but then another thought hit her. If it had been, she'd now made it much harder for him to steal it.

"You did," she replied. "So you'd better keep it safe," she added. "If anything happened to it, you'd be the number one suspect, wouldn't you?" she added with a smile, as if she were joking.

Chapter Eighteen

›››—————————————→

She filed out of the library with James. They said nothing as they walked down the hallway, waiting until they could be certain they would not be overheard. They paused at the sound of rapid footsteps coming up behind them. It was Professor Parks.

"Dr. Philipps wanted me to give you this," he said, eyes on Merry. He held out a sheet of paper. "He's already made a start on some of the pages he photographed on his phone." He paused. "It's all rather intriguing."

"Thanks," said Merry, holding out her hand. She took the paper from the professor. With a nod, Parks strode back to the muniments room, leaving Merry and James alone in the hallway.

They read the words together, so that they sounded like some kind of invocation:

*T*his is the tale of a warrior bold, who comes from far away, from vale of green through deadly cold, seen by bird and watcher fey. Though spoken of in stories hidden, the warrior comes when time is right. By whispered words are they now bidden, through darkness deeper than the night. The warrior saves both man and king, fighting through the deathly knell uniting foes with golden ring, this is their story, read it well . . .

"There's a lot about death, isn't there?" observed James. "I seem to remember the first bit he translated said something about *many have tried, many have died . . .*" He gave Merry a meaningful look.

"Yes," she replied vaguely. "Something like that."

"And now all this *deadly cold* and *deathly knell*."

"Mm. Let's read the next bit," said Merry quickly, hiding behind her curiosity, and they read on:

The warrior seeks the ancient path where emperor walked with queen, far away from home and hearth into realms unseen. Where legions marched with armor bright and old stones marked the way, where watchers saw who have the sight but nothing did they say. And grievers waited in their home for the warrior brave to come into their land alone from far beyond the grave.

Merry stared at the words, heart pounding. *The ancient path . . . where emperor walked with queen . . . Where legions marched.* Roman legions . . . The Roman road, Sarn Helen! It had to be! She struggled to tamp down her excitement, to keep her face bland. She felt bad, especially after James had so cleverly helped her outmaneuver his parents, but the instinct that made her think the book was dangerous made her want to keep James well away from its enchantments and riddles. *She* had no choice. She'd found it, and her family needed whatever treasures it promised. James had his own issues to deal with.

"More intrigue," she mused. "Right then, I'd better get back. And you need a chance to think. Decision time tonight."

James nodded. They walked in silence to the huge oak door, each preoccupied. James opened it for her.

"Call me! As soon as you've made up your mind," said Merry.

"I will. So keep your phone on!"

She laughed. "I never break a promise. 'Specially not to you!"

"Be careful," he said, eyes grave. "Whatever it is you're up to."

It was the first time he'd cautioned her, slowed her down. Normally they egged each other on to greater risks. Maybe he had the same instincts about the book as she did.

"Don't worry about me," she answered, trying to sound light. "I'll be fine."

Chapter Nineteen

>>>———————————————>

Merry got home five minutes before her parents.

"Those roads," exclaimed Elinor, hefting Gawain on her hip as she got him out of the car. "Still banks of snow on either side where the snowplows've been. Like the Cresta Run!"

Merry laughed. "Welcome home!" She paused. "I've got some news."

Sitting at the kitchen table ten minutes later, she told them about selling the book, showed them the contract James had written out.

Caradoc Owen opened his eyes wide. "You moved fast, didn't you?"

"Might have consulted us, darling," said her mother.

"There wasn't time," said Merry. "Dr. Philipps was leaving. I wanted to get this sorted. Sixty-seven thousand pounds, Mam! It'll pay off the mortgage!"

"Brilliant, *cariad*!" exclaimed her father, coming around and dragging Merry to her feet, crushing her in a bear hug.

"It *is* brilliant," said Elinor carefully, "but we haven't got it yet. If I understand you right," she said to Merry, "we can hope to get it within twelve months, if the museum raises enough money."

Merry nodded. She felt a flicker of irritation. Her mother *was* right, but this was a dampener they didn't need. To see her father joyous again had been wonderful, but short-lived. His smile had already faded.

"Seven thousand pounds will buy us time, but your mother's right. We're not out of trouble yet."

"Maybe we could have gotten more selling it to someone else, another museum, just waiting a while to drum up interest," said Elinor. "It seems to me that you've been a bit hasty."

"Maybe I have; maybe we could have waited and gotten more money. But I saw a chance and I took it!" she cried. Upset by her mother's criticism, worried she would say too much, Merry strode across the kitchen and walked out, slamming the door behind her.

She headed past the barn and the stables to the bench in the top field. She sat down heavily and gazed across the valley. She thought about the intruder, about him hitting her, leaving her lying in the snow just a hundred yards away. She could easily have died of hypothermia and the attacker must have known that, but he'd just left her there. That's how ruthless and psychopathic he was. All he cared about was the book, not a living, breathing person. If she told her parents about him, then they'd understand her urgency . . . but that would shatter her mother's peace of mind, send her father into a kind of dangerous vigilance, and curb her own freedoms. All for nothing. She'd gotten rid of the book. She felt sure he wouldn't come back again.

Her mother wanted more money and faster. The book spoke of treasures. Now Merry knew where to go to look for them. For some reason, it had fallen to her to protect her family, and more than that, to save their heritage, so she'd stay silent, take the flak.

She looked up to see her father walking toward her. He sat down beside her. He said nothing for a while, then he put his hand on her shoulder, turned her to face him.

"You did well, *cariad*," he said.

Merry nodded.

"Why don't you clear off for a bit, go for a ride?"

Merry smiled. "Yeah, Da. Think I just might."

Chapter Twenty

Under-exercised over the past few days, Jacintha was fresh and keen.

Merry rode across her family's fields onto the common lands, onto a short stretch of tarmacked road that took her higher up the hillside, then onto the high plain and the rough track of the old Roman road, Sarn Helen . . . *Where emperor walked with queen.*

Merry loved the story of the road, built by the Roman emperor and governor of Britain, Magnus Maximus, at the request of his wife, Helen, nearly seventeen hundred years ago. The story of Maximus's love for Helen, and how they met, was one of the stories of the *Mabinogion*.

On stormy nights, as a young girl, Merry had sat in her father's arms in the rocking chair in her bedroom, the wind whistling through the oak tree as he told her the tales. He told them so well and they felt so real that when she woke in the morning she felt as though she'd been there.

"The Dream of Macsen Wledig," Maximus's name in Welsh, was Merry's favorite tale. Macsen Wledig, emperor of Rome, dreamed one night of a lovely maiden in a far-off land. When he woke, he sent his men all over the earth to search for her. After many trials, they found her in a rich castle in Wales, daughter of a chieftain. They led the emperor to her. Everything Macsen Wledig found was exactly as in his dream. The maiden, whose name was Helen, fell in love with and married him. And he built her this road so she could travel faster and more easily to visit her family.

Feeling a pulse of excitement, Merry rode the ancient path. She couldn't quite get over it, the thought that back in the year AD 383, Helen and Macsen walked this road, shared this same view. It was as if the road were a thread of time connecting her with Helen, with Macsen, with a thousand other forgotten travelers who never made the history books.

Here be dragons, thought Merry, the line popping into her head, making her laugh. Welsh dragons, maybe . . . Riding deeper into this wilderness, it *did* feel as if she had crossed a border.

Dense forests flanked the lower hills, giving way to the sparse moorland grass on the bleak plain where the snow still lay unthawed. It was a remote, inaccessible path, a byway through the savage hills, connecting the lush valleys on either side of the pass.

After a few minutes she came up to the standing stone, Maen Llia, placed there by Neolithic people nearly five thousand years ago. It was a huge, hexagonal sliver of rock, about eleven feet tall, nearly as wide, but less than two feet thick. Her mother liked to paint pictures of the stone and they'd picnicked here a few times. Elinor had told Merry that the rock was believed to have some strange inner warmth. Merry reined in Jacintha and reached out to touch the stone. Despite being aligned north-south, despite the cold, the side of the rock was warm to her touch. Like it was alive.

This part of the Beacons had always felt mysterious to her. She was aware that there was much she didn't know about her homeland, secrets, mysteries . . . things that went beyond science and logic.

Merry urged Jacintha on farther along Sarn Helen; then she headed off the road, approaching the cleft in the valley where a shallow stream ran. She looked up, shielding her eyes against the lowering sun. It was only a small stream, not promising. She couldn't imagine it pooling into anything deep enough to swim in. But as she looked something about it caught her eye. It glistened silver against the emerald grass. She felt her blood quicken.

She rode closer. The ground grew rougher beside the stream, lots of rocks and stones, so she dismounted and led Jacintha by a long loose rein, allowing her to pick her own way. They walked higher. The air cooled. The gurgling of the running water, the sharp calls of a curlew, punctuated the rhythmic puffing of Merry and her pony.

The stream disappeared into a copse of trees. Merry reached into her backpack, took out a rope, and tethered Jacintha to a tree on the edge of the copse.

"I'll be back soon," she said, patting the mare's neck. Jacintha was warm from the effort of climbing. Merry didn't want to leave her for long or she could get chilled.

She turned and pushed her way through the bushes. Thorns scratched her hands, drawing pinpricks of blood. A bird flew overhead and landed on a high branch. But Merry was looking down, and didn't see the nightingale.

The ground sloped steeply to the unseen stream. She slipped and landed on her bottom, muddying her jeans. She got up, pushed on, emerged into a small clearing.

And there was the stream, pooling out before her, bordered by marshy, spongy grass. In which were spooling coils of color. She'd seen these before; her father had told her what they were: petroleum seeps, where liquid or gas hydrocarbons escape the lower geological layers through fractures and fissures in the rock, then slowly ooze or bubble up to the surface. He'd told her how sometimes these could ignite, burning away in an eternal flame. Early peoples thought it was the work of magic; they were drawn to these places and terrified by them. Merry suddenly thought of the *Mabinogion*, of the tree that burned on one side and was green leaf on the other. Maybe it was a petroleum seep, just like this one, burning . . .

Her heart began to pound. She reached down, touched the coils of rainbow-colored ooze, shimmering. She looked up, and off to the right, hidden from the hillside by the thicket, was a waterfall. A small one, only five feet or so, not enough to attract attention in a country with many more dazzling specimens, but the water fell perfectly straight, just like a veil.

There is a cave where the green turns blue, where the earth beside does shimmer. A veil of water guards it well, of its secrets not a glimmer.

She fell silent. She thought she felt something. A quickening of the air. Hands trembling, without thinking what she was doing, just following some sudden compulsion, she took off her boots, her muddy jeans, her helmet and eye patch, her jacket. Wearing just her T-shirt and underwear, she walked into the water.

The cold was like an assault. She forced herself on. Quickly the water deepened. And became colder still. She sank down to her chest, swam against the current to the waterfall. The water, *the veil*, was thick; it was hard to see anything beyond it. Heart racing, she dived and swam underneath the falling water. And came up into a cave.

It was dark. The water was a deep, midnight blue. Merry wished she had a headlamp. She wished she had a wet suit. She was chilled already. She knew she wasn't prepared.

There is a hole in the stone of sand at the back in the gushing flow; follow it through to another land and all treasures will you know. Twenty strokes have many tried, turning them to blue, of those venturers many have died, only the strong pass through.

She paused, swam to stay still in the running water.

Two urges warred inside her: one, never to turn from a challenge, and two, to heed her father's ruthless mantra—Proper Prior Planning Prevents Piss-Poor Performance—the creed of the SAS. She could not afford Piss-Poor Performance in the mountains with the sun going down.

But she had to find out if there was a hole in the back of the sandstone cave. There was nothing above the waterline. She sank back under the water, pushed forward in a powerful breaststroke. Her eye had adjusted and she could just about make out the back of the cave about fifteen feet away. She kicked on, fighting the current, which seemed to be getting stronger. Maybe she was getting weaker, she thought. Chilled and tired. She pushed on till she could touch the sandstone wall at the back of the cave. Rising up out of the water, she traced her hands over the rock, trying to grip on as the water gushed against her. No hole.

It *had* to be here. She felt sure. She dropped down, sucked in a deep breath, went under. Holding her arms in front of her, she kicked out as hard as she could, fingers tracking the wall all the way to the bottom. Then there was nothing—a gap. Her heart lurched. She'd found the hole.

She came up for air, sucked in another breath, pushed down again, kicked hard, hands out in front, protecting her head. She found the hole again, traced it down to just above the floor of the pool. It must have been around five feet high and six across. *This* was it, she knew with a blood-deep certainty. This *was* the riddle pool, leading to the other land, leading to treasures. But the current was pushing her back into the cave, away from the hole, and she needed to breathe. She let the current take her back, out from under the waterfall, to the other side. She rose into the frigid air, gasping, exultant.

She kicked something hard in the water, on the bed of the pool. Curious, she dropped down into the water, felt around for it. Her fingers closed around a long, smooth object. She drew it out of the water, gasped. Dropped it in horror. *Many have died* . . . She'd seen enough medical diagrams in her biology module to know the thigh bone she held in her hand belonged to a human.

That should have warned her, slowed her down, but Merry was on a high, exultant with her find and driven by her mother's fears and the sense that time was running out. So many people knew about the book. Dr. Philipps had done the translation himself. He would be bound to come searching, and send a younger, fitter person into this same pool, to make this same discovery. Merry had sold the book, but she felt overwhelmingly that the treasures it referred to were *hers*. Her family's. If she found them, then maybe she could secure the future of their farm forever. If she got to them in time . . .

She plunged back into the deeper water, swam under the waterfall, came up into the cave. She breathed deeply, trying to get in as much oxygen as possible. Then she dived underwater, pushed down. Into the hole.

Merry reached up and felt rock pressing down through the water: It was a tunnel. She swam on, staying deep, wary of bumping her head, the current pressing against her.

Twenty strokes have many tried, turning them to blue.

How many could she manage before she turned blue? She struck out in a powerful breaststroke. *One, two, three.* With every stroke the current seemed to grow stronger. *Four, five, six.* She had to fight harder. *Seven, eight, nine.* She was cold, she was tiring. *Ten, eleven, twelve.* The flickers of fear began. *Thirteen, fourteen, fifteen.* Fear became terror. *Sixteen, seventeen, eighteen . . .* Oxygen gone. Vision blurring, body spasming. *Many have died . . .* Decide or die!

She jackknifed, let the current spin her back around. It ran with her, pushing her along, but she still had to stay low or risk bashing her head on the rock ceiling. The current ran so fast it was like nothing she had ever felt. Where was the air? Couldn't last much more. Dizzy, so dizzy . . . Was this what dying felt like?

Chapter Twenty-One

>>>————————————>

James de Courcy stood in his room, looking out across the valley to Nanteos Farm. Black clouds gathered on the horizon. It would snow again soon, he reckoned.

He would not go to Bali. He would leave home, return to Manchester, find the cheapest studio apartment he could. He'd saved up some birthday and Christmas money. He called it his slush fund. It wasn't much, but it would see him through for a few weeks and that had to be enough. He would then turn sixteen, and if Man U signed him, and please, please, God, he prayed they would, then he could pay his own way.

His parents would rage against him. Might even disinherit him. But it was now or never. He could only be a soccer player when he was young. This was not the path his parents wanted him to take, but it was *his* path, *his* life.

He took out his phone, called Merry. Now he'd made up his mind, he had to tell her immediately, as if telling her would start it all. The phone rang and rang but Merry did not answer. The call went through to voice mail. James hung up, mystified and annoyed. He called again ten minutes later, but again the phone just rang and rang and then went straight to voice mail.

James chucked the phone on his bed, frustrated. Merry had promised she would keep her phone on her.

Don't worry about me, she'd said. But he had then. And he did now. Even more so.

He strode to his window, looked out again. Great black clouds covered the sky, stealing the daylight. Ice stones pummeled down; he could see them far below ricocheting off the grass.

He called Merry's house line. Her mother answered.

"Hi, Mrs. Owen," he said, trying to keep his voice casual. "It's James here. Could I speak to Merry, please?"

"Sorry, James," replied Elinor. "She went out riding a few hours ago."

"In this?" asked James, his fears suddenly growing.

"Well, I don't know where she went, or if she checked the forecast. She was in a bit of a mood, I must say," observed Elinor. "Blowing off steam, I think."

"Thanks, Mrs. Owen," said James. He hung up. He had a sudden feeling he knew where Merry might have gone: legions marching, an emperor and queen . . . In a blast of shock, he knew. *The Roman road.*

There was no good reason why Merry wouldn't answer her phone. Unless she was hurt, or injured. All his instincts told him something was very wrong.

He ran down the stairs to the boot room at the back of the castle where all the keys were kept and grabbed the keys to the Land Rover. He ran out, jumped in, started up the car, and accelerated along the road across the de Courcy parkland.

The hail drummed onto the windshield, cutting visibility. The tires lost their bite on the tarmac. James felt as if he were coasting on a layer of ice. Crashing wouldn't help Merry. Cursing, he eased off the accelerator. The headlights picked out the hedgerows enclosing the narrow road. Stunted trees bent in the wind. James swept his eyes back and forth, seeking, as he drove on, muscling the Land Rover over the rough ground as he left the tarmac and headed along the old Roman road. Looming through the darkness and the hail, he soon saw the standing stone gleaming in the wash of his headlights. Hailstones bounced off it. Something was moving through the darkness beyond it.

It was Merry. She was slumped over her pony, her soaked hair hanging down.

"Merry!" shouted James.

He screeched to a halt, leaped from the Land Rover, walked toward her and her pony. He wanted to run, but that would alarm Jacintha. He swallowed the sound in his throat, a half cry.

"Hey, Merry, hey, Jac, I've come to take you home. Easy there, easy now," he crooned, taking Jacintha's reins, leading her to the Land Rover. He let go of the pony and pulled Merry off.

She mumbled something in protest. "It's okay, Merry. I'm going to get you inside the car, get you warm," he said. With one hand, he opened the rear passenger door, then clambered inside with Merry in his arms. He reached forward, turned on the engine and the heated seats, and ramped up the heating as high as it would go; then he just held Merry, rubbing her back, giving her the heat from his own body, willing her warm, fighting the hypothermia he knew could kill.

"It's all right, Merry," he said. "You're safe now. I've got you."

She tried to say something but could hardly move her lips. James gazed around frantically. He knew he should drive, should get her home, but he felt that if he let go of her he could lose her.

"C'mon, Merry," he said, rubbing her back harder. "Stay awake, hang on in there."

He grabbed his phone, called her home.

Caradoc Owen answered.

"Get your Land Rover!" James said, trying not to shout. "Hitch the horse trailer. Merry's in trouble. We're near Maen Llia."

"I'm on my way," said Caradoc. He didn't ask how James knew, or any other time-wasting questions. The fear in James's voice told him all he needed to know.

Chapter Twenty-Two

>>>———————————→

Twenty minutes later, James saw a wash of headlights sweep over the car.

"Your father's here now," he said to Merry.

He watched Caradoc Owen pull up, leap from his car, and sprint across to them. He threw open the door, glanced briefly at James.

"Thank you," he said, then grabbed Merry. "I'll take her now," he said. "Load Jacintha for me, will you."

Her father's voice was calm, but James could see the fear in his eyes. Her father was battle trained, medically skilled, he was the best person to take Merry, but James still didn't want to let her go.

"You can come in the car with us," said Caradoc, rethinking. "You can hold her, keep her warm. Just turn off your engine, load Jacintha, and get in," he said, then he hauled Merry out and ran with her through the hail to his own Land Rover.

James jumped out and caught hold of the pony, who'd stood outside the whole time, as if keeping vigil on her mistress.

"C'mon, Jac," he said. He loaded her quickly, secured the trailer door, turned off the engine of his own car, ran back to the Owens' Land Rover, and jumped in the backseat beside Merry as Caradoc accelerated into the night.

*   *   *

They arrived at Nanteos Farm after a terrifying drive. James knew that much faster, or much slower, might have been equally lethal.

Caradoc ran into the farmhouse, Merry in his arms. James followed behind.

"Upstairs," said Elinor, her face pinched and white. Seren Morgan was with her. James was glad. The healer was considered as good as most doctors for just about everything, save surgery. Caradoc took the stairs two at a time.

James, desperate for something to do, went back out into the hail, released Jacintha from her trailer, and led her to the stables. He made sure she had food and water, then went back to the farmhouse.

He stood in the silent kitchen, glancing up at the ceiling as if he might see through the bricks and the mortar. He desperately wanted to go up but knew he'd be in the way, and might not even be welcome. He stayed where he was, suddenly shivering as if from a remnant of Merry's chill.

At last he heard heavy footsteps on the stairs, and Caradoc Owen appeared in the kitchen.

"Between Seren and Elinor, Merry's in good hands," he said. "They're warming her up. She's conscious still."

James nodded, swallowed the lump in his throat.

Caradoc blew out a breath and ran his hands over his face in a rare display of emotion, then he studied James, his face hard and unreadable.

"First of all," he said, moving closer to James, "I want to thank you." He put a hand on James's arm, left it there. "Second of all, I'm going to make us some tea, and you're going to tell me what happened."

James nodded. Suddenly exhausted, he sat down at the kitchen table. He had just one sip of tea before his phone rang.

His mother. He took the call.

"James!" she yelled in his ear. "What the hell is going on? Dinner was served ten minutes ago. No sign of you. We asked Mrs. B if she'd seen you and she finally let on that she'd seen you go tearing off in the Land Rover well over an hour ago. Where the hell are you? Please tell me you haven't been driving on the public roads . . ."

"Actually, Ma, I have. Merry was in trouble. I had to go and—"

His mother cut him off. "That wretched girl again! You'd risk a criminal prosecution, a criminal record, to go off on some wild-goose chase to rescue her? Are you mad?" she screamed.

James couldn't listen to any more. He hung up, glanced at Caradoc, who'd clearly heard every word. He could see the muscles tense in the man's jaw.

James got to his feet. "I'd better go."

Caradoc nodded. "Let me check on Merry again, then I'll drive you home."

"I need to get the Land Rover back."

"I'll drive you there instead. You can tell me on the way."

Chapter Twenty-Three

Fourteen hours later, Merry awoke in her bed, an electric blanket hot beneath her, another electric blanket hot on top of her, and what felt like a mountain of duvets pressing down on her. Sun streamed through her primrose-sprigged curtains. There was a stink of garlic. It seemed to be coming from her. With the smell came the memories: water, cold, Jacintha, James. She felt pretty certain he'd saved her life. She felt a swell of emotion wash over her. Gratitude, something else she couldn't name, but also pure, ice-cold terror.

Despite the electric blankets and the duvets swaddling her, she felt like she'd never erase that memory of cold, of drowning, of being trapped underneath the mountain in that small, dark cave, water below and water above, in her nostrils, in her mouth, that awful current fighting her, then, at last, maybe saving her.

She pushed it from her mind. She couldn't think about it, wouldn't think about it. Would seek refuge in denial for as long as she could.

Seeking distraction, she turned on her phone.

Multiple texts from James, all on the same theme:

How are you? Text me as soon as you wake up.

She texted him back. She remembered Bali, wondered if he had gone.

I'm up. How am I ever going to thank you.

A text came straight back. So he couldn't be on the plane to Bali. She smiled.

You'll never need to.

She smiled again.

Maybe a lifetime's supply of soccer balls?
Deal! Anything u need? Head-to-toe thermals? Padded cell? I can order online . . .
Ha v funny. So no Bali?
No Bali.

Merry hit *call*.

James picked up.

There was laughter in his voice, a kind of relieved delight. "Thought that might get you."

"James," said Merry, letting out a huge breath. "Joking aside, what can I say? Without you . . ."

There was a silence on the phone for a long, awkward moment.

"Let's not talk about it now," James finally said. "You're okay, I take it? That's all that matters."

"I'm fine. I've felt better, but I'm fine. So what I want to know is, what about Bali? Did they all go? Are you home alone?"

"Pretty much. Pa and I are hardly speaking. Ma's sticking rigidly to his side. They went apoplectic at my driving on public roads. It was the last straw for them."

They'd gone apoplectic too because he'd done it for Merry. They were blaming her for everything, though James had no intention of laying that on her.

"They've got it all mapped out for me," he continued. "They want me to go back to school, forget soccer, go to university, train to be a lawyer like my father so that I can run the estate when I inherit one day. I reckon I can do all that at any age. But I can only play soccer now, when I'm young. I've told them that a million times but it doesn't make any difference. It's not fitting, it's not what they expect of me. It's not what they'll allow."

Merry said nothing, just listened to James, to the sadness that still seeped through the words he was obviously trying to speak so emotionlessly. Like a news anchor.

"So what's the point of going to Bali with them and having this discussion over and over? It's going nowhere. I'm not going to change my mind. They're not going to shift. I know the next step will be to throw me out, disinherit me. So I decided I might as well leave now."

"Oh, James." Merry knew how he loved his home, how, despite everything, he loved his parents and sister. Knew what this was costing him.

"So where are you going to go?"

"To a studio apartment in Manchester. I've already found one online, booked myself in. And yes, before you say anything, it's a bit of a comedown, but that's not the point. When I'm sixteen, if I'm good enough, Man U will sign me and I'll have enough money to rent a decent place, to be independent. If Man U don't sign me, I'll find a club lower down the divisions who will. I'm not giving up."

Merry could hear a new, cold determination in his voice, admired him the more for it.

"When will you find out if they'll sign you?"

"Not long. A week or so, I reckon."

"How's it looking?"

"Put it this way: I've got one shot. I'm giving it everything."

Merry felt a surge of emotion. James was risking everything. Had the courage to do it. "You'll get there, James. I know you will."

At the other end of the line, she could almost sense James smiling.

"So, Merry Owen, are you going to tell me what the heck happened out there in the mountains? Your father gave me the third degree but I couldn't really tell him much."

Risking everything too, she thought. Strange how their lives seemed to be running in parallel now, despite the massive gulf between them when they were born.

She had one shot too. "I tried something stupid, I—"

She glanced up, saw her parents standing at the door, Gawain in her father's arms. They were smiling at her like they'd never smiled before, looks of joy, relief, tenderness, and a kind of profound sorrow mixed in.

"James," she said softly, "hang on in there. Do what you have to do. Ring me later. I've got to go now, my parents are here."

"Be careful, will you?" said James. "It'd be kind of lonely if something happened to you."

Another silence, full of things left unsaid, hovered between them.

"I will," said Merry, then hung up.

Chapter Twenty-Four

Merry spent two more days in bed. Trapped by exhaustion, she could only lie there and try not to hear her father on the phone, pleading with the bank manager for more time, trying to disguise his desperation as he negotiated a sale price for the mare, asking the antiques dealer if he couldn't do more to shift their heirlooms . . . She could also hear Professor Parks visiting, could hear the veiled desperation in her mother's questions: *Found anything yet? Anything valuable?* And Parks's clipped answers: *Nothing yet. Takes time. Digs are painstaking, Mrs. Owen.* Then a heavy pause and in a different tone: *How is your daughter? I hear she was in a bad way. What was she doing?* And her mother's answer: *Thank you, Professor Parks. On the mend.*

Lying in her bed, Merry frowned. She'd bet Parks was curious. Had he made the connection between the Roman legions and Sarn Helen? She could only hope and pray that he had not.

May I pop in to see her, say hello? Parks had asked.

Merry froze but her mother sailed quickly to her rescue. *Oh no, I don't think so, Professor Parks. She needs her rest.* That was followed soon after by the sound of the firm closing of the back door.

Seren also came to visit. Unlike Parks, she was allowed to see the patient. *Her* patient.

Merry was sitting up in bed, reading, when there was a knock on her door.

"It's me, Seren. Your mother sent me up."

"Come in," called Merry.

The old lady shut the door behind her, came to stand by the bed. Seren was short, no more than five foot two, but her straight-backed posture and her quiet power always made her seem bigger. She wore her usual uniform of tight gray bun, tweed skirt, warm jumper, and stern face.

"How are you?" she asked, peering down.

"Getting better," replied Merry with a smile. "Thanks to you and Mam."

The healer snorted. "No thanks to your own stupidity."

Merry blinked. "That's a bit harsh."

"No, it's not. What *on earth* were you up to?" she asked with a flash of anger.

Merry looked away.

"You can't lie to me," snapped Seren. "It's something to do with that book, isn't it?"

Glancing at her, Merry wondered what the healer *saw*.

"You don't know anything about the book," she snapped back, going on the offensive. "You haven't even seen it!"

"Quite. Might have been nice if you'd shown it to me. Neighborly."

Merry winced. "I'm sorry, I . . ." Her words trailed off. She couldn't lie, but she couldn't tell the truth either.

"Got rid of it with what one might call indecent haste . . . ," continued Seren. "Only sensible thing you've done."

"Oh, thanks. Glad I got *something* right."

"Would have been better still if you'd never found it."

"You can't blame all this on *a book*!"

"Oh yes I can! Why d'you think it was buried?"

"Because somebody loved it? Wanted it with them in the afterlife?"

"Maybe. Or maybe they just wanted to keep it out of harm's way, far from those they loved."

Merry jolted. That's what part of her thought too, but she wasn't going to admit it. "It's just a *book*, Seren. You talk about it as if it's got some kind of awful power."

"You know it has!" blazed the healer, bending down so that her weathered face was close to Merry's. "You've already acted on it. I know you have, and look what happened. It nearly cost you your life!"

Twice over, thought Merry.

"But I survived," she replied, suppressing a shudder.

"This time," retorted Seren. "Thanks to James. You might not be so lucky the next."

Chapter Twenty-Five

On the third day, Elinor pronounced Merry fit enough to resume normal life. Fit enough to interrogate.

It was a Monday evening. It was shepherd's pie, Merry's favorite. Gawain had been put to bed, so there were no distractions.

"Right," said Elinor, resting her chin on her steepled fingers. Her hair hung down in long curtains, dark against her white skin. She looked like an older, tired Snow White for whom the fairy-tale ending hadn't quite happened.

"What was going on that night, Merry?" she asked softly. "And please don't evade us any longer. No spinning. You scared the hell out of us. I'd like some answers."

Merry took a sip of her lemonade. She'd been preparing for this, practicing the lies. What choice did she have? Tell the truth and blow any chance she had of finding the treasures, the secrets? There was no guarantee the museum *would* manage to raise sixty thousand pounds for the book. They hadn't even paid them the seven thousand pounds yet. She *had* to find these other treasures . . .

She gave a long, drawn-out shrug. "Thing is, I'm not sure. I remember riding out, past Sarn Helen, past Maen Llia, in the day, and I remember riding back that way and it was dark and I was cold and it was hailing and then James rang me, I think I spoke to him. I think I dropped my phone . . . and then James appeared and then Da was there." She took the time to look both her father and her mother in the eye, one after the other, so she couldn't be accused of evasion. "What happened in between is a blur. I just remember water, lots of water, and the cold." She shivered, fell silent as the memories hit her.

Elinor eyed her daughter, weighing her words with a soft frown. "Seren warned us that you might not remember everything. Said it can happen with hypothermia."

"Look, d'you mind if I go to bed now?" asked Merry. She rubbed her arms as goose bumps rose. Her parents could see that she wasn't faking it.

Elinor nodded. "Okay. Up you go."

Merry peeled off her clothes, pulled on her warm flannel pj's and thick socks, and got into bed. The inquisition, brief as it was, had brought it all back. She felt confused and torn in a way she never had before. She should be feeling better now, she should be moving on. What had happened had happened. It was in the past. Over. She should leave it alone. But the treasures were still out there, calling to her almost. And worse too, it felt as something outside herself would not let it go, would not let *her* go. Was it like the curse of Tutankhamen? Was it the chieftain avenging himself for the desecration of his tomb? She felt like she was infected, like the water in the riddle pool had seeped into her blood.

Chapter Twenty-Six

On Tuesday morning, Merry found herself alone at last as her parents and Gawain headed off to Brecon to see if the antiques dealer had managed to sell the old silver photo frames and set of chairs they'd taken to him the previous week.

In the ringing silence of the farmhouse, she thought over what had happened in the riddle pool. She *had* been lucky to survive, she knew that. She had tried to swim through to whatever wonders lay hidden and she had failed. Spectacularly.

But there were two responses to failure: give up, or try harder. The first was not in her nature. Time for a new plan . . .

She rose to her feet in one quick, smooth movement. She made a phone call, loaded a backpack, pulled on her waterproof jacket and boots, and set out.

She took her knife. She thought she'd be safe now, but she still liked to have it on her. The press announcement had gone out as promised. She'd seen no sign of anyone suspicious. Hadn't felt as if anyone was watching her . . . but she couldn't know for sure. She still stopped, still turned circles, thought it was a new habit she wouldn't lose.

She got to the Black Castle, to the drawbridge. Crossing the moat, she felt she was walking back hundreds of years.

The courtyard echoed to her steps. Merry paused at the giant door and rapped the lion's head knocker against the solid oak. Nothing. She opened the door and stepped inside the Great Hall.

"Mrs. Baskerville? It's Merry," she called out, breaking the heavy silence that hung like a living hush, like something holding its breath.

Heavy footsteps echoed up the far staircase. Mrs. Baskerville heaved into view.

"Sorry, *bach*!" she panted. *Bach* was a term of endearment. It meant "little one" in Welsh. Mrs. Baskerville had referred to Merry as *bach* since she was a baby and saw no reason to change now. She gave Merry a shrewd look. "Shouldn't you be in bed resting?"

"Any more rest would kill me! I'm fine!" Merry declared.

The housekeeper spluttered with laughter. "Now, what was it you wanted to ask me?"

"I was wondering if I might use the pool. Today and for the next few weeks."

"I'd have thought you'd have had enough of water for the time being."

"Not really," replied Merry, trying to smile blandly, give nothing away.

The housekeeper blew out a breath. "There's no key. Just a keypad. One zero six six is the code. Whatever you do, don't drown and *don't* get caught. Check with me first in case the earl or countess are in residence."

"When are they coming back?"

"Ten days. With Lady Alicia. Goodness alone knows when Lord James'll be back," she added wistfully.

Merry gave her a sympathetic glance. Mrs. Baskerville had known James since he was born.

"Criminal, if you ask me," muttered the housekeeper just loud enough to be heard. "Have you spoken to him?"

"Every day," replied Merry.

"Any news?

"Not yet," replied Merry.

She thanked the housekeeper and headed out again. She thought about James, wondered if he was lonely. Maybe today would bring the news he yearned to hear, the offer from Manchester United that would make it all worthwhile. She crossed her fingers, sent out a silent prayer.

Merry followed the path of stones that led from the castle to the copse of fir trees that hid the swimming pool complex and green-house. She reached down, grabbed a couple of handfuls of stones, and filled her pockets.

She skirted the copse, inhaling the crisp smell of damp pine, and eyed the big wood-and-glass structure, the vaulted roof. It was huge. She tapped in the code on the control panel, pushed through. The door closed with a soft hiss.

Inside it was deliciously warm. The sweet smell of cedar filled the air. The water filter murmured gently. No reek of bleach and mold, no screaming babies with leaking diapers like in the town pool.

She stripped off in the cozy changing room, removed her eye patch and laid it on her pile of clothes. The stone floor was warm underfoot; low lights cast a golden glow and clean white towels hung on heated rails. She pulled on her swimsuit, then put her jacket back on. She did up the buttons on the pockets so the stones wouldn't fall out, put on her goggles, and walked from the changing room to the edge of the pool.

A shaft of sunlight pierced the clouds and shone through the glass ceiling into the pool, dappling the water. This pool was about as welcoming as water got. But she couldn't go in. She was breathing fast, adrenaline surging. She wasn't scared. She was terrified. The memory of what had happened, of her near-drowning, had gone deep into her body. This wasn't a mentally generated fear that she could fight with reason and logic. It was her body's own fear.

She stood on the side of the gorgeous pool, forcing her breathing to slow. She felt a burn of misery and anger that one of her major pleasures had been turned into terror.

She knew what to do . . . *Face your fears; get back on the horse; get back in the water* . . . She took a breath and dived . . .

The memories hit her. The dark cave, the low roof, the current, so strong, pushing her as she battled it back. Panic rose and she wanted to open her mouth and gulp. She fought it down but she managed only three strokes underwater before she had to surface, gasping, heart hammering. She tried again but her body, so long something she thought she could control, defied her. It did not want to go under the water. So she stayed on the surface, forced herself to keep swimming. She was like a beginner, gasping, splashing, panic tiring her. She carried on, muscles burning.

Her father had told her there is nothing more tiring than terror. It's why in the army you have to be super fit. She *was* super fit. And she was exhausted. She vowed to do twenty lengths before she would allow herself to get out.

Back and forth in the blood-warm water, the heavy jacket weighing her down. She counted off the lengths. At twenty, legs rubbery, she stepped from the pool, walked to the changing room, stood under the power shower. This was water her body could handle. She stood there for a long time, letting the water wash away the memories.

Caradoc, Elinor, and Gawain were still out when Merry returned home, and she was glad of it. She had time to compose herself, time to veil another set of lies—*What have you been up to? Oh, just went for a walk*—something innocuous in case she had been seen. After all, the valley had plenty of eyes and mouths.

Merry washed her swimsuit, wrung it out, and hung it to dry in her bedroom on the inside of the door, dangling off the handle. She didn't want an interrogation if her mother found it. She grabbed a couple of Welsh cakes and brewed up a cup of coffee and settled down at the PC.

She Googled *underwater swimming*, picked a web link written by a former US Navy SEAL. If it was good enough for the guys who got Osama Bin Laden, it was good enough for her.

She clicked on a YouTube demo of the SEAL and his underwater technique.

"Lesson one: Save energy." He used a combination of modified breaststroke with a dolphin kick at the end and a hard downward arm push rather than a typical breaststroke lateral one. *"Minimize*

strokes," he said. *"Underwater swimming should be no more taxing than walking while holding your breath."*

Merry snorted at that one. She had a long way to go.

"Lesson two: Do not hyperventilate before going under. You CANNOT increase your oxygen levels by taking additional deep breaths before swimming underwater. Instead you are reducing your levels of CO_2 and so increasing the danger of shallow-water blackout. Doing strenuous exercise before swimming underwater could also have the same effect because that could make you hyperventilate too. One big inhale/exhale and one last inhale is all you need."

Merry filed that away. Thank you, Google.

There was a last word of warning: *Do NOT do this alone. Many people have died trying.*

That was the only piece of his advice that Merry did not plan to follow.

Chapter Twenty-Seven

➤➤➤━━━━━━━━━━━━━➤

Merry's parents and Gawain arrived home in a sudden cloudburst bearing newspaper-clad bundles of take-out fish and chips.

"Oooh, delicious!" exclaimed Merry. "I'm starving."

"Good!" declared her mother. "You've got your rosy cheeks and your appetite back. Good to see."

That'd be the exercise, thought Merry.

Caradoc scooped the mail off the doormat, opened it on the way to the table.

"Yes!" he roared, making them all jump.

He brandished a piece of paper in the air. "Check for seven thousand pounds, made out by the National Museum of Wales!" He pulled Merry into a familiar bear hug.

Merry smiled. "It's a start."

"With what you've set in motion it'll be a finish too," her father added. "We'll pay off our mortgage by the end of the year!"

"*If* it goes according to plan," replied Elinor. She managed a small smile, but Merry could see her mother still lived in fear of losing their home and all that went with it. And was still judging what she saw as Merry's rashness.

"I wonder how Professor Parks is getting on?" said Merry, with a frown.

"Well, you know he came round, asking after you. Which was nice," added Elinor, "but he hadn't found anything."

Merry didn't say she'd heard him come visiting; didn't want her parents to know she'd also heard her father on the phone, heard them arguing with the bank about how they were going to pay that month's mortgage and the arrears.

"I might just go and take a look at the dig after lunch," said Merry.

"Be a bit careful, *cariad*," cautioned her father.

She didn't think to ask what he meant.

It had stopped raining but drops continued to plop from the branches onto the forest floor.

The fallen tree still lay prone. Merry could see no sign of Professor Parks. She crept up behind the tree and peered over the huge trunk.

The burial mound was covered in a lattice of crisscrossing fine ropes, with labeled sticks protruding from each square. It all looked very professional. And clinical. Merry felt a lurch. The chieftain would hate this.

"I wasn't expecting visitors," said a voice.

Merry let out a yell and wheeled around. Professor Parks stood behind her. Just four feet away.

"You startled me!" she said.

"You shouldn't go creeping around, then, should you?" he replied evenly.

"It was you who crept up on me." She frowned. "How'd you do that?"

"You walk on the outside of your feet, rolling forward slowly."

"Really? And why would you know that?"

Parks laughed. "I stalk deer in the Scottish Highlands. Stealth is everything."

Merry filed that away for later. "Found anything yet?"

"Digs are slow and painstaking and made more so by spectators. Look, I'm sorry," said Parks, sounding anything but, "I thought I'd made it clear. We cannot afford to have the site contaminated. Again. With respect, *Merry*."

"Contaminated? You make it sound like a crime scene."

"It's not dissimilar. I'm searching for evidence in a forensic manner."

"And there's a dead body. We know that much."

"We *assume* that much," corrected Parks.

"It's a *burial* mound!"

"But there could be more than one dead body, Merry. Ever think of that?"

Merry shuddered. One dead chieftain was bad enough.

"I'll leave you to it," she replied, turning and walking away.

She headed home through the dripping forest. She walked normally, and then she tried Parks's trick, rolling forward on the outside of her feet. It took a while to get right, but it worked! A useful skill, she thought. If you were a hunter.

Merry's Easter vacation had officially begun, so she had lots of free time. Every day, she'd tell her parents she was off for a run and head over to the Black Castle. They were used to her going off on hill runs for hours so it didn't strike them as odd and they didn't question her. Part of her felt bad at the deceit, but a stronger part of her had become obsessed by her plan.

Thanks to the SEAL's tips, at the end of a week, she was able do fifty yards without a breath; the same distance the SEALs had to do as part of their selection. But in the de Courcys' pool there was no current to fight. And that bothered her. She wanted to swim with more weight. She needed something like a fully weighted jacket. But what?

She found it as she checked in with Mrs. Baskerville the next day.

"They're back tomorrow," said Mrs. Baskerville. "So make the most of it."

Merry nodded. "I will, thanks." She paused, plowed on before she could change her mind. "Heard anything from James?"

For the last few days, she hadn't texted him. Or called. For his sake, she couldn't keep asking him what was happening with Manchester United, if they'd made him an offer. Or not. When he had good news, he'd let her know. She just had to wait and believe.

"He texts me every so often to tell me he's fine," the housekeeper said. "Hasn't come home once." Her eyes misted over. "Don't think he will neither."

Merry gave a sad smile. "He's following his dreams. That has to be a good thing."

Mrs. Baskerville turned on her with a hard look. "That's what you think at sixteen. Let me tell you, not at sixty."

"But he *is* sixteen, or almost!" protested Merry.

"And is that what you were doing too, chasing your dreams when you got hypothermia out on the mountains?" demanded Mrs. Baskerville, hands on hips.

Merry bit her lip, didn't answer.

"Yes. Thought so, though God knows what you were dreaming of out there! There's a price to chasing your dreams. And you nearly paid it in full, from what I hear," she added, more softly now.

"But I didn't," replied Merry just as softly. "I'm here now."

"Hmm. I don't like any of it," said the housekeeper. "Off you go then, and do whatever it is you're doing, you with your secrets . . ."

As she bustled away, indignant and worried, Merry's eye turned to Sir Lancelot in the Great Hall. To his chain mail. Mrs. Baskerville's fears had rattled her. She felt she needed to train harder, to prepare better. Sir Lancelot had the answer.

Quietly, she slid the chain mail off his wooden body and pulled it on herself. It was finely wrought and loose, allowing her to move, but it was *heavy*. Merry reckoned it weighed a good twenty-five pounds. She clunked out of the Black Castle, along the stone path.

Inside the pool house, she removed it, changed into her swimsuit, pulled her shirt back on, then slid the chain mail over it. The cotton would stop the metal cutting into her skin. She eased into the pool. The chain mail dragged her down in the water, just as she wanted. She felt a brief flutter of panic, then reminded herself she could climb out at any time, that she was fine, that she could do this.

She counted out the lengths. She managed ten, then, blowing hard, heart pounding, she took a break. After a few minutes, she started her underwater training. It was tough but she pushed on. Tired, she resolved to do another few lengths underwater when something made her pause: a disturbance in the air.

She surfaced and looked up into the astonished and furious face of the Countess de Courcy.

Merry climbed out of the pool, clinking and dripping, her blond hair hanging to her waist. She removed her goggles. Her eye patch wasn't in reach and she saw the countess flinch at the scarred-over empty socket of her left eye. Anne de Courcy briefly covered her mouth with her hand; then she composed herself. She planted her hands on her skinny hips and almost spat out her words.

"Merry Owen! What the *hell* do you think you are doing?"

Merry's first thought was, *What the hell are you doing back home?*

She paused, stood straight. She needed to get her breath back, but she refused to let the countess think she was nervous, or intimidated in any way. She held her head high.

"Swim training," she answered.

"In *my* pool?" The countess paused theatrically. "In *my* chain mail? Does Mrs. Baskerville know about this?"

"Course not."

"Oh, I suppose James gave you the code, did he?"

"No, he did not. The door wasn't closed properly. I just had to push it open." The lie came easily. The last thing she wanted was to get James or Mrs. B in trouble.

She slipped out of the chain mail, let it clink to the ground.

"After having helped yourself to my chain mail. Mrs. Baskerville forgot what day we were coming back on. It would seem she is forgetting her duties altogether."

The countess reached out one manicured finger and poked Merry in the chest. "You know you were a fool not to sell that book to me . . . silly girl that you are."

Merry's heart began to pound, but she kept her face impassive.

"I'd have written you a check for sixty thousand there and then," continued the countess in her oh-so-carefully-cultivated upper-class accent. "That kind of money's not easy for pony breeders to come up with, is it?"

Merry's fury rose up in her. She struggled to keep it under control. Anne de Courcy's eyes were sneering; she was enjoying this, enjoying the power her money gave her and the pain it could cause.

But Merry was taller than the countess, and much, much stronger.

"Over my dead body," she said.

The countess laughed. "You're lucky the wolfhounds didn't catch you trespassing or else there'd be more than a dead stallion in the Owen family."

Merry felt as if she were watching herself. Her control snapped. She reached out, grabbed the countess, and pushed her hard.

Into the pool.

The countess went in with a shriek, came up spluttering and cursing.

"Get out, Merry Owen! And stay away from James!" she screamed, her Welsh accent resurfacing at the same time. "You're damaged goods, you are. I don't want you consorting with our family! You're nothing but a bad influence on him!"

Merry grabbed her clothes and ran home, the sound of the countess's scream and the echoes of her parting words playing over in her mind. There'd be a cost to what she'd done, but she didn't care.

Even so, she struggled to sleep that night. She thought only of the black water, the evil cold of the cave behind the waterfall.

It was time to go back in.

Chapter Twenty-Eight

>>>>———————————————————>

Merry woke late. She sat up in bed, heart already pounding with adrenaline. She pulled on her eye patch, strapped on her watch. She made breakfast, porridge with whole milk and honey, then organized herself. Her father was already out on the farm; her mother had taken Gawain to baby gym in Brecon. Alone, unsupervised, she stashed supplies in her backpack: Welsh cakes, a thermos of milky, sugary tea, her headlamp. Jacintha's tethering rope. A small towel, a super-warm fleece. She stared at her phone. If she took it, she'd be told off for not answering it. If she left it, and got into trouble, needed help . . . She grabbed it with a scowl, shoved it into the backpack. She added her knife and a leg strap to her pack, grabbed her catapult and stones for luck—James had given her them as a present after she'd lost her eye. He'd handpicked the stones in the river, she remembered, called them "lucky stones." Then she plaited her hair and pinned it up. Last thing she needed was mouthfuls of hair choking her.

She let herself out. She didn't need to lock the door anymore. She'd made sure that everyone knew the book was long gone.

Jacintha picked up on her nerves. She tossed her head and snorted as Merry pulled the halter onto her, fashioning the tethering rope into reins. Grabbing a handful of mane, she vaulted onto her pony, who gave a halfhearted shimmy. It would never have dislodged Merry. Jacintha was just making a point: *Why are you jumpy? What are we going to do? And if it's scary, why are we going to do it?*

"Because," murmured Merry, walking her pony to the gate, opening the latch, and guiding her through. "Because we have to."

Under the sun, in the fresh breeze blowing down from the mountains, Merry rode out. She moved through a trot to a slow, loping canter and back to a trot or walk where the terrain grew rougher.

The good weather had brought out the walkers. They were scattered like Day-Glo sheep across the green of the lowlands. She could see groups of them heading up Pen y Fan mountain as well. And a runner too, moving swiftly along the hillside some distance away, fit enough to keep pace with her and Jacintha.

Along Sarn Helen she rode, past Maen Llia. She reined in her pony and paused to touch the standing stone. It was warm and Merry smiled. A good omen. Up the sloping, rough track. She dismounted, walked Jacintha to the copse, through the gap in the dense bushes. She tethered her to a sturdy trunk, hidden from view, she thought.

Jacintha looked around, eyes wide, nostrils flared. She didn't want to be in this place again. Merry tried to calm her. She rubbed her pony's neck, leaned down, breathed into her nose, and saw in her pony's eyes fear and worry.

"I'll be back soon. I promise!" she murmured, wondering as she said the words if she could make such a promise.

She removed her eye patch, stripped down to her swimsuit. She put away her clothes, stacking them inside a plastic bag in the backpack, protected if it rained. She pulled on her headlamp, took out her knife, and strapped it to her thigh. She took one last look around and pushed through the final barrier of bushes.

She looked at the pool, and the memories rushed back. Her body wanted to seize up. She tamped down the fear, focused on her training, on faith, and the iron will of her own belief.

The book had guided her here.

One way or another, it had nearly killed her. Twice.

It had warned her clearly enough: *Only the strong pass through.* But she *was* strong. Stronger than ever. She just had to believe she was strong enough.

Merry strode into the water. It was black, pierced by shards of sunlight cutting through the trees. None of the sun's warmth seemed to have reached it. Bitterly cold, it felt as if it came from the dark heart of the mountain, somewhere beyond the touch of the sun.

Her heart began to race. The water clenched around her legs like bands of steel. She walked in deeper. She switched on her headlamp and launched forward into a powerful breaststroke, kicking against the current. She dived under the waterfall, surfaced, and swam to the end of the cave. Damp walls gleamed in the headlamp's beam. Trapped air hung fetid with decay.

She recalled the lessons of the Navy SEAL. She inhaled, exhaled, took one further deep breath and down she went, underwater, hands exploring the wall till she found the emptiness of the hole.

Fighting the current, she kicked out. Passed through it. She could see the outlines of a tunnel, the same dimensions as the hole, stretching away into darkness.

Heart racing, she counted the strokes. *One, two, three* . . . the far-ther she went, the stronger the current became. She pushed on, her long, smooth breaststroke with the hard downward arm thrust at the end, the frog kick of her legs morphing into a dolphin flick. *Minimize the stroke number, minimize the energy output, stay calm.* The SEAL's voice. Yeah, right.

Ten, eleven, twelve . . . the current was so strong. Another eight to go. She fought her way forward. Still the beam of her headlamp showed only blackness ahead. *Thirteen, fourteen, fifteen* . . . her mus-cles began to burn. Her stroke became ragged. Her lungs screamed for air.

Just a few more strokes! She forced her body on. *Sixteen, seventeen, eighteen.* Darkness stretched ahead, unbroken. Keep going or turn back?

She *had* to find out what lay beyond, what treasures . . . She forced herself on, dredging up every last reserve of courage and strength. *Nineteen, twenty* . . . Still nothing, no light, no air. *Twenty-one, twenty-two* . . . Her lungs were burning, her brain was screaming, *Open your mouth, breathe.* She fought it, battled on, another stroke . . . Something ahead, a lightening. One more stroke . . . She was fading, strength nearly gone. *Strong,* she thought, *strong* . . .

Her body contorted itself into one last stroke: *twenty-five.* She saw light. She raised her arm. Felt air.

Chapter Twenty-Nine

Merry surfaced, gasping, almost delirious with relief. In the gloom, she gazed around.

She was in a pool, in a cave, identical to the one she had just left.

The relief turned to confusion. It *had* to be the one she'd just struggled so hard to leave. But how could it be?

Dazed, she swam on toward the source of light. Flickering at the edge of the mouth of the cave was the waterfall. She wondered if her brain *had* been starved of oxygen and if she hadn't gone forward, but backward in some weird way. She exited the cave, blinking in the sudden brightness. Her feet slipped on the smooth pebbles as she walked through the mossy shallows.

She paused, looked around. She felt a crushing disappointment. She had gotten nowhere. She'd risked her life to end up back where she started. How was that *possible*?

Yet it was odd. It was the same place but somehow different. The bushes lining the banks of the stream looked thicker, more impenetrable. She'd be scratched to bits getting through in her swimsuit. She shivered.

She needed the fleece in her backpack, a cup of her sugary tea. She pushed through the thicket, exclaiming sharply as the thorns raked her skin. Why had it been so much easier coming through in the other direction? And where *was* her backpack?

It was gone. Jacintha was gone. The trees were different. There were more of them. The smell was different. *Greener.* She was going mad. Jacintha must have broken free, galloped home without her.

She stumbled downhill through the undergrowth, feeling horribly exposed in her swimsuit. Without her eye patch. Should have come out onto open ground by now. Too many trees. Too many bushes. This was a forest, not a copse! Heart pounding. Something was *very* wrong. She ran on. Froze.

Thirty feet from her, picking something from the forest floor, was an old lady wearing a long dress and a weird bonnet. The woman straightened. Her face creased in concern.

Standing in her swimsuit, Merry felt naked, but what was worse was not having her eye patch. She didn't allow anyone to see the ruined socket underneath. Not her mother, not her father. Only Gawain had seen it when he pulled off the patch one day when tugging her hair, though he hadn't minded one bit. In twenty-four hours, first the countess and now this stranger had seen her exposed.

"Who are you? Where are your robes?!" demanded the woman in Welsh.

Merry wasn't fluent, but understood enough. She could tell too that the woman was more bothered by her near nakedness than by her eye. She replied in English; her Welsh wasn't good enough.

"Someone stole them." She wondered about Jacintha. "And maybe they took my pony too. I left her tethered."

"There are thieves abroad. And worse," replied the woman in an odd, stilted English. She shook her head. "Come, quickly, you would not want the Earl de Courcy and his men to find you disrobed so."

"His *men*?"

The old lady gave her an odd look. "Let us not tarry, girl." She picked up a basket and, with her other hand, grabbed Merry's arm. "Come."

Merry felt light-headed, disconnected, as though she were stuck in a dream. She let the old lady hurry her along. The wood seemed to go on forever. Merry gazed around in disbelief. Finally they emerged from the trees beside a tethered pony—black but not Jacintha—and a ragged cart.

Merry gazed around. She couldn't breathe. There was Sarn Helen, cutting along the high plain, and the standing stone, Maen Llia. But where there should be just the rolling grasses of the plain, there were thick clumps of trees. And no telephone poles, no tarmac cutting through the valley like a black scar. The scene swirled before her. Merry let out a sob as dizziness closed in.

Swaying motion, clicking hooves, rough blanket covering her. Smelling of herbs and the oily, animal tang of unbleached wool. Almost gagging, Merry came around. Pushed off the blanket. She was lying in a cart being pulled by the black pony and driven by the old lady.

She sat up, wrapped the blanket around her, scrambled forward, balancing precariously on the swaying cart.

"Where am I?" she hissed at the old woman, looking around desperately.

There was the Black Castle, standing in stark isolation. But all the laurel bushes, all James's mother's soft landscaping, were gone. Her eye swept to the other side of the valley. But where her home should have been, there was another house, a different, smaller, less

144

well-tended house. The extension her father had built was gone. She rubbed her eyes.

"Where am I? What is this?" she yelled, confusion making her wild. "Take me home! Now! I am Merry Owen! Take me home!" She felt the need to say who she was, as if saying it would make sense of what was happening.

"Merry Owen?" asked the woman. "The Owens of Nanteos Farm?"

"Of course! Caradoc Owen is my father."

"Glyndŵr Owen, you mean. And Rhiannon is your mother?"

"No!" screamed Merry. "Elinor is my mother. Caradoc is my father. Gawain is my brother!"

Was *she* mad, or was the woman? Was she kidnapping her? Had she drugged her?

They continued on up the hill, to where Seren's house should be. But this too was different. Seren's house had roses and lavender and quince trees, not firs. And it was two stories, not one. And the stone was whitewashed, not plain. Seren's house had a slate roof, not thatched.

The woman climbed down from the cart, tethered her pony. "Come on, girl. Get within before you catch your death."

"This is Seren's house!" shouted Merry.

The woman scowled at Merry. "It is *my* house, girl, and I am Mair, not Seren."

Merry looked at the woman in horror. She must be demented or lying.

Piercing the silence, a distant hound gave a bloodcurdling call. Merry shivered, pulled the blanket tighter. But driven by curiosity and by the cold, and by a desperate desire to see Seren, Merry got down from the cart and followed the woman inside.

The door shut. A bolt slid home. Then another.

Merry let out a low moan. "This is wrong," she said. "This is Seren's cottage, Ty Gwyn," she repeated. This was where she spent two hours each week, sitting at the kitchen table as Seren taught her botany. Only it wasn't.

The woman shook her head. She bent over a trunk, pulled out a bundle. "Put these on," she said, handing Merry a pale linen shirt, a brown wool tunic, and a shawl.

Merry looked at them in puzzlement. "These look like they belong in a museum."

The healer gave her a look of sheer incomprehension. "They are serviceable and warm and better than nakedness!"

Merry pulled on the clothes. They were rough against her skin, but she immediately began to warm up.

She looked around, her mind rebelling at what she saw. At what she did not see. Where the terra-cotta-tiled floor should have been was a rough stone floor, with gaps revealing the earth below. Where the oven should have been was a huge open hearth where hunks of wood burned. A basic-looking oven was built into the side.

Her mind spun. She could *not* be seeing what was before her. She must be concussed, oxygen-starved, mad in some unknown, terrifying way. *Had she died?* Another wave of dizziness broke over her. She reached out, grabbed the rough-hewn table, steadied herself. Sucking in deep breaths, desperately trying to get back to herself, to *normal*, she watched the woman busying herself.

She took a log and fed the fire; then she swung a large, iron kettle, suspended on an iron arm, over the flames. She took a stick, stuck its tip into the fire till it caught; then she lit a thick candle. A horrible stench wafted up.

Merry wrinkled her nose.

The woman, Mair, paused, planted her hands on her hips, eyed Merry with a mocking look. "Used to expensive beeswax candles, are you?" she asked.

Merry shook her head. Nothing made sense. "What's that made from, then?" she asked, nodding at the candle, desperate to get her bearings, to understand even a bit of what seemed to be going on in this alien but familiar place. "Why does it stink of rotting fish?"

"Tallow. And glycerine," said the woman. "Not what *fine ladies* have to put up with," she added tartly. She poured a thick broth from a pot on the fire into a cup, and handed it to Merry. "Drink."

"It might be poison," said Merry belligerently.

The old lady narrowed her eyes. "It might be. An herbalist must know the killing plants as well as those that cure."

She bent forward toward Merry, anger in her eyes.

"You'd be dead already if I wished it. That's if the earl and his men hadn't gotten you first . . ."

Her voice tailed off as a great bugling of horns sounded in the valley, followed by the pounding of galloping hooves.

Merry put down the cup and crossed to the window. Where there should have been glass there was just a thin sheet of pale linen. It was hard to see through, but she could see enough.

"What the . . ."

A troop of men and a sole woman, all of them in costume, were riding with a pack of wolfhounds, pursuing a herd of Welsh Mountain ponies that galloped from them in terror. Merry shuddered. This was how her stallion had died, pursued by the earl's wolfhounds. *This can't be happening.*

The ponies got to the stream. The stallion led them across, the mares followed, but two of the foals couldn't make it. They were small, the water deep and fast. The dogs got them as they struggled in the current. One of the mares stumbled. The men drew back their spears and threw. The mare took a spear in her flank.

The surviving ponies jumped a stone wall and galloped on. A wild-looking man with long fair hair came running out of what should have been *her* house, had it not been smaller, different. Then a woman and two children rushed out.

The man was shaking his fist, shouting at the hunters, gesticulating at the fleeing ponies. One of the riders reined in, drew back his whip, and lashed at the protester. Merry watched as the fair-haired man grabbed the whipcord and pulled his attacker off his horse. Quickly, and brutally, some of the other hunters leaped from their horses and began to beat the man. He fought back ferociously, though he was heavily outnumbered. It took a while for his attackers to drive him to the ground with boots and fists.

Merry wheeled from the window, ran to the door. She hauled back the heavy bolts, rushed out, preparing to scream at them to stop. A rough hand slammed over her mouth.

"Silence! Fool!" hissed the old lady. "Want to get yourself whipped or worse?"

Mair's fear was real, and contagious. Merry shook her head and the old lady removed her hand. The escaping ponies galloped by, tails streaming out behind them as they fled up the hill to safety.

Merry turned back to the huntsmen and their victim on the ground. With a sense of horror, confusion, and disbelief, she watched the scene unfold.

"This is our king, vermin," yelled one of the velvet-clad huntsmen, so loudly his clipped tones carried up the hill. "You would order him off your land?"

"What, this peasant is the owner of this land?" asked another man, incredulous. He looked huge, with an elaborate plumed hat, a fur-and-velvet jacket, a riot of scarlet and ruffles. He had a broad face with small, beady eyes. His horse was huge and black, one of the finest Merry had seen. He was very obviously the leader of this weird pack. He looked vaguely familiar. Were they actors? wondered Merry.

"Blame the Black Prince, my Liege," the first man replied. "This man's forebear saved his life at the Battle of Crécy. In return, he was granted this farmhouse and this land."

"Saved the life of his prince, did he?" asked the big man. "Well, a healthy precedent, one might say," he added, provoking a chorus of laughter. He eyed the man on the ground and his voice turned harsh. "You will remain in the Earl de Courcy's dungeons while we decide your fate. If it weren't for your sporting forebear I'd have decreed already."

"Your Majesty, you must forgive me," said the man, getting to his feet, wiping the blood from his face. "I did not know it was you.

All I knew was that these ponies were on my land, where they should be safe from the reach of the Black Castle."

"Your land?" boomed the huge man. "There is no land in the kingdom that cannot become mine if it is my wish!"

"But, Your Majesty," the man continued, "there is a pledge! The Black Prince himself decreed—"

"Silence!" screamed the first man. "Do not dare to address His Majesty. To the dungeons! And if you break your silence again, your woman and children will join you!"

The fair-haired man said no more. Merry watched him being dragged off, hands bound, the rope tied to one of the mounted horses. Four men on horseback accompanied him, while the other five and the one woman dug their spurs into their mounts and galloped off after the ponies, who now had a sizeable lead.

The farmer's wife and children, one of whom had a small bow, were weeping, calling out to the tethered man, and pleading with the hunters. Who ignored them.

Mair hurried Merry back into the darkness of her cottage as the hunting party thundered by. Peering through a crack in the door, Merry saw the woman was dressed in lush green velvet, with a lavishly feathered hat, and rode a magnificent black Arab horse.

She turned to the old lady, whose face had gone pale. "Who *are* those men and that woman? Why are they in costume? Why are they hunting ponies on my land and who was the man who tried to stop them? What's all this talk of king and majesty? Is this some weird *movie*?"

"*Movie?* What in the name of God is a *movie*? And that land . . ." The old lady glowered at her. "That's Longbowman *Owen's* land!"

"Exactly," replied Merry.

The old woman shook her head and carried on, her voice low and slow, as if she were conversing with an idiot. "As for those hunters, that's the Earl and Countess de Courcy and their men-at-arms, and as you can see, they're doing the king's bidding, with the king himself alongside."

"What king? What bidding?"

"King Henry, of course!" exclaimed the woman, losing patience. "That was the *king* riding by! They're following his command. *Kill all the wild ponies below fifteen hands high.* He thinks it'll improve his stock of warhorses," she added bitterly.

"Warhorses?" mouthed Merry.

"Warhorses," snapped back the woman. "These Welsh ponies are deemed too small. So they're hunted down, speared, fed to those wretched hounds."

Merry felt her world spinning. She took a step backward, steadied herself against the door. The huge man on the horse, the square face, the small but imperious eyes . . . she *had* seen him before. In history books . . .

Now she understood the riddle of her book.

As the lost tale of the *Mabinogion* had prophesied, she had *followed through.*

Into sixteenth-century Wales.

Into the brutal kingdom of Henry VIII.

Chapter Thirty

>>>———————————————————→

It was her world but not her world. She was five hundred years away from home. The question raging in her head, shouting for an answer, was: *How do I get home?* Her book said nothing about getting back, just *passing through* . . . But for the moment, all she could think of was her ancestor being dragged off to the dungeons.

"What will happen to Longbowman Owen?" she asked.

"He'll be beaten, thrown into de Courcy's dungeon on some false charge. Let's pray it is not insulting his king."

"What happens if he *is* found guilty? If he *is* said to have insulted his king?"

"That's treason," Mair said almost in a whisper. "And they hang traitors."

"You have to stop them!" cried Merry.

The old woman sat down heavily on a bench by the table. She twisted arthritic fingers together, seemingly debating with herself. "I will try," she said at last. "I shall write to the Bishop of St. David's, seek his help. He can intervene with the king, or with his henchman, Thomas Cromwell. And the de Courcys owe me. I saved the countess's life once when she cut her arm."

Merry nodded. No antibiotics in this time. A septic cut would be a death sentence.

"I'll seek an audience," Mair was saying, "but the earl is a cruel man who hates the Owens and covets their land. He's burning up with ancient wrongs he thinks it's time to right."

"When his land was given to the longbowman at the Battle of Crécy," murmured Merry.

The old woman's eyes flared in surprise. "How did you know that?"

Merry just shook her head.

The woman gave her a probing look but continued. "The earl will want to seize his chance. He may petition the king to have Longbowman Owen dragged off to the Tower of London."

Merry felt a coldness seep through her. She walked to the window, gazed across the valley and beyond to the Beacons, to the forested slopes where the river ran, where the water pooled, where escape lay. She felt a strange fever of indecision: desperate to go, compelled to stay.

She'd swum the riddle pool, survived when many had died. She had strength and she had knowledge. If her ancestor was hanged, or died in the dungeons, a victim of the de Courcys' violent henchmen, then perhaps she would never be born . . . Who knew if the line continued through the two children she'd seen? This was a harsh time. Many children didn't make it to adulthood. Many women didn't survive childbirth . . .

Across the valley lay the Black Castle, more stark and impenetrable than ever.

Only it wasn't.

Not if you knew a secret way in.

Merry looked out at the gathering night. Darkness would hide her but it would make finding her way back to the cave horribly difficult.

"I have to go," she said, making up her mind.

"Wait," said Mair. She moved to her pantry, took out an earthenware jar, poured a stream of thin gold liquid into a rough mug.

"Here. Mallow juice and honey. To restore." She gave Merry a mocking smile. "Not to kill."

Merry sat down on the bench. The old woman stood watching her, warming her back by the fire. Merry eyed her over the rim of the mug.

"I believe you. Not because I think you could not kill but because I think you're telling the truth."

She sipped. The drink was sweet, with a slight taste of roots.

"Maybe I am. Maybe I'm not. You should be careful who you trust."

Merry looked at her thoughtfully. "I am" was all she said.

The woman turned away, bustled in her pantry, returned with a pewter plate.

"You should eat too," she said, offering it to Merry.

"Thank you." Merry felt half starving, half sick with fear, but she ate. She needed to.

The bread was dark and grainy, the cheese rich.

The old lady went into a side room and came back with Merry's headlamp, sheathed knife, and thigh strap. She removed the knife from the sheath.

"Never seen anything so fine," she said, turning the handle so the firelight glinted off lethal steel.

"Good, isn't it?"

"I'm wondering why a girl with your aristocratic bearing carries such a blade?"

"I'm no aristo."

"*Not used to tallow candles.* Only aristocrats and the church have beeswax. *Tall and well fed.* Like a girl of noble birth." Mair paused, put down the knife, and took Merry's hand in hers. She turned it, tracing her fingers over the palm.

"What, you a palmist?" asked Merry.

The woman laughed. "Don't need palms to see!"

Merry felt a punch of realization. This woman was Seren's ancestor. A healer who had the *sight*, just like all those who had gone before.

"No, I'm looking at these calluses . . . wondering how a fine lady got them. If you weren't female, I'd say you had archer's hands."

Merry smiled but said nothing.

"The hands, the knife, the lost eye . . ." The old woman's gaze went far away. Then it snapped back to Merry. "Are you some kind of warrior?"

Merry reached for her knife, sheathed it, and strapped it to her thigh, where the short wool tunic just about covered it. She pulled on her headlamp but kept it turned off.

"Just a traveler," she said.

Then she slipped out into the closing night.

Chapter Thirty-One

The valley was drenched with moonlight. It reflected off the black granite of the castle, shimmered on the stream, and silvered the dew-laced grass.

Slipping from copse to copse, keeping low, Merry moved through the night. She kept the weight on the outside of her feet, just as Professor Parks had taught her. *A useful skill, for a hunter.* She had a sense that in this time, it was a straight choice—that if you weren't a hunter, you could only be prey.

She scanned left to right in a wide arc.

There was no sign that anyone else was around. No more birds erupted from their roosts. No twigs cracked. No movement except for the trees swaying in the breeze and sheep shifting on the hillside. She guessed that nights in the sixteenth century saw everyone tucked up in cottage or castle. Everyone save the predators, the wild animals, the thieves and vagabonds. And her.

Suddenly, just as she was emerging from one thicket and moving off into the open, she got a sense of something. Of *someone.* She reached down, unsheathed her knife.

She turned full circle, checking the darkness behind, the moonlit grass in front. She could see no one, hear nothing save the soft soughing of the wind through the leaves. But she could not shake this sense of another presence. She could feel it in the goose bumps on her arms and the hair rising on the back of her neck.

She turned again, saw nothing. She was probably spooking herself with all these thoughts of vagabonds and wolves.

She hurried on. Made it to the stream, leaped it cleanly, hurried for the cover of trees. She'd always felt the Black Castle had eyes. Now more than ever the arrow slits seemed to be looking back at her.

Suddenly, two flaming torches bobbed around one side of the castle. Night watchmen! The earl would have had men patrolling, especially with King Henry staying. The torches moved down the hill. Toward her.

She dropped to the ground. One of the things her father had told her when they played hide-and-seek was that it's the flash of a pale face or hands or movement that gives you away. So she stayed still, face pressed into the damp earth, breath so soft her back hardly rose or fell.

She could hear the faint chatter of the men coming closer, the cadences of Welsh. They came to within a hundred yards of her, then, very gradually, they moved away again. Merry stayed where she was, not yet daring to move. The dew had soaked her woolen shift and she began to shiver. She raised her head, scanned left to right. The torches were far away in the distance, a faint glow, growing fainter.

Merry got to her feet and hurried over the grassland toward the cover of the forest. Trees everywhere, so many more than in her time. *Better cover*, said the voice in her head. This new voice she hadn't known existed.

High above, an owl hooted. The soft whoosh of its wings passed overhead. She glanced up, saw its outline silhouetted against the moon.

Inside the forest, the darkness was intense. Only narrow shards of moonlight cut through. She had her headlamp but the night watchmen and their flaming torches had stood out like beacons. So would even the modest beam of a flashlight. They'd taught her a useful lesson. She'd go in darkness. Even though it made navigating much more difficult.

She knew where the tunnel was in her time, but the forest and the darkness changed everything. She could easily miss it or spend hours going around in circles, or twist her ankle down a fox hole, or tumble on roots and break her leg. Her bare feet were already bleeding, cut by briars and sharp stones.

She paused, gave her eye time to adjust, tried to feel the forest around her, to sense the hidden hazards.

Constantly she felt the ripples of fear. *Fear is good*, said the new voice. *Fear keeps you alive.*

She moved deeper into the forest. Branches snagged her woolen shawl. One raked her cheek, drawing blood. She winced. She had one good eye. A thorn could rip it in the darkness.

Arms raised, protecting her face, she searched for the mound and the gorse bush that hid the tunnel in her time. But she couldn't find it. She began to feel a wave of panic. She feared she was going around in circles. Her arms were lacerated with cuts from the brambles.

She had to take a risk. She turned on her headlamp. Its beam lit the thicket ahead. She hunted quickly, helped by the light. Then she saw it. The huge gorse bush. Even bigger than in her time. She turned off the light, squatted down, listened to the night, waited for her eye to readjust to darkness.

She heard nothing human, just the wind and the creaking of trees.

She felt sure there was no watchman guarding the tunnels. Only the inner circle of family and retainers would have known that they existed. That was their whole purpose. Emergency and secret routes to and from the castle. Built in an age when war parties were a way of life. Waiting no more, she crawled in under the thorny branches.

The coconut smell of the yellow flowers filled the air as she pushed through into the mouth of the tunnel. She straightened, extended her arms, spread her fingers, found the tunnel wall. Using it as a guide, she made her way along the narrow passage. She didn't turn on her headlamp, just in case anyone did happen to be there. Darkness was her best protection.

There was a sound, like a footstep. She froze, listened, but there was nothing. It must have been the echo of her own bare feet slapping against the stone floor. She continued on, skin bristling with fear, ears straining for a sound that never came.

After a few minutes she slowed. She had a sense of something before her, blocking her way, moments before her fingers touched wood. They probed for the door handle, closed on cold metal. She muttered a silent prayer and turned the handle.

It moved! But with a horrible groan of ungreased metal. She paused, heart racing. But there was nothing; no approaching footsteps, no shouts of inquiry. Cautiously, she turned the handle farther. It moved silently now, till with a click it opened into the bowels of the castle. Into the dungeons.

Wood burned in a brazier, casting out scant warmth and a meager light that hardly penetrated the gloom. There was no chimney, so the smoke hung heavy, stinging Merry's eye. She wanted to cough, swallowed saliva instead. She looked around, scanning, listening. It didn't seem like anyone was there. She pulled the door shut behind her.

On tiptoe, she slunk through the vaulted jail, searching for her ancestor. All eight cells were empty.

Maybe he lay shackled in a cart rumbling toward the Tower of London. Maybe he was dead already. Apart from the loss to his wife and children, Merry couldn't begin to work out what that might mean for her *own* family. Only knew that it would be beyond bad.

She began to shake with rage and despair. Her teeth chattered in the cold. And then she heard a sound. Rusty metal groaning. She spun around. The door to the dungeons was opening again. Somebody was coming in.

Chapter Thirty-Two

Merry glanced around wildly. There was nowhere to hide and no other exit. She turned and ran up the stairs into the body of the castle.

Around and around the narrow staircase, hugging the dank walls. Candles fixed to wall sconces, between pockets of darkness. She slunk from one to the next, heart and mind racing.

Who had followed her into the tunnel? And were they following her now? She had to find somewhere to hide. She hurried on up. She thought she could hear footsteps behind her but couldn't be sure.

She came out into the servants' area, in her time the cheery domain of Mrs. Baskerville, outfitted with gleaming fridges and freezers and all the modern conveniences of a contemporary kitchen. Now it was dingy and gloomy. She could hear the clatter of plates and pans in the big old kitchen, and voices arguing in Welsh. She tiptoed past, on up the servants' narrow staircase, up to the bedroom floors. The priest hole, she thought. She could wait in there till everyone went to sleep, then sneak out. She padded down the hallway, paused at the corner, breathing hard.

Male voices. Coming up the main staircase. Heading her way. She froze. Where now?

Then a door opened behind her. Trapping her. Merry wheeled around and came face-to-face with an elaborately dressed woman with blond ringlets and a fancy lace head covering.

"Why are you loitering?" demanded the lady. Merry opened her mouth to say something when the woman cut in. "Follow me!" she commanded, wrinkling her face with distaste as she eyed Merry up and down. Her gaze lingered, but only briefly, on Merry's ruined eye. This was an age where physical imperfections, marrings and scarrings, pox marks and shriveled limbs were not uncommon. "I've been waiting *ages* for a maid to come and see to my chamber pot," complained the woman, stalking back into her room.

Merry nodded her head and hurried in after her. In her linen shirt, tunic, and shawl, and bare feet, she must have looked like a particularly ragged servant. Just right for emptying chamber pots.

An unpleasant stink hit Merry. No wonder Little Miss Ringlets was so impatient.

"Go on, then! Take it!" ordered the woman.

Merry located the smell. Under the bed, of course. She hurried across the wooden floor and crouched down just as she heard other footsteps approach. And pause at the open door.

"Everything to your liking, Lady Bess?" asked a cool, clipped voice.

"Why, perfectly fine, thank you, Lord de Courcy," replied the woman coquettishly.

"Excellent. We shall see you for the feast, then. We have His Majesty's favorite—*spiced swan*."

"Ooh, how delicious! Mine too," gushed the lady.

Merry kept her head bowed. She was terrified that the earl

would recognize she was not one of his servants. Her hands trembled as she gripped the stinking chamber pot. She felt eyes on her back and waited, heart hammering. But the earl and his companion moved on. Merry blew out her breath, waiting until their voices had faded. She got up, nodded to the lady, and scurried out of the room.

The door shut behind her. Listening hard, adrenaline pumping, Merry crept along the empty hallway. She'd find somewhere to dump the bedpan, then hide in the priest hole. She crept past the watching portraits and realized with a jolt that most of the faces she was used to seeing were yet to be born. Their places were occupied by lushly woven tapestries.

She paused in front of what she thought was the right tapestry, pushed it aside, and searched for the tiny ridge in the paneling. With the right amount of pressure, a concealed door would pop open, revealing the tiny hiding place inside. But there was no ridge. She searched under other tapestries and portraits, getting desperate as the seconds ticked by, but there was no priest hole. Then she realized: It hadn't been built! Wouldn't be built until Henry's daughter, Elizabeth, became queen. She'd have to find somewhere else to hide, or try to get out now.

She rounded a corner, headed toward the servants' staircase, then pulled up abruptly, nearly sloshing the contents of the chamber pot over herself. Someone was coming up. She could hear their footsteps, their labored breath.

She turned and rushed back in the direction she had come, looking for a room to hide in. But each one seemed to be occupied. She could hear murmured conversations, some in English, others in

French, coming through the heavy oak doors. She hurried on. There was just one room left at the far end of the hallway.

The red room. James had shown it to her once, when his parents were out—said it had always been occupied by the earl and countess. Merry paused, ear to the door. She heard nothing: no aristocratic conversation between husband and wife; no instructions to a servant; no industrious clattering of maids cleaning.

She opened the door, ducked inside, closed it. She blew out a breath and looked around.

The room was richly furnished, with lavish scarlet curtains and a heavily carved four-poster bed. The floor was sprinkled with lavender and rosemary.

Merry hurried across the scattered herbs, which released their scent into the air. She pushed the chamber pot deep under the bed. As she was straightening up, there was a knock on the door.

"My Lady?" called a voice.

Oh God, not again. Where to hide now? Under the bed with the chamber pot? No, she'd be spotted if the maid went to retrieve it, which, given the smell, she was bound to. She spun around wildly, spotted the wardrobe, tiptoed rapidly across the lavender and rosemary, ducked inside, and pulled the door shut just as the bedroom door opened.

Crouched in the darkness, she heard a voice curse in Welsh. There was a tiny crack in the wood. Merry put her eye to it and peered out. A maid was hauling out the chamber pot. Picking it up, she hurried out the way she'd come. Merry moved her hand to wipe a bead of sweat off her lip. Her fingers hit metal, a lever perhaps, because there was a slight click and something popped open against

Merry's arm. It was a drawer, velvet-lined. Her fingers explored the soft surface. She felt rings, a selection, some smooth, some jeweled. One hooked itself onto her forefinger. She held it to the crack in the wood. In the darkness, it gleamed gold.

She thought of the book, of its promise of treasures. Her family could do with whatever treasures she could find. Surely it would be all right taking just this one . . . ?

She pushed the ring onto her finger.

A great gong sounded.

It was time for the royal feast.

She'd failed to find and free her ancestor. She had to believe he would be okay, that she shouldn't in any case interfere with history more than she already had.

It was time to escape.

Chapter Thirty-Three

>>>>————————————————————►

Wearing her Tudor treasure, Merry crept out of the wardrobe and listened at the door. She heard footsteps and chatter and a swishing of silk as lords and ladies and maybe even the king passed by and headed downstairs to the Great Hall, to their dinner.

Merry still had no idea who had followed her or if they were still attempting to follow her, but she couldn't hide any longer. Everyone, both noble and lowborn, would be occupied with the feast. Now was her best chance of escape.

She gave it five minutes, hoping that everyone would now be at the dinner; then she hurried down the main staircase, past the watching portraits. If anyone saw her, all she could do was run. She could hear the sound of the banquet booming out of the Great Hall. Raucous laughter, the clanging of metal plates, some kind of twanging string instrument, probably a mandolin.

She crept toward the door by the staircase that led to the kitchen area—her route out, via the dungeons. She pulled it open a few inches. A procession of servants was rushing up, carrying huge platters of food and jugs of steaming wine. She closed the door. They'd spot her as an interloper.

She hurried back to the main part of the castle, turned a corner, and almost collided with an elderly man dressed in velvets and frills.

He was leaning against the wall with a lost look on his face. Merry recoiled, waiting for him to shout, grab her, or react in any way. But he just blinked in surprise. Merry could see his eyes were covered in filmy white cataracts. Whoever he was, he seemed trapped inside his own dementia.

"The feast," he said in a reedy voice. "Why aren't you there? Will you take me back in?" He pointed vaguely with a trembling hand.

Merry realized he probably couldn't see her threadbare clothes, her bare feet. She put on her best aristocratic voice.

"Er, yes, of course. But I must first have some fresh air," she said, hurrying off toward the front door.

She was committed now. She strode purposefully toward the door, hauled it open.

A blast of cold air hit her. The full moon lit the courtyard, which had a stable block in one corner. It looked beautiful, eerie, and, best of all, deserted. Merry closed the huge door behind her and hurried across the cobbles. They were cold, slippery underfoot with the evening dew.

And there was the drawbridge. Thankfully it was down and the portcullis was raised. She rushed on. Then the castle door crashed open just as she reached the stables. Merry spun around. The old man teetered out. Two women hurried after him, calling him. They were focused on him but they'd see her any second, especially if she darted to the drawbridge. She ducked inside the stables.

Heart pounding, she breathed in the smell of horse and manure and wet straw. She could hear no signs of humans, but that didn't mean there weren't grooms sleeping in the hayloft. She blinked in the darkness, waited for her vision to adjust. Stiffened. She could feel eyes on her. There was a low snort.

She saw a dark face above the half door to a stall. The dished head, the black eyes blazing with intelligence and curiosity and just a touch of indignation. It was the Arab horse. The one she'd seen the countess riding on the hunt. The horse snorted again. Merry moved closer, offered him her palm to sniff.

Don't give me away, please, she thought. She heard footsteps outside on the cobbles, the plaintive voice of the old man, and the two women arguing with him.

"She's out here," the old man was saying. "Fresh air. She needed fresh air."

"Come on, Father," said a crisp but loving voice. "There's no one here. Look around."

"Excuse me, my Lady," came a voice. "I think he's right. I saw someone slip into the stables."

Merry felt a wave of panic. She'd be discovered. Again. And this time she would not be able to explain herself, pretend to be a groom. She had to get away. And quickly. She pulled back the bolt to the horse's door, eased into the stall.

Trying to slow her breathing, summoning calm, Merry reached up to stroke him. She should go slow to win him over, but she didn't have time. They'd be here in seconds. She had to escape *now*.

She took the bridle hanging outside his stall and slipped it on him. She was distracted by the task, trying not to let the metal bit jangle. She didn't hear the soft whisper of skirts.

As she buckled the bridle, a hand grabbed her arm. Merry gasped in terror, turned.

The lady of the hunt stood there, lavish in velvet and rubies, her eyes narrowed in fury.

"Who are you and what are you doing in my stable?" she demanded.

Merry knew those eyes. She'd seen them in her portrait—five hundred years into the future.

Chapter Thirty-Four

It was Catherine, the twelfth Countess de Courcy. The elderly man, who had to be her father, stood behind her, frowning. A maid stood beside him, holding on to him as if he might fall.

Merry's brain raced. She played for time. "Lady de Courcy. I beg your leave." That was how they spoke, wasn't it? Merry had read Shakespeare.

"You beg my leave. To do what? To steal my stallion? We *hang* horse thieves!" spat the countess, voice dripping venom. She lifted her head, opened her mouth to call out.

Merry lunged forward, stuck her hand over the countess's mouth, choking off her words. She struggled, tried to get the countess's hand off her, but the viselike grip remained. Merry was taller than the countess, heavier, more muscled. She could have taken her down, but the countess would scream. She *had* to keep her hand over her mouth. Thankfully the countess was handicapped by her elaborate dress. Merry kicked out, hit the side of her knee. The countess bit her hand and yelped as she fell to the floor, but she took Merry with her. The maid started screaming as Merry and the countess wrestled in the straw.

"Help! Help! Thief! Attacker!" Then she joined in, grabbing her, viciously kicking Merry while the countess grabbed her arm and clung on like a limpet.

Merry took the kicks, ignored them. There was a much greater threat.

The stallion, enraged by the screaming, by the invasion of his stall, reared and stamped, then lowered his head to them, teeth bared.

Desperately, Merry grabbed the countess's hand and yanked it, breaking her grip.

"Thief! Thief! Here in the stables!" yelled the maid again.

Merry jumped up, sent the maid flying with a two-handed push to her chest, kicked the countess in the knee again, caught the stallion's reins, and rushed from the stall, past the old man, who flailed out an arm, trying to grab her.

Leading the furious horse, Merry ran from the stables into the courtyard.

Alerted by the countess's screams and curses, men streamed from the castle into the courtyard. Grabbing the stallion's mane, Merry vaulted onto his back. She squeezed her legs.

"Go!" she urged.

He shot into an instant bolt, accelerated out of the courtyard, under the portcullis, across the wooden drawbridge. Merry leaned forward onto his neck, twined her fingers in his mane. If she fell off, she'd be caught. She needed all her riding skills and more. This horse was bigger and much more powerful than Jacintha. And she didn't know his whims and fancies, what spooked or scared him, if he bucked or reared.

The night was an explosion of sound: her horse's pounding hooves, men shouting, the countess and her maid screaming. Then, around the corner of the castle, came the guards with their flaming torches. Running at her.

The stallion spooked, shied away, and then slipped on the wet grass. Merry lurched to one side, nearly came off, then shot forward, desperately bracing herself against the stallion's neck. By some miracle she stayed on and he kept his feet. She kicked him on, away from the flaming torches, and he accelerated down the hill, wild with the adrenaline of flight. She knew they'd be followed but they had a head start and the Arab had to be the fastest horse in the stables.

She leaned lower across his neck, urging him ever faster, gripping his mane and his reins. Then, in the moonlight, the boundary wall loomed.

"Easy now, easy, need to slow," she murmured. He was well trained, but Merry had to haul back on the reins. Hard to do bareback. Merry felt his muscles bunching; then he launched. They flew over the wall, landing solidly.

And then through the darkness came the baying of hounds.

Terror flooded Merry's veins, and the horse's. He lengthened his stride, galloped faster still. Merry guided him across the land to the void of darkness that was the forest. She slowed to a canter, then a trot, as they rode under the canopy. The thunder of his hooves softened on the pine-needled floor. Shards of moonlight cut through the trees, lighting the path just enough.

She could hear the dogs baying behind her, as if crying out to each other: *This way, this way!*

At last, she saw a break in the trees and came out onto the common lands, onto Sarn Helen. She pushed the stallion into a gallop. It was horribly risky. He could step into a rabbit hole and fall and in minutes the dogs would be upon them, but if they went any slower the dogs would get them anyway. All or nothing . . .

She raced on, saw the fold in the hillside and the forest that concealed the pool. She didn't glance around, just entered the wood, praying they had a good enough lead. But then a dog bayed, horribly close, and she had no more time for thought.

Branches ripped at her clothes, scraped her face, caught her hair. She lay low on the horse's neck, trying to avoid the worst of them, but she had to keep looking up to check her bearings.

She felt the ground falling away; then she heard the sound of running water, and they emerged from the trees onto the grassy bank. The pool lay before them, black water glinting in the moonlight. And behind it, the waterfall.

The stallion hesitated for the first time, ears flickering, calculating. She had to let him go free. She slipped from his back, quickly removed his bridle so he wouldn't get trapped by flailing reins catching a branch. She leaned in, kissed his neck. "Thank you," she breathed. Above the rush and tumble of the waterfall came the baying of the hounds. "Now go!" she urged.

He needed no encouragement. He plunged into the stream, cantered across, jumped up onto the far bank, and galloped off into the trees.

Merry dropped the bridle, strode into the stream and toward the waterfall, just as a massive wolfhound burst through the trees, hurtled down the slope, and leaped into the stream after her.

Merry dived under the waterfall, came up into the cave, took one deep breath, then kicked under again. The current took her into the blackness.

Chapter Thirty-Five

Merry was dragged by the gushing current through the tunnel. This way, the river ran terrifyingly fast. There was no need to fight, to stroke your way desperately to the other side. You just had to ride it, avoid smashing into the roof or the walls. One hand reaching forward, the other hand protecting her head, Merry raced along. Seconds later, the river spat her out, up into the cave, pulled her through the waterfall, delivered her into the shallows.

She sucked in air, walked on trembling legs up onto the bank.

Was she home? Was this the twenty-first century or some other time?

Then, above the roar of the waterfall, she heard a howl behind her.

Fear stabbed at her.

She turned to see the huge wolfhound, half drowned but still snarling, vibrating with bloodlust, standing just feet away. Merry could see him gather himself, about to leap. She pulled her knife from its strap, unsheathed it, gripped the blade in her fingers, and threw.

The knife sailed through the air and embedded itself in the wolfhound's chest. With a hideous howl, the beast fell to the ground, lashing back and forth. Merry waited until it stopped moving; then she reached out, pulled her knife from its body.

Her fingers were slippery with blood. She studied the moonlit darkness, waiting to see if more wolfhounds would emerge. None did. They must have drowned, or managed to stay on the other side. She rubbed her hand on her tunic, shoved the knife back into its strap around her thigh.

A sudden whinny pierced the air. Merry burst out laughing. Joy and a wild relief surged through her. She'd know that call anywhere.

Jacintha!

She was home.

Merry rushed through the trees to where Jacintha was tethered. The mare snorted at her, as if to say, *Where the hell have you been?* She stroked her knuckles up and down her forehead, just as the mare liked. Merry wondered how long she'd been away. She rummaged in her pack, pulled out her phone. It still had a slight charge. She checked the time. Midnight. It had been only half a day, a few hours of the night, but it felt so much longer. She quickly changed into her own clothes, squashed Mair's woolen ones into her pack. Then she untethered Jacintha, vaulted up on her back, and set off for home.

She crossed the common lands, glancing right and left, but nobody was around. No one to witness the Welsh Mountain pony with her black-clad rider moving silently through the night. They passed like ghosts through the darkness.

As she crossed onto her own lands, Merry gazed across the valley at the Black Castle looming through the moonlight. She shuddered. Just hours ago. Five hundred years ago.

She felt a wave of dizziness so intense she nearly fell off. Grasping Jacintha's mane, she walked her to the field near the barn where the rest of the herd grazed. She slipped from her pony's back, put her arms around Jacintha's neck, and, for a minute, just held on. Then, worrying about what on earth she'd say to her parents if they were still up, she headed for the farmhouse.

She saw with relief that there were no lights on. Her parents had probably gone to bed early, assumed she'd gone out on one of her many long expeditions on Jacintha. They had reluctantly allowed her the same freedoms as before, though she knew they worried. She blew out a breath and let herself in.

She tiptoed up the stairs, past her parents' bedroom. She could hear the soft sounds of their breathing. She peered through the open door into Gawain's bedroom. He lay sleeping on his back, arms thrown out. She felt a stab of emotion, thought of her ancestor. He was long-since dead, but had he lived? Had he survived the day and night that she had just lived through?

Exhausted, she headed on into her own room. Closed the door softly. Cold, still trembling with the shock and terror of it all, Merry undressed and pulled on pajamas. She paused just long enough to drain the water from the glass on her bedside table and remove her eye patch; then she got into bed and pulled the covers over her head like she was hiding from the world.

She was home.

She'd escaped the sixteenth century.

On her finger the golden ring gleamed.

An unbreakable link to the past.

Chapter Thirty-Six

Radio playing. Distant dogs barking. Ponies whinnying. Merry woke shouting, her head full of wolfhounds, huntsmen, the drowning river. *The river of time.* She gazed around wildly, saw the stenciled wardrobe, her primrose-sprigged curtains. *Home.* She felt an overwhelming surge of relief. And disbelief. Had she imagined it all?

She pulled off the covers, tried to get out of bed. Winced. Everything hurt. Her cuts stung like fury. They were all the evidence she needed. She limped across the wooden floors. She was starving, but first she'd have to see to her injuries.

The bathroom was empty. She hurried in, stripped, got under the shower.

Her legs, arms, feet, hands, and face were latticed with cuts and scratches. She swore as the hot water sluiced over them. She shampooed her hair and tried to pick out bits of bramble and twig that had caught in it. She practically unearthed a bird's nest.

She got out, toweled herself dry, daubed her cuts with antiseptic and covered them with adhesive bandages, apart from the ones on her face. They'd heal better in the air.

Pulling on her dressing gown, she hurried back to her room, dressed in soft, baggy cargo pants and a long-sleeve T-shirt. She slipped a woolen cardigan on top to make sure no bandages were visible through the thin fabric. She toed her feet into her Uggs and was just about to go downstairs when she saw the ring glinting on her finger.

She felt a lurch. *You stole*, she chided herself. *You had reason*, the new voice answered. She pulled off the ring, hid it in her bedside table.

"Merry! It's gone ten. Are you ill?" asked her mother when she appeared in the kitchen. "And your face! My God, Merry! Did someone attack you?"

Merry shook her head. Well, other than the countess . . . "No one, Mam, don't worry. I just went out riding on Jacintha, got carried away. You know what I'm like with time . . . Night fell and I was in the forest."

"Luckily for you, your father and I went to bed early. He assured me you'd be fine even though I wanted to go out and look for you. He heard you come in, though. God only knows what time."

"Sorry," said Merry, inadequately. On impulse, she went over to her mother, kissed her cheek.

Elinor smiled. "I expect you're hungry, Spinner?"

Merry nodded. "Starving!"

Her mother made pancakes, busying herself at the stove. Gawain sat in his high chair scrunching up a plastic book.

Merry ate three pancakes with sugar and lemon juice, washed down with a mug of milky coffee and a glass of water.

She felt stronger.

Then her father appeared in the doorway. "Merry Seren Owen! What time did you—?" He crossed the kitchen in two paces. "What the hell happened to your face? Who hurt you?"

"No one." She shook her head. "Thornbushes, Da."

Caradoc made a harrumphing sound. "And the look in your eye . . . where does that come from?"

"What look?" asked Merry warily.

"You look frightened, *cariad*. And something else . . . Like you've had a very, very close shave."

Merry forced herself to meet his gaze. "No one hurt me."

They *could* have, they *nearly* did. She thought of the huntsmen, the wolfhounds, the knife . . . She shuddered, hoped her father didn't see it. She got up, hugged him, comforted by his bulk, by the security of him. But then she thought of her ancestor. If he had been killed that day, could the tentacles of time reach forward, claim her father too? She pushed down the memories, tried to reason them away. Five hundred years ago. Long gone. Her father was safe. They were all safe.

So why didn't she feel it?

Chapter Thirty-Seven

Merry could hardly drag herself through her chores for the rest of the day. Her body ached and she was exhausted. It was a kind of delayed shock, she knew that. Her mind kept turning back to the River of Time, as she now called it, to the Black Castle, thinking of being hunted, of being prey . . . She'd find herself staring into space, teeth clenched, hands fisted, seeing not what was before her but what was five hundred years ago. She avoided her parents, exhausted too by the effort of lying, of concealing, of smiling and pretending everything was normal.

She went to her bedroom at eight o'clock, pleading a headache. She closed herself in, sat on her bed in the sudden, throbbing silence. She opened her bedside table, pulled out the ring. Turned it over in her hands, studying it. It was a signet ring made of rich rose gold—Welsh gold, of course. On the outside, she could see the motto of the de Courcys: *Avis la Fin.* Look to the End. It was odd; instead of the two phoenixes that they now had, there was only one. She turned the ring around in her hands, studying the inside. There was a number, in Roman numerals. MDXX. She Googled it on her phone, worked it out: 1520. She whistled through her teeth. Nearly five hundred years old.

It was beautiful but she didn't want it anymore. It gave her the same feeling her book had: that she wasn't the rightful owner. She had taken the book in innocence and had nearly paid a very high price for it. She knew with some deep instinct that she would pay a higher price for taking this ring in full knowledge of what she was doing.

She shut it away again, pulled her curtains, then slipped under the covers.

She could almost feel the ring, lying there next to her, just inches away. It was like a link in a chain connecting her to the past, to the sixteenth century. As she lay in the darkness, she cast her mind back, felt just a pale version of the terror that had almost consumed her. But what was almost worse was the feeling that the past had somehow gotten into her blood, as if swimming through the River of Time had contaminated her in some way, infected her, because some small part of her, the part that spoke with the new voice, that walked on the outside of its feet, *wanted* to go back.

But the Merry she had known for all her life, the Merry she had been, that girl did not want to go back. Under any circumstances. *That* Merry knew what she should do: get rid of the ring. Neutralize it in the same way she had neutralized the book. As she fell asleep, she thought up a plan, intending to carry it out the next day. She reckoned she'd worked it all out, a way to keep her and her family safe and sever the link with the past. She didn't give a thought to the law of unintended consequences, to the chain of events the ring and her plan would unleash. If she had known, she would have taken it to the top of the north face of Pen y Fan and thrown it to the winds.

The next morning, making the most of her free time during the wonderfully long Easter holidays, Merry headed out after breakfast.

"Going for a walk," she told her mother.

"What's with the backpack?" Elinor asked.

"Just being practical. Warm layer, bottle of water," improvised Merry. She hurried from the kitchen before her mother could check.

She headed for the burial mound. Using the trick Parks had taught her, she crept up to it, rolling on the outside of her feet, moving silently as she had when she walked through the Tudor night. She kept pausing, turning full circle, checking he was not hiding behind a bush, but there was no sign of him.

She waited and watched some distance away from the burial mound. She circled it, checked from all angles, waited and watched, but there was no sign of Parks. It was a Saturday, she didn't expect him to be working, but she was taking no chances.

Just to be sure, she called out, "Professor Parks? It's Merry. Come to say hello. You'd better come out if you're hiding somewhere. I don't want to contaminate the scene!"

Her words just echoed away through the trees. She waited, half expecting Parks to step from some concealing thicket with a frown and a sharp comment.

But after the minutes ticked by, Merry felt sure she was alone.

She walked up the mound, eyed the squares marked out by strings on sticks. She pulled off her backpack and sat cross-legged on the forest floor. She opened the pack, took out Mair's shawl, still damp, and cut off a small piece, big enough to wrap the ring in. She rubbed it in the loose soil. She scored its wool fibers with a pair of scissors till it looked rough and threadbare. Then she rolled the ring in the tattered fabric, got to her feet, and walked up to the mound.

She studied the neat little squares, trying to work out where Parks would dig next. There was one that looked half excavated and she chose that. She pushed the cloth in deep but not too deep, just an inch or so, reckoning he'd find it within a day or two. Then she tried to smooth out the top layer. She sat back, studied her handiwork. *It'll do*, she thought. Then, glancing around to make sure Parks hadn't crept up on her, she backed away.

"I'm sorry, chieftain," she whispered, as if he might hear. "Just doing what I need to do."

She'd hoped to feel a sense of relief. She'd gotten rid of the ring. She'd severed that link to the past. But that night in bed, she had the same strange yearning, the same strange fear that she would go back. She saw it in brilliant detail, the Tudor kingdom she had entered, the world she had left behind. Every time she closed her eye, she would see it on the inside of her eyelid, more lifelike than the world outside her bedroom window.

Merry tried to live a normal life. She texted James, but he texted back that he had no news. He was training, doing his best, waiting . . .

Robbed of her searching, deprived of her swim training, with no James to burn the days, Merry felt oddly purposeless. She still felt the strange yearning, the sense of contamination, the desire to go back to the past. She felt as if she had unfinished business there.

She found herself heading out to Sarn Helen, to the smooth ground of the old Roman road where she could gallop. She would lean down across Jacintha's neck and urge her on: Run, *run like the wind*, and her pony would lengthen her stride and gallop so fast Merry felt like they were flying over the wild mountains.

Every time she took Jacintha out, she would remember how on the Arab stallion she had galloped for her life.

She rode out for four days in a row, in sun and rain. All the time she felt as if she were waiting for something to happen. Waiting for Professor Parks to discover the ring and bring it to them—the treasure that would save their farm forever. But Parks didn't come. And Merry began to have a jittery feeling, as if something were happening, something she couldn't see, wouldn't see, until it was too late.

Chapter Thirty-Eight

While Merry was out riding, James arrived back at the Black Castle. He had an exhausting reunion with his parents and his sister, Lady Alicia. They switched between delight at seeing him and anger at what they described as his desertion. Then there was the inevitable interrogation with its mixture of threats and bribery. After two emotional hours, he was rescued by the arrival of Dr. Philipps, who brought with him some fascinating news. Now more eager than ever to see Merry, James extracted himself from his family's clutches, headed to his room, and texted her.

> Can I come round?
> **You're back???**
> For a few days.
> **Perfect timing! Everyone's out. I just got back from riding. Come when you can.**
> On my way.

He found her outside at the stables, cleaning tack, when he turned up twenty minutes later, puffing hard. He glanced at his watch, smiled.

"Almost a personal best. Probably would have been if I hadn't trained so hard yesterday."

"What was special about yesterday?"

"Let's go and sit on your bench," he replied. He didn't need to rest. He just didn't want to blurt out his news standing here by the stables.

They walked together across the grass and sat down side by side.

"Like I said," James began, angling his body toward Merry. "I had a hard day's training. Then, at the end of it, the manager called me into his office." James tried to talk normally, but all he wanted to do was yell out his news. "They want to sign me when I turn sixteen. They've offered me a contract."

Merry shouted out, grabbed him, pulled him to his feet and into a hug. He hugged her back.

"That is amaaazing! James, I am so happy for you." Merry released him and he saw she had a tear in her eye.

"I did it, Merry," he said quietly.

"You did it, James," she echoed. "I am so proud of you."

He nodded, felt suddenly bashful. "Thanks," he said, cheeks reddening. They both sat down again.

"I'm guessing they're not quite so happy at home."

"Could say that. But I had to tell them face-to-face, and tomorrow's my birthday too. It seemed wrong not to be at home."

"So what's going to happen, then?"

"I'll sign. Even if my parents disinherit me."

"They won't."

James gave a brooding look toward the Black Castle. "Who knows? They're lurching between threats and persuasion at the moment."

He held out his hand, twisted it so that a glint of rose gold caught the light.

"My mother just gave me this, in advance of my birthday. The de Courcy signet ring. You know the drill, every son and heir gets one at sixteen. It marks him as an adult, ready to fight, ready to go to war, ready to assume the responsibilities that go with the privilege of being the lord of the Black Castle."

Merry reached out, grabbed his hand, studied the ring on his little finger. "But it's different!" she exclaimed. "It's not like the normal de Courcy crest!"

"No, it's not," agreed James. "This one's an antique. From 1520."

"1520," repeated Merry, looking away, her voice barely a whisper. She turned back to James. "Where did she get it from, your mother?"

"She was very coy about that," replied James. "You know what she's like, trying to buy bits of the castle's history—like she tried to buy your book," he added with a half smile. "So she was very pleased to find this. She has a network of antique dealers on the lookout. I guess she got lucky," he concluded.

Merry said nothing. She just looked away again, her face hard. James was having difficulty keeping up with her. She'd been over-joyed by his news; now she was brooding like something truly terrible had happened. What the heck was going on in her head?

"And there's something else," James said, hoping to shift her mood back to sunny.

"Full of news today, aren't you!" said Merry. "What is it?"

"It'll blow your mind. It blew mine."

"Go on!"

"Dr. Philipps just paid us a visit. He—"

"He's come back?" Merry interrupted. "Was Professor Parks with him?"

James shook his head. "Surprisingly, not this time. Apparently he went to London a few days ago on some urgent business."

Merry swore. "Bit my lip," she explained.

James carried on. "Anyway, Dr. Philipps discovered something in an old Welsh text he unearthed. He was pretty excited about it."

"And . . ."

"You know that King Henry, Henry VIII, stayed with us . . ."

"Oh, yes. I know," Merry responded with some bitterness.

James glanced at her. It was a strange reaction.

"Well, apparently he asked for a tourney to be held. Archery, of course, and jousting, which he also loved, and falconry. We used to supply him with peregrine falcons from the Beacons. And this is where it gets deeply weird." James paused, kept his gaze on Merry. "He called for a longbow contest. And he called upon the pledge that your ancestor made to the Black Prince. That each generation of Owens furnishes him with a longbowman, if their king asks for one. And King Henry did."

Merry began to look odd.

"Thing is, your ancestor, the man of the house at the time, was, er, apparently in prison." James hesitated just as Merry spoke out.

"Your dungeons!" she exclaimed.

"How'd you know that?"

"Just guessing," Merry said. "After all, your dungeons are the only prison hereabouts, and they're notorious."

James frowned. "Want to hear the story?"

"Sorry. It wasn't you," said Merry.

James raised his eyebrows. "No. It wasn't. Anyway, your ancestor couldn't honor the pledge, so the king declared that unless an Owen came forward to compete in the tourney, a longbowman who was skilled enough to fight for him in time of war, that Nanteos Farm and all your lands would be confiscated."

Merry gasped. "D'you know what happened? I'm assuming someone came forward."

"Someone *did* come along. An Owen, given away at birth. Just in time, they came back and entered the competition. And this is where it gets truly spooky. It was a woman! They called her the angel warrior. There are legends about her."

Merry said nothing. Ashen-faced, she just stared across the valley.

"And there's more," said James. "It was predicted in your book!"

"What d'you mean?" asked Merry, turning back to him.

James pulled a crumpled piece of paper from his shorts pocket.

"Dr. Philipps just gave me this. He was beyond excited at this point! It's a translation of one of the pages. Listen . . .

" '*There will come, it is foretold, from a kingdom long away, an angel warrior young and bold, though warned against by watcher fey. With skillful eye and hair of gold, with bow and arrow does she fight, to save the land of families old and triumph under kingly sight. But foes remain and freedom's lost and family betrays its own. The Traveler does find to cost and must flee to lands and worlds unknown . . .*' "

James watched in shock as Merry rushed away and retched. He waited till she had composed herself, then he walked up, reached out, touched her shoulder. She turned, offered him a weak smile.

"You all right?" he asked.

"Something I ate."

"Seemed like something I said."

"Must have had too much sugar."

"What is it, Merry? You turned white, looked like you'd seen a ghost," he said, searching her face.

Merry walked back to the bench, sat down heavily.

"You look so troubled," said James, sitting down beside her and gripping her arm. "What's going on? Let me help you! I'll do anything. You know that!"

But Merry shook her head. "No," she said. "No one can help me."

Chapter Thirty-Nine

She'd known somehow that she'd have to go back. That she was infected. Contaminated. She'd feared that she'd *want* to. She'd never thought that she'd *have* to. She was the only one who could save her ancestors and her own family's heritage.

But could she really risk being spotted by the countess and arrested as a horse thief? *We hang horse thieves . . .*

She let out a sob, felt the nausea rising, braced her hands on her thighs, sucked in deep breaths, fought it down.

She stood at her window and watched James heading back across the green acres to the Black Castle. She'd hurt him, she knew. She hated pushing him away, keeping this from him, but it was the last thing he needed. What she was doing was beyond dangerous. She would risk her life but not his, especially now, when all of his dreams were beginning to come true.

This was her destiny. It was as if she'd been meant to find the book. It was the key to saving her family, both *then* and *now* . . .

Everything in it had been leading to this moment, when she'd learned what she had to do. No wonder she'd felt bound to the past, as if somehow she couldn't escape it. Her fate had been written nearly a thousand years before she was born. She'd never be free unless she fulfilled it.

She would swim through the River of Time. Again.

She would answer the king's summons.

She would fight in the longbow tourney.

And she would have to win.

There'd be a cost to going back, Merry had no doubt of that, but she felt too that there'd be a terrible price to pay if she stayed. She didn't know how exactly, just that her family would pay. She'd have to trust her instinct. There was no manual for this. No one she could ask, no past lesson to learn from.

She knew she had to go now, before she changed her mind, before time ran out and the cost fell due. *Think. Plan.* What did she need?

She wished she could take her own longbow, knew she could not. She'd never be able to swim through the river with it. She'd have to use whatever bow she could find. But if it was a typical longbow of the time, the pull would be far too great for her. All she could do was hope to find a bow with a lesser pull. Then, with a sinking heart, she remembered something her father had once told her. Tudor archers were required to shoot their arrows huge distances: a minimum practice range of two hundred and twenty yards. That was much farther than she was used to. She'd need a much more powerful bow to do that, a bow with a draw weight that she wouldn't be able to manage, strong as she was.

She thought furiously. There must be a way around it. She cast her mind back to everything her father had told her about the period. Bow, arrow, string, archer . . . Then an idea rocketed into her brain.

She couldn't take her bow or arrows, but she *could* take her strings. Modern strings were made of something called "fast flight." It was much less yielding than the hemp and linen strings that

Henry VIII's archers would have used, and also a lot thinner. It would propel the arrows much faster. Much farther.

Feeling a throb of excitement, she hurried to the tallboy to get her strings. Three. All of different lengths. At least one of them should fit whatever bow she managed to get hold of. She coiled them in her hand. Now she felt she had a chance. *There's just one problem*, said the voice in her head. *Modern strings put the bow under much greater strain.* There was a real risk that with modern strings, a Tudor bow would break. Merry silenced the voice. Lightning never strikes twice in the same place, she told herself.

She wrapped a Danish in tinfoil and grabbed a small plastic bottle of water. She took them upstairs to her room and packed them inside the waterproof backpack her father had given her last Christmas. She'd swim with it strapped tight to her back. Designed for hill running, it was lightweight, slim fit, and 100 percent waterproof. It would need to be. She took her coiled strings, wrapped them in a plastic bag just in case, and pushed them deep inside the pack. The headlamp went in next, then her catapult and lucky stones. A weapon if she needed one, and a souvenir of James. She added her knife and leg strap.

She moved fast, not allowing herself to linger over anything, not allowing herself to feel.

She changed into her swimsuit and pulled on her skins over it: leggings and long-sleeve T-shirt. She added a long-sleeve fleece, plaited her hair, pulled on her black beanie. Then she dug around for the box she kept in her chest of drawers with all her odds and ends, the box she'd nearly thrown away many times but for some reason had kept, even though she never used what lay inside.

She opened it up. Shining back at her was a sapphire-blue eye. She disinfected it by pouring over a dilution of hydrogen peroxide from the first-aid box; then she dried it with a clean towel, put it back in its box, and zipped it inside the backpack.

Now she was ready. She wanted to see her parents and Gawain one more time. But they were out and it was not to be. She took pen and paper and she wrote a note for them. *I may be gone a few days. PLEASE do not worry. I'll be quite safe.* That much was a lie, but what else could she say? *Please just wait calmly for me. I love you all.* They were the hardest words she had ever written. She wanted to cry but the tears would not come.

She hurried downstairs, pulled on a thin pair of water shoes. She could run and swim in them. She slipped out of the back door. Didn't turn around, didn't allow herself to look back.

The sun had dipped behind the mountains, but there was still plenty of light. It was eerily quiet. It seemed as if the whole countryside was becalmed, waiting for something to happen. Waiting for her.

Merry couldn't take Jacintha this time. She had no idea how long she'd be away. So she walked through the fields, skirting the hedgerows, trying to stay out of sight. She wanted to run but needed to save her energy for what lay ahead. Her pulse raced. She knew she was doing the right thing, but she was still terrified. Her mind was full of warring thoughts about her family now . . . and her family then, about leaving James with hurt and anger in his eyes when all he had wanted to do was help.

As she headed up toward the forest, storm clouds blew in on a freshening wind, darkening the day prematurely. It was even gloomier once she was under the thick canopy of leaves. She didn't worry now about being seen or heard. She made no effort to move stealthily. Twigs cracked under her feet and roosting birds erupted from the branches overhead. Caught up in her own thoughts, she didn't hear the soft, persistent sounds of pursuit.

Night had fallen by the time Merry reached the pool. Flickers of moonlight forked through the canopy of dark leaves and danced on the black water. It looked eerily beautiful. And sinister.

Merry drank from the bottle in her backpack. She took out the Danish, wolfed it down. She knew she shouldn't eat before the swim but she was tired and hungry and she needed energy. She gave herself a few minutes for the pastry to settle, but hanging around didn't help her nerves. She stripped down to her swimsuit, tightly rolled her clothes and just managed to fit them into her pack. She pulled on her headlamp, switched it on, then walked into the coiling water. It swirled around her thighs as she waded deeper, pushing her back like it didn't want her there.

Stay calm, preserve oxygen. She called to mind once again the lessons of the Navy SEAL. Despite the cold, despite the fear, she willed herself to relax. She pushed deeper until her feet were swept from under her. She launched forward in a butterfly stroke, under the waterfall, into the cave. She breathed in, out, in again, then she propelled herself forward and down into the tunnel.

She kicked hard, pushing through the darkness, fighting one more battle with the River of Time.

Chapter Forty

>>>>————————→

James watched Merry Owen walk into the pool, dive under the waterfall, and disappear. He could hardly believe his eyes.

What the *heck* was she doing? Was this some weird feat of fitness and daring? Hike miles through the hills, then go caving in the dark in freezing black water? Was it some weird initiation ceremony, done for someone else's benefit? He'd had a strange sense as he'd been following her that someone else was around, but every time he'd turned and looked he'd seen nothing. But whatever stunt Merry was pulling, swimming in caves in the dark was dangerous. He'd seen enough rescue helicopters in this part of Wales. Too often, they flew away with the bodies of dead cavers.

He couldn't wait any longer. He kicked off his sneakers, pulled off his jeans and sweatshirt, then, cursing loudly, he waded in. The water was *freezing*. Merry must be out of her mind. He pushed in deeper, till the current swept him off his feet. He swam forward, breaststroked through the waterfall, flinching as the icy water pummeled him. He came up into the cave. The darkness closed around him like a physical force. There was no sign of Merry, just the swirling water. But then he could have sworn he saw a flicker of light ahead, underneath the water.

Feeling the first stabs of fear, he puffed in and out. When he had a good lungful of breath, he dived under and he swam. He kept his eyes open, seeking the light again. After a few strokes he saw it, some way ahead. It lit up the contours of a hole in the cave wall. There must be a tunnel beyond. He tried to catch up with it but the current seemed to be fighting him, and getting stronger. He kicked down and forward, calling on all his strength.

He swam through the hole, into the tunnel. The distant light blinked through the darkness. Against all instinct, all sense, he followed it.

He pushed on, stroke after increasingly difficult stroke against the racing, freezing water. Fighting the cold and the current was using up all his breath. He was tiring. His lungs started to burn. He knew he should turn back, but the light flickered on ahead of him, leading him deeper.

If Merry could do it, he would too. *Anything is possible . . .*

His lungs were on fire. Oxygen and strength burned out. Close to drowning. He screamed inside, dragged up one last reserve of strength. He kicked out, lunged forward. His fingers fought through water, felt air.

He erupted up into another cave. Opened his mouth, rasped in desperate breaths until he had enough strength to swim on. There was another waterfall ahead. He swam toward it, through it, out into an open pool. He staggered into the shallows, gasping, almost retching. He got to a bank, crawled out and collapsed. He was dimly aware that there was no light. That Merry and her headlamp had disappeared.

Disoriented, shivering in his underwear, James got up. He gazed around. It was a clear night, lit by a half moon and stars that seemed to be shining brighter than normal. It was strange, but the bank here looked just like the one on the other side. The forest was different, though, denser and bigger.

He searched for his clothes and sneakers. Couldn't find them anywhere. Was this Merry's idea of a joke? Half drown him, then hide his clothes and give him hypothermia? It didn't seem like her and it made no sense.

He pushed through the trees, straining to see in the darkness, searching for Merry, but there were no flickers of light, no sign of her. It was as if she'd vanished into the night.

James hurried on. Branches scratched him. His arms and legs were bleeding when he emerged from the trees. He looked around in the moonlight, trying to get his bearings. The stark face of Pen y Fan was there in the distance, and he reckoned the rough ground ahead led to Maen Llia and Sarn Helen. And the way home. Yet it was different, he could have sworn. More trees, more bushes. *Wilder.*

He thought he caught a glimpse of someone, far ahead, moving fast across the open ground. It had to be Merry. He set off in the same direction, breaking into a run, desperate to warm up.

He ran on but got no closer to the runner, which was odd. He was super-fit from soccer training. Maybe it wasn't Merry. Maybe it was a Welsh Mountain pony. All he could see were glimpses of movement in the distance.

His bare feet still felt frozen and hurt like hell when he stepped on loose stones but he didn't care. Pain meant he was still alive.

He ran on down the hillside, across the common lands, and there, finally, was the Nanteos valley. Rising up on the hillside opposite, in all its sinister majesty, was his home, the Black Castle. Only different. No soft landscaping. No ranks of laurel bushes.

James shook his head. He must have damaged his brain during the swim. Or he was hallucinating. Feeling as if he were in a nightmare, desperate to wake up, James ran on toward his home. As he approached the drawbridge, a strange man loomed from the darkness and accosted him in Welsh.

"Who the heck are you?" asked James warily. He took a few steps back.

The man broke into English. "Watchman," he declared.

"We don't have any watchmen," James said carefully, as if talking to a madman.

"I am the Black Castle's watchman," the man repeated belligerently, taking a step closer.

"This is my home!" said James. A new wave of fear pulsed through him but he held his ground. "This is my family's castle. What are you doing here? And what's with the costume?" he added, eyeing the man's weird baggy woolen smock, rough leggings, woolen hood.

"Your home?" asked the man with a look of disbelief.

"Yes. My home. Now I'm going inside and you'd better get lost," said James. He was freezing, desperate to get inside and call the police—have this weird stranger arrested.

The man grabbed his arm. James kicked him hard in the shin, earned himself a punch in the stomach, found himself gripped in a headlock. Shouting and struggling, he was dragged across the drawbridge, beneath the portcullis, across the cobblestoned courtyard, and into his home.

The man released him in the Great Hall. James stood, hands fisted by his sides, numb with shock. Portraits, but none of his family. No rich Persian carpets, just flagstones strewn with rushes and straw and sprinkled with dried flowers. Different furniture. Different smell. No jasmine and furniture polish. Instead, wood smoke and lavender. A fire burning in the great hearth.

Two tall men in white tights, codpieces, and indecently short and ornate pleated jackets swaggered up. Both of them wore rapiers in metal sheaths attached to belts. Both had trim beards: one black, the other red. The black-haired one had a vicious scar running down his cheek from the outer corner of his eye to his mouth. The red-haired one had a puppy face that would have made him look friendly were it not for the hard look in his eyes and the sword.

"Who's this scoundrel, Aeron?" he asked the watchman. He turned to James before the man could answer, firing off another question. "Where are your clothes, boy?"

James felt his guts turn to liquid. He wanted to shut his eyes and wake up in his bed. He did shut them for a moment, then opened them again quickly.

He stood as straight and tall as he could.

"I am James de Courcy. Who are *you*? What are you doing in my house? And where are my parents?"

"Your parents?" asked the scarred man sardonically, turning to the other with a raised eyebrow.

"The earl and countess. My parents!" shouted James.

The watchman snorted disbelief.

"The countess is much too young to be your mother," mused the scarred man. He spoke softly but James could feel the violence pulsing just under the surface.

"I am Lord James de Courcy, son of the earl and countess. Where are they?" James repeated. He felt that, above all, he must stay calm. Or fake it. That he must not show fear.

The puppy-faced man twisted and stared at the portraits rising up the staircase from the Great Hall. He turned back and murmured:

"The nose . . ."

The scarred man scrutinized James again. "Has the mark . . ." He reached out, grabbed James's arm with almost invisible speed. "Come with me. You too," he added to the watchman.

James, shivering, was led to the drawing room. The scarred man knocked, was called in with an imperious: *Come*. A female voice; a stranger's voice.

They walked in. The drawing room. Familiar yet unfamiliar. James's eyes fixed on a woman sitting by the fire. She was embroidering a tapestry. Her black hair was plaited and pinned up with an elaborate band of jewels and fur. And she was also wearing a costume: a full-length gown of green and gold velvet, with huge, dangling sleeves and skirts.

The woman put down her embroidery, got up, turned to face him. James gasped, struggled for words, could not speak.

The woman's winged eyebrows arched even higher.

"Brioc, Cranog? What have we here?" she asked.

"Begging your leave, my Lady," said the scar-faced Brioc. "The watchman found him wandering around." He paused, pushed the man forward. "Aeron, tell Lady de Courcy."

"Found 'im outside, my Lady. 'E seems to think he owns the place. *His family's castle* and a load of nonsense."

The stranger, the *countess*, approached James. "Who are you? Why are you near naked and what are you doing roaming around my castle, claiming it for yourself?"

James blinked. He knew the woman. He'd seen her before. On the wall. Immortalized in a portrait. She was his *ancestor*. The twelfth Countess de Courcy. But here she was. Alive. Standing in front of him. Near enough to touch.

It was impossible! But it was happening. He'd been in this very room just hours ago. In that time all the lights had been removed. The subtle heating concealed inside bookcases and cabinets had been removed. All the furniture had been removed and replaced. It wasn't possible. Unless, his mind raced madly . . .

He thought of Merry. Her sudden interest in history. In Henry VIII. He thought of the legend, of the angel warrior who'd saved her family. And Merry's violent reaction to it.

Then the truth hit him. The angel warrior was *Merry*. She'd traveled through time to save her ancestors. And he'd followed her. Back to the sixteenth century.

Chapter Forty-One

The twelfth countess, who had died nearly five hundred years earlier, took a step closer to James.

She stood, very much alive, beautiful head angled to one side, scrutinizing him.

"So who are you?" she asked, voice edged with curiosity.

James sucked in a breath. If he spoke the truth, he knew it would end badly. He glanced at the men standing guard. The scarred man's right hand rested lightly on the ornate silver handle of his rapier. His eyes were fixed on James.

"I am Lord James de Courcy, your ladyship," he announced with the simple sincerity of truth.

"And I'm the king of England," muttered the red-haired man.

"I swear on my life that I am James de Courcy," James declared. Despite his terror, despite his exhaustion, his brain still worked. He offered his hand to the countess. He pointed to the signet ring, stamped with the de Courcy crest of the phoenix rampant, *Avis la Fin* engraved below.

The countess grabbed his hand, studied the ring. Studied him. Her eyes opened wide.

"You have the ring, the crest. *Our* crest. It's just like the earl's ring! And you have the nose," she pronounced, looking to her armed men for confirmation. They nodded back, reluctantly. James, who had always hated his nose, now gave thanks for it.

"A kinsman," declared the countess, letting go of James's hand. "From where?" She grabbed his chin, turned his face this way and that, scrutinizing him. James submitted to the examination. He knew instinctively that all that kept him from the men with the rapiers was the countess's belief.

"You're not one of the French de Courcys, are you, with your dark coloring? You look French."

Thank God for his mother's insistence on his learning French at school. He excelled in the language, spoke it fluently.

"*Oui, Madame la Comtesse,*" answered James in his flawless French accent.

"But what are you doing here? Where are your parents? Your servants? You cannot possibly have come alone."

James thought wildly. "My parents stayed in France, thank goodness. I wanted to see this country, have an adventure. I came with my servants by sea. There was a great gale. We were shipwrecked." He paused, closed his eyes as if it were all too much, and concocted the next piece of his story. "Only a few of us survived. We made our way across land. I sought to find the sanctuary of my kinsmen."

"Begging your leave, my Lady," cut in the scarred man. "When he was brought to us he was asking where his parents were, as if he expected them to be here."

The countess turned to James, eyebrows raised.

James, trapped in the lie, had to come up with a better one.

"We were attacked at night," he said, rubbing his head. "I was beaten. Everything, even my clothes were taken. I managed to flee but I could not find the rest of my party. Then . . ." He struggled for words, swayed in the sudden heat from the fire. "I'm confused, disoriented . . ." He felt the countess leading him to a chaise longue, calling for hot broth and robes.

Cranog, the red-haired man, hurried off, leaving Brioc keeping watch.

"You were beaten, kinsman. Were you hurt badly?" asked the countess with sudden maternal concern.

James nodded. Conveniently he sported a collection of bruises from soccer. He could see the countess noticing them.

"But you must have walked for days. You are exhausted!" she exclaimed.

Like Merry before him, the rigors of the crossing caught up with him, and, helplessly, James passed out.

Chapter Forty-Two

Merry couldn't quite believe she had made it back again, even though history said that she had. She felt even more terrified by the old world this time, knowing some of what it had in store for her.

One battle at a time, she told herself. First, disguise yourself.

She unzipped her backpack and took out the box containing her glass eye. Feeling squeamish, as she always did when handling it, she pushed it into place. Then she stepped from her wet swimsuit and pulled on her warm clothes.

She glanced around, feeling that someone was near. Maybe she was just paranoid. She took her knife from her backpack. Looked around again. She couldn't see anyone, but her instincts were screaming at her. *Time to get away.*

She ran through the forest, out onto the open land. She paused, scanned the landscape. No one.

She ran down toward Sarn Helen, picking up speed. She wanted to get to Mair's, get to safety, get out of the night.

She reached Nanteos, saw the massive edifice of the Black Castle looming in the moonlight. She ran along the valley, up the hill to Ty Gwyn.

An owl hooted. Merry jumped. She half expected the earl's men to be lurking behind every clump of trees.

She glanced over her shoulder, then knocked quietly on Mair's door.

"Mair. It's me. Merry . . ." She waited, shifting from one foot to the other, growing cold. Growing worried. Silence. She knocked again, louder, listened hard.

Footsteps, heavy, coming closer.

"Mair! It's me. Merry," she whispered again. She pulled off her pack, sheathed her knife, realizing she probably looked terrifying.

The rusty sound of bolts drawing back. The old woman stood at the door in a worn nightdress, white hair streaming down her back like a ghost. Or a witch. She carried the stinking fish-whiff tallow candle, which cast a pool of light around her. Beyond, there was darkness.

The healer eyed Merry, looked past her. She seemed to be debating something, biting her lip, her eyes anxious and flickering.

At last she beckoned Merry in.

"Thank you," breathed Merry, hurrying inside. She stood, waiting, uncertain of her welcome as Mair pushed shut the door, slid home the bolts.

Merry pulled off her beanie, gripped it in her hand. Water dripped from it to the rough stone floor.

"They say you are a horse thief," Mair declared, holding her candle to Merry's face. "A prized Arab stallion was stolen." She spoke slowly, like a judge gearing up to pass sentence. "There's a price on the head of the one-eyed bandit. Ten sovereigns."

Merry said nothing, just stood, clutching her hat, waiting.

"They hang thieves!" hissed Mair with a sudden, shocking

passion, as if Merry's silent impassivity were too much to bear. "And they hang those who give them shelter."

Merry swallowed. She hadn't thought of that. Did the healer plan to turn her in or turn her away? She could fight, she could run, but she needed help and the old woman was the only one here to give it to her.

"I have two eyes," said Merry.

Mair barked out a laugh, surprising Merry. "So you have!" The laughter faded. "How?"

Merry swayed. She was tired, cold, and desperate. She wanted to sit down; she wanted to get on with what she came for.

"It's a long story."

"I'm a patient woman," said Mair, finally gesturing at the table and stool.

Relieved, Merry sat. The fire was banked for the night, no flames, just glowing embers, but Merry was grateful for even their scant warmth.

"You've woken me," said Mair, taking a poker, prodding the flames into life before adding two thick logs. Then she took a stool and sat opposite Merry. "I won't get back to sleep again this night. I have time for a story or two."

A sudden wind kicked up, howling against the cottage.

"First I need to ask you, what news of Longbowman Owen?" said Merry. "Did they kill him?"

Mair made the sign of the cross, shaking her head violently. "God have mercy, no they did not."

Merry scratched her chin. Where had he been when she went

searching for him? Was he being interrogated in some other part of the castle?

"Where is he now?" she asked.

"He languishes in de Courcy's dungeon. Pending the king's decision. His family fears he will hang."

"Damn the king!"

"Careful, girl! If anyone heard, you'd be joining him at the gallows."

Merry sucked in a breath. She'd have to learn to bite her tongue in this time.

"In that case," she said, her voice low, determined, more of a declaration than a request, "I need a longbow. One that's my height, not too powerful a draw. And flight arrows made for the bow."

"*You?* A war bow! What for?"

"It's a long—"

"God in his heaven! No more *long story* excuses!" exclaimed the healer. "One more time and I'll cast you out!"

Merry couldn't think of anything to say.

"How old are you?" demanded Mair.

"Fifteen."

"And you want a bow?"

"I do."

"What for?"

"For the king's tourney."

"What tourney?"

"The tourney where he asks for the Owen family to fulfill their pledge. Where he asks for a longbowman to come forward."

"He hasn't asked for any such tourney."

"He will."

"How do you know?" asked Mair, eyes wide, all signs of tiredness gone.

"Does it matter?" replied Merry. "All I need is a longbow so that I can honor the pledge."

"But you're not an Owen, girl!"

"Oh, but I am!" She paused, emotions rising. "I saw Longbowman Owen's daughter run out to him when the king's men took him away. Even from a distance I could see the resemblance. I looked like her, at her age, when I had both my eyes . . ."

Mair tilted her head, studied Merry. "You weren't born like that?"

"No," said Merry. "I lost my eye in a longbow accident three years ago."

"Why would you play with a longbow?" asked Mair, frowning.

"I don't *play* with one. I've *trained* since I was five years old to shoot the longbow. Every generation of Owens has a longbowman."

"Glyndŵr Owen."

"Yes. And now me. I am the longbow girl." Merry leaned toward the old woman. Her words came out slow and heavy and deliberate. She *had* to make Mair understand. And believe.

"There will be a tourney. The king will call the Owens on their pledge. I will answer it."

"If you are a longbow girl as you claim, then where's your bow?"

Merry felt waves of exhaustion hit her, the sheer, grinding weariness of accumulated lies.

"And how can there be two bowmen?" continued Mair. "Or one bowman and one *longbow girl* at the same time?"

Merry gave a hollow laugh. It was time for the truth. "That's just it. We're not at the same time. You want a long story? I'll give you one."

In the flickering light of the fire, Merry told her tale.

Mair sat and listened, fists clenching and relaxing, clenching and relaxing, like a heart beating. Outside the wind roared down off the Beacons, just as it always had, just as it always would.

The tallow candle burned down as Merry talked. When she finished, she simply sat, palms turned upward on her thighs. She'd risked it all. She could be turned out as a raving lunatic. She could be betrayed. There was the bounty on her head.

Mair said nothing. She just looked from Merry to the fire and back, eyes restless as the flames. Finally she spoke. Her voice was faint, as if she were talking to herself.

"How can I trust you?"

"What? You want *proof*?"

"Not for my heart, not for my soul, but for my mind . . ."

Merry got up, paced around the kitchen. "First, the de Courcys will declare a tourney. Wait and see." She was angry. She hadn't come here, left her home, risked everything, to be doubted. "Second, there's a brick here, in your hearth, three up, four across." Merry hoped this wasn't a recent addition. Seren had shown it to her when she was a child, told her it was where the Morgan family had always kept the few valuables they'd possessed.

"Take it out and there's a hiding place," she continued, and knew from the flare of Mair's eyes she was right, that the hiding place was there now. "You have a leather book, a healer's book of remedies and herbs and recipes dating back hundreds of years, even from this time."

Merry fell silent. She sat down, rocked her body back and forth. It was too much, too much. What doesn't kill us doesn't always make us stronger . . . but she felt she had no strength left. "A longbow girl," murmured the old lady. "From another time." She reached out, touched Merry's shoulder as if to prove to herself she was flesh and blood. Merry looked up, met her gaze. The woman seemed to see the truth in it, for she nodded and went to stoke the fire. "Forgive me and my doubts," she said to the flames.

Then she turned back to Merry.

"I've saved someone in every family in the Beacons and beyond. They all owe me. You'll have your bow by the end of the morrow. Now you must rest. You may sleep on the pallet I keep in my herb room."

Mair gave Merry a rough woolen blanket; then she disappeared into a small room next to the kitchen.

Merry felt spent, purged, beyond exhaustion. She pulled the pallet bed from the herb room, pushed it close to the fire. She took out her glass eye, put it in its box, lay down on the straw mattress, pulled the blanket over her, and fell fast asleep.

The healer did not try to sleep.

The girl of her visions had returned. The girl with the hands of an archer. The longbow girl from another time.

Chapter Forty-Three

Exhausted, feverish, head spinning, James awoke. He had the sense that something was very wrong. Lying flat, cocooned in sheets and blankets, still half asleep, he blinked a few times. Then a few more. Above him was a rich red canopy. Around him were four elaborately carved posts draped with green velvet. He sat up, looked around, heart racing. He was lying in what was his own bedroom, or should have been, in a four-poster bed. It all came careering back: following Merry, the river, the swim, that awful drowning swim, the castle, his home. Only not. Not for nearly five hundred years.

He swung his legs around, pushed aside the velvet drapes, put his feet on the floor. Onto *rushes*.

He looked down at his body. He was wearing a nightgown! Who had put this on him? He had no memory of that, or of being put to bed . . .

Weak light filtered through a gap in the curtained windows. It was morning. He was desperate to pee. But where? He knew there'd be no converted en suite bathroom. There wouldn't even be a loo down the hall. They didn't exist. What there would be, somewhere, was a chamber pot.

James got down on his hands and knees on the sharp rushes and peered under the bed. Spotted the pot, hauled it out.

Seconds after he had finished, there was a knock at the door and before he could speak, a man came in carrying a huge bundle of what looked like cloth and a dead animal. The man with the black beard and the horrible scar. Brioc. He must have been waiting outside, listening . . .

The man nodded to James, gave a curt bow, but his eyes were hard and watchful.

"You have awoken, Lord James."

"So it would seem."

"I took the liberty of collecting some clothes for you." Brioc raised the bundle in his arms. "The countess asked me to take some of the earl's vestments," he added with a frown of distaste, as if this were really quite inappropriate.

"Good," said James. "Er, thank you."

He eyed the weird collection of items the man was now laying out at the foot of the four-poster bed: linen, velvet, and lace; frills, pleats, embroidery . . . and tights! God, if his mates at school could see him . . . if Merry could see him . . . He felt a sharp pang of fury with Merry for not telling him the truth, mixed in with fear for her. Where was she now? With her ancestors?

The man was nodding at the clothes. James hesitated; he really didn't know where to start.

"Used to a body servant, are we?" asked Brioc.

James swallowed, forced himself to nod. Anything to convince the man he was a typical sixteenth-century lord who did nothing, not even dress himself, was good.

It must have taken ten minutes for the man to dress him, an almost unbearably intimate process. James shut his eyes and pretended it wasn't happening. Finally, after securing scores of tiny buttons and multiple laces, Brioc spoke.

"Would you like to check yourself in the glass?" he asked, nodding to a corner of the room.

Next to the wall was a small freestanding mirror. James tilted it up and down, blinking at his reflection. Doublet, jerkin, leggings, delicate black leather shoes . . . codpiece. He looked ridiculous. He looked like one of the portraits. Like a sixteenth-century de Courcy. And that, he suspected, might be just enough to save his life.

James walked down the stairs. Brioc prowled by his side, the courtier warrior, velveted, scarred, armed. His silver rapier dangled from an ornate black belt, stabbing the air behind him as he walked. On the other side of his belt lurked a dagger in a leather sheath. Death at either hand.

At the far end of the Great Hall stood a group of similarly dressed men. They fell silent as he and Brioc approached, watchful eyes narrowed in suspicion.

Brioc paused by the drawing room door, knocked, coughed, and was summoned by the countess with her imperious "Come!"

He opened the door, gestured James inside.

The countess lounged in her chair by the fire, flanked by two wolfhounds. They pushed to their feet and eyed James speculatively. Teeth, swords, daggers . . .

"Thank you, Brioc," said the countess, with a careless smile.

Brioc seemed to devour the smile. James noted that, noted everything. Fear heightened his perception. He supposed if you were sufficiently afraid you would be almost numb and notice nothing. He was quite a few notches down from that, a sort of amber terror, not full-on red. He feared what *might* happen, not what was happening now.

Brioc glanced at James, as if to say, *Behave or you'll have me to answer to,* then spun around and strode from the room.

His footsteps echoed away, then stopped. Eavesdropping on the other side of the door, thought James.

The countess tilted up her head. "Come, let me see you," she commanded.

James approached across the long drawing room. The wolfhounds set up a low growl.

"Zeus! Apollo! Desist!" ordered the countess.

James hid a smile. So like his father's wolfhounds, even down to the names.

"Something is amusing?"

"No, reassuring," replied James, reaching out his hands to let the wolfhounds get his scent. "My father has wolfhounds. Four of them."

"Ah, a real de Courcy," declared the countess. "You miss him."

"More than you could imagine . . ."

The countess gave him a smile of sympathy, then her expression changed and she ran a practiced eye up and down him.

"That's a bit more fitting. You're almost my husband's size. He's just a bit taller and broader than you."

"Where is he?" asked James, glancing around as if an angry earl might burst into the room at any moment. He would be much harder to fool than his wife . . .

"Hunting with His Majesty. Wild boar in the forest of Brecon. They rested overnight in our lodge there. They return today. I am

216

sure my husband will be intrigued to meet you. To hear your story," she added, head to one side. Mistrust or plain curiosity, James couldn't tell.

The countess indicated the chair opposite her with a gracious sweep of her velvet-clad arm. "Now, sit, please. Was your room comfortable?"

"Very, thank you," said James, sitting down on the ridiculous pleated skirtlike thing, rearranging it under him.

"Good. The green room is the chamber given to the heir, to the next earl." Her mood seemed to change and she gave a slight, sad smile. "I am hopeful God will bless us, but so far he has not. Just like King Henry himself. Though he does at least have a daughter."

James nodded: the future Queen Elizabeth. He opened his mouth to say that, rapidly changed his mind.

"You will have a son," he said instead. "I am sure of it." James could have described him: dark-haired, long-nosed, a smile of mischief; the thirteenth earl . . . he'd lived with the portrait of the boy for sixteen years.

"I live in hope," the countess replied wistfully. "Now, since you are rested," she declared, her voice light again, "I want to hear more of your incredible story."

She leaned toward a small table, her heavy clothes making the movement stiff, picked up a large golden bell, and rang it vigorously. Rubies dangled from her ears, glittering as they caught the light.

A few moments later, a lady, well dressed but not so richly as the countess, hurried in.

"Bring food for my kinsman."

The lady bobbed, then scurried out, closing the door softly behind her.

The countess took a large pewter jug from the table beside her, filled a goblet, handed it to James. He took a sip. Watered-down red wine, spiced with cloves and cinnamon and gently heated. It was warm and soothing. James cautioned himself to just have a little. He needed his wits about him.

He took up his story again, the boat journey, the shipwreck, his long, cold journey from the coast. The attackers who stole his clothes. His arrival at the castle.

The maid came back in with a plate of chicken drumsticks and some kind of pie.

The countess gestured. "Eat. You must be famished."

There were no knives or forks, so James picked up the food with his hands.

"You're lucky my watchmen didn't run you through," mused the countess. "Creeping about the castle grounds at night."

"Why would they?" asked James, swallowing a mouthful of chicken. "I must have looked like a drowned rat!"

"Robbery, of course. They probably thought you swam the moat."

"I wouldn't want to swim in that moat, not with all the ca—" James cut himself short. Did carp exist in this time? Were they in the moat?

"The carp?" said the countess. "Yes, well, we *do* have carp, huge ones. Not very appealing to swim with. We *eat* them, roasted with prunes." She paused and her face grew serious. "But you'd be surprised what people do when they're desperate."

"It'd be a brave or stupid person who tried to rob this castle, what with the moat, the portcullis, and all the armed men."

"Brave, stupid, both, but the castle *has* been robbed," fumed the countess.

"What was taken?" asked James.

"Zephyr!"

"Who's Zephyr?" asked James.

"My beautiful Arab stallion!" declared the countess, eyes flashing with temper. "Stolen!"

James gulped his wine, felt the heat rush through him. "And any ideas who might have taken him?" he asked, aiming for casual.

"Oh yes! I know *exactly* who stole him."

"Who?"

"The English-speaking *witch*!"

"Witch?"

"With one eye. I caught her in the act of stealing him, challenged her. She fought me. Fought like the devil. She only *just* made her escape." The countess fidgeted in her chair, reliving the scene. "She must have put a spell on Zephyr; it is only *I* who can ride him! And he is so fleet they outran all my men on their chargers." She took a sip of wine, slammed down her goblet with a bang that slopped red wine onto the table. It dripped like blood onto the rush-covered wooden floor.

"But don't worry," she said, with a smile. "We'll catch her, sooner or later. You can't exactly hide an Arab stallion forever. People will notice him. People will talk. He has our brand on him, besides. And *she* can hardly hide, the one-eyed witch."

James bent over his goblet of mulled wine. He pretended to

breathe in the wafting odors. He took a sip, swallowed the lump in his throat. Only when he felt his face was clear of all emotion did he look up.

"What will you do with her," he asked, "if you catch her?"

"She'll hang, of course. Like all horse thieves." The countess leaned forward toward the fire, rubbed her hands, and spoke into the flames. "Or maybe she'll burn, for witchcraft . . ."

Chapter Forty-Four

The fire spat and crackled in the Black Castle's huge hearth. A sudden wind roared down the chimney, whipping up the flames.

Oh, Merry, thought James, his stomach churning. *What have you done?*

The countess peered at James, concern creasing her beautiful face.

"You look ill, kinsman!"

James improvised. "It's my head. When I was attacked I fell and hit it."

"You are concussed!" declared the countess, alarmed. "What year is it?"

"Er." James tugged at his eyebrow. "Oh God, I don't know."

"You are indeed concussed," pronounced the countess. "The year is 1537."

Ah, thought James, summoning up his history.

"It's coming back," he said. "His Majesty dissolved the monasteries last year, didn't he?"

The countess nodded, looked wary but pleased. "The Suppression Act, it is called."

James gave a wry smile. He'd bet that the de Courcys had benefitted from that, as King Henry had shared a little of his priceless plunder.

"He had a busy year," continued James, trying to keep his voice neutral. "His Majesty also beheaded his wife, Anne Boleyn, last year, if I remember rightly."

The countess pursed her lips. "We don't speak of that."

"And more happily," James continued quickly, "His Majesty recently married Jane Seymour."

He could have added that Jane Seymour, the new queen, would go on to die in childbirth in October of this year, but then he'd be hanged and eviscerated as a traitor for voicing terrible thoughts.

"Your memory is good now, I see. And you are well informed," noted the countess, with just the slightest tone of wariness.

Best to appear friendly and very slightly stupid, the hapless victim of too much aristocratic interbreeding, thought James.

"Oh, you can thank my mother for that," he declared, waving his hand. "She likes to keep up on all the gossip." That much was true. The delivery of her weekly copy of *Hello!* was a treasured moment.

"Gossip can be dangerous," cautioned the countess, eyes hardening with a sharp intelligence.

Enemy, James reminded himself.

"Now," said the countess, breaking into a broad smile in a dizzying change of mood, "tell me about your home. I've never been to France, though I'd love to."

Was she testing him, wondered James, or just curious?

"Well, it has a moat like this, with carp," he began with forced enthusiasm, "though my mother would never eat them, and it has twelve turrets," he continued confidently. The previous year he and his family had gone to a château in Normandy. His father had said that it had once belonged to the French branch of the de Courcys.

"It is built of . . ."

James spent ten minutes describing Château de Clermont in great detail before being interrupted by the sound of a horn: far off but insistent.

"His Majesty!" yelled the countess, springing to her feet. "I must ensure that all is ready."

James stood too. A wave of adrenaline rushed through him. The king would arrive. Declare the tournament. And Merry would come. The one-eyed witch, the horse thief, would be walking right into a trap.

James followed the countess into the Great Hall. Men-at-arms, rapiers bouncing at their thighs, materialized out of doorways. Maids poured out of the servants' areas, scurrying through the Great Hall with panicked gestures. The great tide bore James out of the Castle, into the courtyard where maids and grooms and courtiers and countess were forming up, ready to greet their king.

Trumpets sounded. Drums beat. Hooves stamped as a cavalcade of horsemen came clattering over the drawbridge.

Finely dressed courtiers in scarlets and blues and greens rode high-stepping destriers with extravagant manes and lavish trappers. Servants in dull-colored clothes were being dragged along by wolfhounds on heavy chains. Huge gold-and-red pennants bearing images of unicorns, leopards, and falcons fluttered in the breeze.

James knew immediately which mounted figure was the king. He recognized him from the history books but he would have picked him out anyway. He could feel the power pumping from the man as he glanced around, smiling beneficently, the regal king returning victorious from the hunt. He could see it in the watchful and frightened eyes of the audience.

This was pure, absolute power.

The king reined in his horse in front of the countess. She lowered her gaze respectfully. As she curtsied, her crimson sleeves draped to the ground. She couldn't keep her hands still. They fluttered and danced, and the dangling sleeves swept the cold afternoon air, orchestrating her words as she addressed her king:

"Welcome back to the Black Castle, Your Majesty."

The king dismounted. James watched, transfixed, not quite believing that here in his own castle stood Henry VIII. Legendary king. Religious renegade. Wife killer.

He was every bit as big as his reputation. He stood feet planted, powerful legs braced, huge chest puffed out. His face was broad, his lips small and pursed, as if tightly controlling some emotion, possibly impatience. His beard with the drooping mustache gave him a touch of melancholy but it was still, overwhelmingly, a belligerent fighter's face. The widely spaced blue eyes, the direct gaze, the high eyebrows seemingly set in a permanent challenge.

Power corrupts, and James could see its legacy in the king. It would not do to upset this man. As the ghosts of his two murdered wives would attest: one recently beheaded, the other not even married.

Chapter Forty-Five

Merry sat at the kitchen table in the stone cottage. The fire burned away nicely but there was no sign of Mair. Merry wondered where she'd gone. She felt both nauseous and starving. Sick with worry for her parents, who would have discovered her absence and her note. Starving as usual. She was grateful for that little bit of normality. She found herself instinctively reaching for her phone, wanting to text or call James. He always made her feel better. She gave a bitter laugh. He was nearly five hundred years away.

She pushed up, prowled around the little kitchen. She needed to do something. Occupy herself. She ought to get breakfast ready, but there was no fridge stocked with milk and eggs and bacon, no boxes of cereal, no foil-wrapped sticks of butter. She didn't know where to start.

A distant burst of trumpets sounded. She hurried to the door, peered out. When she saw that there was no one around, she walked out, stared in amazement at the spectacle across the valley.

Merry couldn't see faces from this far, but she could see a huge figure on a fine black horse riding at the head of a cavalcade of mounted men, followed by more men on foot leading at least eight wolfhounds. Hordes of people streamed out from under the portcullis of the Black Castle. They scurried around the man, bowing low before him, walking backward as he rode forward. King Henry VIII. The man who held the future of her family in his hands, who would toy with that future, throw it all into peril when he declared the tourney.

Even from a distance, the power of the king and the fear he inspired was obvious—as it had been when he'd ridden past on that first hunt. It rippled across the valley, made the hair on the back of her neck stand on end. The next time she saw him, she'd be close up. How would she fare then, in his presence, with so much at stake . . . so much to do . . .

She prayed the tourney would be soon, for her family's sake, both now and in her time. And for her sake. She didn't want to live too long with this fear.

When the king and his entourage disappeared into the Black Castle, she went back inside the cottage.

Not long afterward, the door swung open behind her. Merry spun around and in one smooth move unsheathed the knife she wore on her thigh strap and brandished it in front of her.

It was Mair. The old woman took two quick paces back, eyes wide. "Put away your weapon," she said quickly.

Merry stared at her blade as if wondering how it got there.

"Sorry," she said, sheathing the knife. She noticed her hand trembling, felt the burn of her own fear and adrenaline. "Seeing the king just now . . . it spooked me."

"Given the whole valley fright."

The old lady closed the door and bolted it. She turned back to Merry.

"Everyone in sound mind is riven with fear. Even, it is said, the earl and countess. Everyone knows what happens to those who fall from grace."

"They lose their heads," murmured Merry.

She felt a jolt run through her as she understood, suddenly, where the expression came from. It was bandied about in her time like it meant nothing. Now it meant everything.

She shivered. "Where've you been, then?" she asked.

Mair smiled and some of the tension left the room. "To find the longbow girl a bow."

"I'd've come with you."

Mair shook her head. "Not garbed like that. Remember, the earl's men are hunting you." She eyed Merry up and down. "You look outlandish."

Lycra and fleece, thought Merry. Twenty-first-century wardrobe essentials that would mark her as an outsider, some kind of weird foreigner, immediately.

"I've laid out some more suitable clothes for you," said Mair, nodding at a small pile on the stool.

"Thank you," said Merry.

"What happened to the others I gave you?"

"I'm sorry. I left them behind. In my time." She didn't add that she'd cut up a bit of the shawl to hide a stolen ring.

Mair made a face, half annoyance, half resignation. "Luck has smiled on you. Got these a few weeks back in payment for healing an archer who'd cut himself making arrows. Nasty infection but I cured it. Change, then we'll eat."

The healer busied herself with a pot and what looked like oats and milk while Merry dressed in the new clothes. Cream woolen leggings, a white linen shirt, a green woolen tunic, heavy, but loose around her shoulders. A brown leather belt.

Mair turned, studied her. "Much better. Now," she said, handing over a wooden pail, "fetch us some water, would you?"

For a fleeting moment, Merry found herself looking around for a tap; then she remembered the well.

"Don't mind my cow," she added. "She's friendly."

Merry unbolted the door and walked outside. She paused for a moment, gazing at the valley. All was quiet now. All the action would be inside the fortress of the Black Castle, far from prying eyes.

Merry spotted the cow. As she approached it, the animal suddenly started at a noise in the copse down the hill. It sounded like a branch snapping. Probably some animal moving around, thought Merry. A big animal. Were there wolves? She hurried to the well to draw up the water.

By the time she returned to the cottage, Mair had set two steaming bowls of porridge on the table. Each was decorated with a clump of honeycomb. It was rich, filling, and delicious. When they'd finished eating, Merry cleared up.

"What now?" she asked.

"We sit and we wait. You can help me pound some herbs if you seek occupation."

Merry smiled her thanks. "I do. Please. Anything."

As she sat in the little room, grinding dried herbs to a powder, using a pestle and mortar, she felt a wave of dizziness, a kind of vertigo of time. She'd done the exact same thing, so many times, sitting right here with Seren alongside her, teaching her about plants and their properties, about what could heal, and what could kill.

Chapter Forty-Six

The hours passed unmarked by any clock. As day sank into night, Mair lit the tallow candles; then she and Merry picked up their knives and started to peel and chop a basket full of vegetables to make a stew.

Merry's thoughts went to her mother and father. What were they doing now? What suffering were they going through, with her missing?

Merry sheathed her knife as the vegetables bubbled in their pot over the fire. As darkness fell, she and Mair sat down to their vegetable stew. Merry wasn't hungry, but she forced herself to eat.

Outside, the spring winds were screaming again, masking the sounds of approach.

The knock at the door made them jump. They exchanged a quick, terrified look.

Mair lifted her finger to her lips, nodded at her side room. Soundlessly, Merry eased back her stool, picked up her plate, spoon, and tankard, slid behind the curtain. She unsheathed her knife and waited.

The old lady went to the door. "Who goes there?" she called out.

"Ivan Evans," came the reply.

Merry hid behind the thin curtain, knife poised, heart pounding. Who was Ivan Evans? A bounty hunter? A friend?

Mair called out, "Just a moment."

Bolts slid back, cold blew in as she opened the door. A reek of blood filled the air.

"I've something for you," said a low male voice. Then there was a chuckle. "Two somethings. A nice bit of lamb, slaughtered just an hour ago." The man paused and his voice lilted up questioningly. "And a war bow for you. Well, for someone who stands five feet seven, I think you said. Most specific you were, according to Farmer Pryce, who I saw coming home from market. I said why is Mair Morgan after a war bow and he said don't ask, just get. So here it is. Been in my family since before my grandfather's time. Bit of a history . . . Bit of a draw . . . but any man worth his salt should be able to manage it, and if he can't, he isn't a man."

Merry pulled a face but she was thrilled. She had a bow!

"Here's an arrow bag too," the man was saying. "Twelve flight arrows, with the goose fletchings trimmed right low. The best. I filed them down, took off as much weight as I could. You asked for long distance. These'll do it."

"Thank you, Farmer Evans. I am much obliged."

"I can't help wondering, though, who it might be for. See, I heard something today . . ." The man's voice trailed off.

"What did you hear?" asked Mair.

"I heard from my brother, you know him, he's footman to the earl, that tonight at the banquet the king will declare a tourney for two days hence. And he will call upon the Owens to honor their pledge. He will call on them to send forth a longbowman."

Behind the curtain, Merry gripped her knife, body rigid with anticipation and fear. So the countdown had begun.

"We will see," Mair replied crisply. "I thank you again, Farmer Evans, and must bid you good night."

Merry listened to their mutual farewells, then, when she heard the door click open, then shut firmly, with the bolts drawn home, she slipped out from behind the curtain.

She glanced at Mair, took the bow the healer held out to her. She felt that familiar surge of power as she held it in her hands.

She stood it next to her. Just slightly longer than she was tall. The perfect length . . . She weighed it in her hands. Only a fractional lack of balance could mean that an arrow loosed over a distance of just fifty yards would either hit the gold or miss by inches. She prayed this bow would shoot true.

She put it down, picked up the arrow bag. She knew that archers in this time did not usually carry quivers. The open top meant that rain could get in. Wet feathers made arrows fly crooked. And in the rough and tumble of battle, arrows could fall out of an open quiver. Nothing would fall from this arrow bag. Made from linen, it was secured with a lace fastening that bound the top closed. It felt resinous to the touch, as if waterproofed with wax. Inside there was a fine wooden frame to space the arrows and widen the bag so that the feathers would not be crushed.

Merry took out a selection of arrows, examined them, balancing them on her outstretched fingers. They *were* light. Wonderfully light. They'd really fly. She pressed her finger to the steel tip. But they could kill too.

Inside the bag were two coiled strings. But Merry wasn't going to use those. She selected her own string from her backpack. Flemish inlaid and fourteen strands, the best the twenty-first century could provide. It would put the bow under huge strain, but it was her only hope for making the distance.

She unbolted the door and walked out into the night. She stood a few paces from the cottage. Mair followed her, holding out a candle, lighting Merry's silent ritual.

First, using her knee to help bend the stave, she strung her bow.

Then she measured the distance from the handle to the string with her right fist.

She heard her father's voice in her head. *Looks about right. Not too highly strung,* cariad . . .

Now to test the draw. She flexed her legs, bent over again, and in the familiar, fluid movement started to straighten up, pulling back the bow at the same time. Her muscles strained and shook. She called up all her strength. Fifty-five pounds or so, she guessed. Five pounds heavier than she was used to, but she *could* do it. She *had* to do it. She pulled it back to its full draw, right to her ear, and she held it there, muscles burning.

It seemed to her like the wood was singing, or screaming maybe. She released it slowly, then unstrung it.

She turned to Mair, to the candle bright in the darkness.

"Now all I need is a target."

Chapter Forty-Seven

The clanging of the gong echoed through the Black Castle. It was time for the feast. Dressed in gleamingly white tights and a red-and-green doublet with a frill that at least offered some level of cover below his hips, James was escorted from his room by the scarred man-at-arms, Brioc.

"No rapier for me?" James asked, eyeing Brioc's weapon.

"Not a man-at-arms, are you?"

"No, but I am a lord."

Brioc shot him a look of disdain. "Come on. Wouldn't do to keep His Majesty waiting . . ."

As James followed the hordes of guests heading into the Great Hall, Brioc suddenly paused and bowed. "My Lord," he said, addressing a tall, hard-faced man whom James immediately recognized as his ancestor, the twelfth earl.

"Who have we here, Brioc?" the earl asked.

James pushed down a quick stab of fear. He could feel instinctively, and see from the look in the man's eyes, that this wasn't one of the useless de Courcy earls. This man was a red-in-tooth-and-claw warrior, and he looked as if he'd have been quite happy to lunge at James with the rapier that hung from his waist.

James gave a slight bow. "I am Lord James de Courcy. Of Château Clermont."

The earl's eyes widened and he subjected James to a quick and ruthless scrutiny. His eyes came to rest on James's hand. He reached out, grabbed it, turned it palm-up.

He reached out his finger, traced it over James's signet ring. And froze. He opened his mouth to speak but his words were drowned out by a sudden peal of trumpets, followed by shouts:

"The king! The king!"

The earl let go of James's hand and bent to whisper something into Brioc's ear. Whatever it was could not have been good. James felt a flash of fear as the man-at-arms turned and gave him a ferocious look.

Then all eyes turned to the king, to Henry VIII as he processed surrounded by his entourage of men-at-arms into the hall. He was draped in velvets and furs, shoulders gigantic, glittering with gold chains and jeweled rings.

The Countess de Courcy appeared and, together with the earl, led the king to the largest table, seating him between them. The countess wore a gown of rose-gold silk and velvet, heavily embroidered, fitted tight over her waist to show off her youthful figure. She was adorned with the de Courcy rubies.

James's heart was hammering. *Now! Get out, now* . . . He began to turn, found himself flanked by Brioc and Cranog, who had suddenly materialized.

"Wrong way, Lord James. Forgetting our etiquette, aren't we?" whispered Cranog. "When His Majesty sits, we sit."

Together the men-at-arms herded James toward one of the two long tables, farthest away from the king, talking, smiling all the while as if it were nothing more than a magnificent social occasion. They took their seats on either side of him. James felt trapped.

Once the king had reached for his first bite of peacock leg, Brioc and Cranog tucked in. The table groaned with meats. There were venison and lamb and chicken but there were also what looked suspiciously like swans. James had no appetite, but he forced himself to eat.

The dining hall fell silent as the king pushed to his feet.

"I would like to thank my gracious hosts, the Earl and Countess de Courcy," he declared. He paused, turned, offered them regal smiles. "We have had a successful few days hunting. We speared two dozen boar and a score of those wretched Welsh Mountain ponies that corrupt the breeding of my warhorses."

There was an eruption of cheers and claps and shouts of approval. James looked around in disbelief. He thought of Merry's ancestor, wondered if some of those ponies might have belonged to him.

Then the king opened his mouth to speak and, as if a spell had been cast, everyone fell silent once more. "Even the fickle Welsh weather has been kind to us, and now this magnificent feast. To offer the smallest reciprocation, I declare a tourney to be held, two days hence." More roars from his minions, more clapping and clashing of goblets.

"We shall have jousting, we shall have pitching the bar, we shall have archery. This part of the world is famed for the prowess of its bowmen. I look forward to seeing it with my own eyes." The king turned to the earl and exchanged what James could only call a conspiratorial look with him.

"On behalf of my hosts, I issue a summons," he declared, his voice booming around the hall. "I call upon the Owen family of Nanteos Farm to send forth a fit and able longbowman. He must enter my contest. He must acquit himself with distinction. He must honor the pledge made by his forebears to the Black Prince."

James felt his heart thudding. The trap for Merry had been set.

The king sat down to tumultuous applause. Guests clapped, and banged the table with fists or pewter tankards, slopping liquid over the wood. The earl was banging the hilt of a dagger against the table, eyes shining with triumph. Then he turned in James's direction, and gave a slight nod to Brioc.

Brioc's hand closed on James's arm.

"I think you had better come with me," he said grimly.

"Why?" asked James with all the belligerence he could muster.

"Because thieves have no place at the king's feast, *Lord* James."

Chapter Forty-Eight

➤

James felt the breath of cold, musty air as they neared the dungeons. Brioc touched his back with the end of his rapier, forcing him down the stairs.

Cranog laughed. "Feel the noose, *Lord* James? Feel it tightening against that noble throat of yours?"

James bit back an answer. His brain seemed to be running at a thousand miles an hour as he tried to navigate this whole new territory. Captivity; sword; men-at-arms; thief; dungeons. What on earth made them think he was a thief? It seemed to have something to do with his ring, but that was impossible.

A fire burned in the lower hallway, casting out scant warmth and coils of smoke that had nowhere to go. A heavy man in rough clothes sat by the fire, half dozing. He jumped to his feet as the trio approached.

James recognized the night watchman.

The man raised his eyebrows in surprise. "The lord James?" he asked.

Cranog gave a derisive laugh. "Thief and liar, more like. Lock him up!"

Brioc prodded him on with his sword toward a cell at the far end of the dungeon, where it was darkest, coldest.

As they passed by empty cells, James saw a sudden movement. A man like a Viking warrior with long, fair hair and a heavy beard got to his feet and gripped the bars with huge hands. *Merry's ancestor.* It had to be. James met his eyes: intelligent, curious, charged with the pent-up fury of a caged animal.

Brioc pushed him on, into an open cell, and pulled shut the door with a clang that echoed through the dungeons. The jailer took a large bunch of keys from a pocket in his tunic and locked him in.

"Pray to your god, *Lord* James," mocked Brioc, grinning at James through the bars.

The puppy-faced Cranog gave a parody of a bow, then turned and, laughing with Brioc, walked away.

James listened to their dying footsteps. He stood in his cell in the sudden, ringing silence. Locked up. A prisoner. No one would come and rescue him. In this time—or his.

He could hear a furtive scrabbling sound: rats. The smell of smoke, damp, and bad food hung in the frigid air. He sat on the rough bench, pulled a thin blanket around his shoulders, and rubbed at his face. How had it come to this? How had this nightmare unfolded? He knew the answer: curiosity and anger that Merry was keeping secrets from him. Now he knew why. For his own good. The six-teenth century was not a playground for the privileged children of the twenty-first. He got up, paced the confines of his cell. Ten steps took him right around.

He would not be that privileged child, then, he decided. He would become someone else, anyone else, whoever he needed to be to survive. And to escape. The first thing he would not do was despair. Merry was out there somewhere, navigating the past, carving the future. So would he. No one was coming to rescue him. He'd have to rescue himself.

Then he remembered. Today was his sixteenth birthday. He was meant to be signing with Manchester United. He felt a rush of fury. He'd followed his dreams, and in some vicious twist of fate it hadn't been his own parents who'd gotten in the way, but his ancestors! But the fury gave him hope and it gave him purpose. No one was going to get in his way. *Somehow*, he would manage to escape and return home.

Chapter Forty-Nine

Time stretched, James had no way of measuring it, but perhaps an hour later he heard footsteps. Brioc and Cranog appeared, carrying flaming torches. Behind them walked the earl. And the countess.

The jailer fumbled with the keys. Fat fingers slow and clumsy. The earl hissed with impatience. "Snap to it, Aeron!"

Finally the jailer had the lock and the door open. Brioc yanked James out into the hallway between the facing rows of cells. James flew forward, steadied himself, glowered at Brioc. Then he turned and faced the earl.

"Who *are* you?" snapped the man.

"Lord James de Courcy."

"So you say," mused the earl with a cold smile. "Shipwrecked, says my wife. A tall story! You're nothing but a thief and an opportunist."

The earl reached out, grabbed James's hand, and yanked off the ring. He turned it so that he could read the inscription inside. He ran his fingers over the rim and his face tightened with fury.

"As I thought."

He drew back his hand and administered a full, backhanded slap to James's face. Like King Henry, he wore large, ornate rings. James felt blood gush down his cheek as the jewels cut through flesh.

He wanted to lunge at the earl, knew that would only bring him more of a beating, so he just stared at his ancestor, steeling himself for whatever came next.

The earl turned to his wife, contempt on his face. "How could you be such a fool as to trust this boy, this impostor!"

"Because I thought he was kin!" exclaimed the countess, uncowed by the earl's ferocity.

"Kin! He's nothing but a thief!" hissed the earl. He held out the ring. "He took you in, you little fool. That's *my* signet ring. The one that disappeared. Somehow this little bastard got in here and stole my ring. It's a good job I came back when I did. Should have thrown him in the dungeons the second he turned up here!"

James's mind raced. How was it possible that *he* had the earl's ring?

"I saw the ring before; he showed it to me when he arrived," protested the countess, green eyes flashing with indignation. "All de Courcy men over sixteen years of age have such rings! I *couldn't* know it was yours!"

"Mine has a tiny nick on the edge that makes it unique!" snapped the earl, holding up the ring, showing the mark to his wife. "You might have thought to be on your guard after Zephyr was stolen right under your nose."

"The one-eyed witch cannot hide for long," the countess declared. "Our agents are searching and they'll find her."

The earl turned back to James. "We haven't suffered thefts here at the Black Castle for many years. Then the one-eyed thief turns up. Then *you* turn up. I don't believe in coincidence."

James tried to shut down his mind, to blank out all thoughts so his face revealed nothing. He just looked back at the earl, into his hard eyes, and he waited.

"Do you know her?" asked the earl. "Are you in league with her?"

James shook his head. "I'm in league with no one."

The earl just looked at him for a while. James could sense the violence in the man. He waited as the blood still gushed from his face. He felt it running down his chest. He prepared himself for another blow. But it didn't come. Instead the earl turned away, addressed the jailer.

"Lock him up. No food. No water. We'll see how well he sticks to his story when the hunger spasms grip."

Chapter Fifty

The next morning, across the valley in the stone cottage, Merry and Mair breakfasted on bread and honey and fresh milk.

"I need to go out," said Merry when they'd finished. "I must practice with the bow."

The old woman eyed her thoughtfully. "You can't stay locked away in here, it's true."

She got up, rummaged around in a drawer. "Here."

She handed Merry a pointed green woolen hat, triangular in shape. "An archer's hat. Plait your hair, tuck it up out of the way. From a distance you'll look like a man."

"Okay. Thank you." Merry took the hat, twisted it in her hands, suddenly nervous. "And there's something else. I want to meet my ancestors. Longbowman Owen's wife and children."

Mair nodded. "Since you'll do battle in their name, it's fitting. And they have a target you'll be able to use." She got up, pulled on her bonnet. "Come on. Let's go now. It's early. Less people about."

Merry quickly plaited her hair, twisted it around her head, wedged it under the hat. It filled the triangular top.

Mair nodded. "Passable," she said, pulling on her shawl.

Merry took the bow, the arrow bag, and her own coiled strings: her twenty-first-century interlopers. Out they went into the bitter wind.

There was no sign of anyone, but still Merry glanced about, turning circles, checking. They hurried down the fields toward Nanteos Farm. Merry kept expecting her parents to come running out, carrying Gawain. She felt a wrenching pain, tried to shove it away.

As they neared the Owens' farmhouse, *her home*, Merry felt a wash of emotions. It was familiar but different. Smaller, less well-kept. Like Mair's cottage, there was pale linen in place of glass in the tiny windows. No white-painted windowsills. Only one door, at the back of the house. No rosebushes, no well-positioned bench. No leisure time to sit and take in the views, thought Merry. The only thing that remained the same was a small herd of Welsh Mountain ponies. There were four mares and two foals corralled in a small field. They looked just like their modern counterparts with their shaggy winter coats, dished heads, intelligent eyes, and powerful bodies on slender legs. Sheep grazed on the other fields and there were rows of something growing in plowed earth.

As they drew closer, Merry could hear weeping coming from the house.

Mair knocked loudly, called out. The weeping stopped. A woman opened the door.

She had lank hair and a face gnarled by distress and streaked with tears. She was flanked by a boy and girl—maybe six and nine, guessed Merry. She stared at them in amazement. Her flesh and blood. *Her ancestors . . .* Both had her own blond hair and blue eyes. And close up, the girl looked even more like Merry had at her age, with two eyes. The emotion bubbled up inside her, threatening to overwhelm her.

The children shuffled up to her, nervous but intrigued. Merry squatted down.

"What's your names, then?" she asked, smiling at them.

The children were too shy to speak. Their mother answered for them.

"Angharad and Gawain. And I'm Rhiannon."

Merry felt another punch of emotion. Gawain, like her baby brother, just a few years older.

"I'm Merry."

She gently eased the girl's hair back from her face and tucked it behind her ear, just like her own mother did to her. She turned to the boy, a waif with huge eyes in his pale, scared face.

Rhiannon was talking to Mair. "My husband languishes in the de Courcy dungeons. He might hang. And now the king has declared a tourney. Tomorrow! He called for us to provide a bowman. Else we forfeit our home. Our lands. Our ponies. Our sheep. Everything. The de Courcys will take it all." Rhiannon started sobbing again, which set off the children. The three of them stood in a sobbing knot.

Merry felt a tightening in her chest. She blew out a breath. It wouldn't happen. She wouldn't *let* it happen.

"Stop!" she said loudly, straightening up. "Enough!"

Rhiannon grabbed her children and stared in shock at Merry. But they all stopped wailing.

"You shall *not* lose your home," declared Merry. "You shall *not* lose your lands. I give you my word."

"How do you know? How can you promise that?" asked Rhiannon despairingly.

"Because I will enter the competition. In your husband's absence."

Rhiannon opened her eyes as wide as they'd go. "But you're a woman! And you're not an Owen."

"Right about the first. Wrong about the second."

Rhiannon squinted at Merry, a mix of hope and recognition dawning. "His sister, Blodwen, was given away at birth. Couldn't afford to keep her. Are you her, come back to us?"

"I am." A necessary lie.

"But you can't shoot a longbow! That takes a man's strength."

Merry shook her head. She held out the bow. "I've trained on bows like this since I was five. I *can* shoot a longbow, and I can do it as accurately as any man!"

Her words were met with silent disbelief.

"I need to practice now. You can watch me, if you like." She needed her ancestors to believe in her. She needed to give them hope. "I assume your husband has a target?"

"He practiced every week before the de Courcys threw him in their dungeons," replied Rhiannon bitterly. "As he is bound to do. It's over there, behind the house."

Merry flinched. The same place her and her father's target stood, five hundred years later.

"I cannot tarry," Mair was saying. "I have jobs to do and a living to earn."

The old woman's face was creased in worry. She walked a few paces away, beckoned Merry to her.

"Practice, I know you must," she said quietly but urgently. "Give them the hope they need, then hurry home. And pray stay out of sight if you see others nearby."

Merry nodded.

"Remember, the Owens will suffer more if they are seen to be harboring the one-eyed horse thief."

Merry reached out and touched the healer's shoulder. "I'll be careful, I promise. They have enough trouble without me adding to it."

Worrying, all too aware of the dangers that seemed to multiply around her, Merry watched Mair set off up the hill. She turned as she felt the girl, Angharad, pulling at her sleeve.

"Shall I walk you to the target?" the girl asked, a hint of boldness in her eyes.

Merry smiled down at her. "That would be very helpful."

Angharad took Merry's hand and led her along. Rhiannon and Gawain followed behind.

"How many summers are you?" Angharad asked, looking up at her.

"I'm fifteen," replied Merry. "How many summers are you?"

"Eleven" came the reply. Merry hid her surprise. Angharad looked smaller, younger.

"Where do you bide?"

"Bide?" replied Merry with a puzzled look.

"*Live.* Your home," explained the girl.

Merry felt another jolt of emotion. She blew out a breath. "Ah, not too far away," she managed to say.

Preoccupied, she didn't notice the man watching from the trees.

Chapter Fifty-One

Longbowman Owen's target was different from the ones Merry used, but the principle was the same: hit dead center! This one was made of a circle of white-painted wood attached to a post that was dug into the ground. In the middle was a black circle about six inches across and inside that a small white circle: the gold.

Merry paced away from it, counting out the yards, looking for any marks in the grass that would reveal the start line.

"Where's your father's start mark?" she asked Angharad.

"He has several. The far one is a long, long way back," replied the girl with a flash of pride.

She strode out, Merry following. At last they came to a scuffed area with a faint streak of white.

"This must be all of two hundred yards," Merry said. She felt a wave of despair.

"Yes, but he uses closer ones too," Angharad added. She pulled Merry back closer to the target. "Hundred yards, this one is," the girl said, pointing at a worn area in the grass.

That was thirty yards more than she trained at, thought Merry. She walked forward another twenty yards. If she were to practice for accuracy, get her eye in, this was as far back as she could go. She could only pray the tourney would focus on shorter range, higher accuracy shooting.

She picked up the unfamiliar bow, weighed it in her hands, tried to get a feel for it. Thicker, heavier, darker wood. It was an old bow, well used, well made. She remembered Ivan Evans's words: *"Bit of a history . . . from before my grandfather's time"* . . . She had the strongest sense that it had gone to war. Maybe even Agincourt . . . just over a hundred years ago.

She gripped it tight. She would use its history, use its strength. As always holding a bow, but today more than ever, she felt the power of the weapon surge through her.

She turned to her ancestors, gave them a brief smile. Their faces remained somber. And disbelieving.

She turned her attention back to her bow. She used her knee on the stave, putting most of her weight onto it, flexed it, strung it with her own fast flight cord.

She twisted, loosened the drawstring on her arrow bag, pulled out an arrow. She flexed it, proved it, nocked it. She braced her legs, bent over and breathed. In one graceful movement, summoning all her power, Merry straightened, pulling back the bow as she did. *Please don't break*, she thought, aware of the almost unbearable tension her string placed on the old bow.

She took a moment with the bow at full extension, eyeing the target and the fields behind. Then she released her string. The bow sprang back to vertical with a massive, explosive force, propelling the arrow into the target.

Merry heard the gasps, heard the words, but she ignored them all. Instead she looked up at the cold mountains, watching impassively, the mountains of her childhood. They'd be the mountains of her old age too, if she survived this.

She pulled her attention back to her bow, to the target. She loosed her remaining arrows. Only then did she turn to her audience.

Now they believed.

Merry continued to practice. She'd hit the black ring and that was a start, but she was not consistently hitting the inner white ring. She had no idea if taking part in the tourney would be enough, or if she had to win. But it seemed to her that winning would be the only sure way to guarantee that her family's pledge was seen to be honored by the hostile earl and his friend the king.

She shot arrow after arrow till her fingers were raw and her muscles trembling.

The ancestors continued to watch. High above a peregrine falcon circled.

Finally, she got three arrows in a row in the inner white ring. She knew if she practiced any more today, her muscles would seize up. She unstrung her bow.

"I'll see you tomorrow," she said to Rhiannon and the children.

They nodded gravely.

"You're like an angel," said Angharad, awestruck.

"No, she's not," said Gawain. "She's like a warrior!"

Angharad laughed. "An angel warrior!"

The words hit Merry like an electric shock. Time, legend, and truth collided. She looked at her three ancestors and felt the burn of a new purpose and strength grow inside her. *This* was what it was all about. *This* was who and what she'd come back for. Maybe even why she'd been born. To their surprise, she grabbed them, hugged them in turn, then, before they could see her tears, she hurried up the hill to Mair's cottage.

Chapter Fifty-Two

—————➤

Merry pushed open the door and froze.

Mair lay on the beaten-earth floor, blood leaking from a wound to her temple.

Merry rushed over to her, fell to her knees.

"Mair, can you hear me?" she asked, taking the old lady's wrist, frantically feeling for a pulse. After a few terrible seconds she found one.

"Oh, thank God. Thank God. You're alive," she said.

No reply. Mair was unconscious. Merry prayed she wasn't in a coma. Was she breathing? Merry held her hand close to the healer's lips, felt the slightest of drafts.

God, what to do? Move her? What if she had a broken back? Merry didn't think so. It looked like Mair had been hit with a blunt object, perhaps taken by surprise by an intruder who crept up on her from behind. Then Merry saw the brick on the ground, the hiding place revealed, and at that moment, Mair murmured and tried to sit up.

Merry reached her arm around the old lady's back, supported her. "It's all right, Mair. I'm here."

"A man," said the healer in a faint voice. "Looking for *you*. He asked me where *Merry* Owen was. And he took my gold coins and my healer's book."

Merry glanced from Mair to the door. She felt a kind of blind fury. Fury that had nowhere to go.

"How long ago?"

"Just now."

Fury that had somewhere to go. "Will you be all right? If I leave you for a bit?"

The healer nodded, struggled to sit.

Merry strung her bow, shouldered her arrow bag, closed the door. She looked across the empty field, past the lowing cow, down to the forest.

Who *was* this man who had attacked Mair and asked for her by name? And where would he flee to? A flock of birds erupted from the treetops as if in answer to her question.

Merry didn't think twice about following the man. About what might happen if she caught him.

She sprinted down to the forest. Paused, listened. Movement, footfalls, branches breaking. She sprinted on, weaving between the trees, jumping fallen logs.

With luck, the thief would be making so much noise he wouldn't hear her, but she'd have to be careful. She paused again, heard something farther down the slope. She glimpsed movement ahead, a hundred yards away. A lithe figure dodging through the trees.

She ran on, gaining. The man was running, not sprinting. He had no idea he was being chased. As Merry closed the gap on him, she could see he was wearing a green woolen tunic, similar to hers. Underneath, he wore dark leggings. But as she got closer still, she could see that the leggings were made not of rough wool, but of *Lycra*.

Her heart lurched. The man was from her time . . .

She stepped on a fallen branch. It snapped with a loud crack. Birds erupted again from the trees, cawing their alarm.

The man froze. Every single fiber of his body seemed to stop moving. One foot in the air, one arm forward. Then he turned.

Merry gasped. It was Professor Parks! She'd had a sense that someone had been following her, both in her time and now. Parks must have tailed her to the pool, watched her swim under the waterfall, swim back through time . . . And swum back too. Then stalked her, listened outside the cottage, heard her describing Mair's hiding place, where she kept her gold coins. Knew everything.

He began to walk toward Merry. His face was set, eyes hard, scanning the forest behind her, as if to check she was alone.

Merry took an arrow from her bag, was about to nock it when Parks stopped. Thirty yards away.

He stood, feet planted wide, facing her full on, making a target of himself in silent mockery of the lethal weapon she held in her hand. He didn't look remotely afraid, or ashamed to have been caught. Instead he grinned at her with what looked like a kind of twisted delight.

"Merry Owen. Who'd have thought it? You and I. *Together*. In King Henry's time?"

He had the beginnings of a beard. It darkened the hollows of his face. He'd always looked vaguely sinister; now he looked frightening. And oddly liberated. As if he'd shrugged off *Professor Parks* and become someone different.

"You were following me all along, weren't you?" said Merry.

"You only just figured that out?" He gave her a contemptuous look. "You really are spectacularly unobservant, aren't you?"

Merry said nothing. She just kept her gaze fixed on him. She could feel her heart thudding.

"And it was you who broke into my home."

Parks laughed. "I didn't even have to break in! You'd left the doors unlocked—you even told me you always did. Quite unbelievable!"

"That's because I don't live in a world with people who steal, who attack," said Merry.

"Actually," sneered Parks, "it would appear that you do. Besides, who are you to lecture me? You stole the signet ring."

"And then you stole it again, flogged it to some antiques dealer."

"Who sold it to the countess . . . Nice little profit, that."

"You're a thief and almost a murderer. You hit me and knocked me out! I could have died of hypothermia out there in the snow."

Parks shrugged. "You got in the way. The snow was unfortunate."

"Why did you want the book so much?"

"I had a feeling it would lead me to some other discovery." Parks stretched his arm out. "I had no idea it would be this." He paused, smiled. "I didn't manage to get the book, but I had the next best thing. You!"

"Me?"

Parks came closer. "I felt sure you were up to something, hunting for something. So I followed you. *Many have died.* Kudos, Merry, for swimming back, for surviving."

"How did *you* manage it?"

"It was *very* tough, even I must admit that, but an oxygen rebreather and flippers proved rather useful." He smiled again. "I followed you back the first time too. Didn't you sense me?"

"It was *you* in the tunnel, following me into the castle!"

"It was indeed. Suicidally risky. I took some little *objets*, souvenirs, couldn't resist . . ." His eyes gleamed at the memory. "Then I went outside again, hid in the forests, waited and watched." He gave Merry a nod of admiration. "Bit of a narrow escape you had that night, galloping off on the Arab horse. If they'd caught you . . ." He made a cutting motion, hand across his throat. "Not even sure you'd have made it as far as the gallows. The men and the dogs hunting you, blood up. You'd have had a far worse fate . . ."

Merry shuddered at the memory. Of being hunted. Of being *prey*.

Parks took another few paces closer.

"Dicing with death again, aren't you, coming back, *horse thief* . . ."

"I did what I needed to do then. And now," replied Merry, anger rising. "But you . . . *you* had no need to attack an old lady, to steal her savings and her book."

Parks narrowed his eyes. "Have you *any* idea what this is like for an archaeologist? A historian? Coming back, to another world, a different time? How could I *not* take things?"

"Taking her treasures is bad enough. But attacking her? You could have killed her!" shouted Merry.

Parks's response was chillingly cold, almost devoid of emotion. "She got in the way."

"Like me. In the snow."

Parks nodded. "Exactly."

Merry stood very still, her body tingling with horror. Was this what a psychopath looked like? Reasonable. Remorseless. Ruthless.

Parks continued to approach. He was just fifteen yards away now. Merry knew she'd have to act. *Nock, mark, draw, loose* . . . Could she do it . . . ?

"You're in my way again," murmured Parks.

Merry nocked her arrow.

"I can read a lot in people's eyes," continued Parks. "Like I can read in yours that you want to shoot me." He gave a half laugh. "Only you haven't got the nerve for it, have you, Merry? It's just an ego thing, this longbow girl affectation." Again he stepped closer.

He was going to rush her, she could see that.

Merry held her bow, the bow she felt sure had gone to war, had more than a few kills to its name . . . She nocked, marked, and drew. She looked at the man, looked at the tree behind him, then she loosed her arrow.

It flew toward Parks, nicked his ear, and embedded itself in the tree with a loud thud.

Parks swore, dropped the book, touched his ear, stared at his bloody fingers with disbelief. A muscle twitched in his cheek. Merry could feel the fury boiling in the man, the violence waiting to erupt.

She nocked another arrow, marked him, drew again. "Put down the gold coins or I'll shoot this one right into you." Her voice and her hand on the bow were steady, but inside she was vibrating with fear.

The blood ran down Parks's neck. He pulled a bag from his tunic and dropped it to the ground.

"One little pathetic victory for you. Enjoy it while you can, *Merry Owen*, because I'll be out here. I'll be watching and waiting and I promise you, I'll make you more than pay for this."

Merry made the arrow twitch. Parks dodged, turned, and sprinted off into the deep of the forest.

Chapter Fifty-Three

➤

Across the valley in the Black Castle dungeons, cold, thirsty, and hungry, James sat on the bare bench, looking through the bars. He'd had a rough night, trying to sleep on the narrow bench with just the thin blanket to cover him. He wondered what time it was. It *felt* like morning, but he had no way of knowing.

He'd have been afraid if he let himself, but he pushed down the flickers of fear every time they stole up on him.

He thought constantly of escape. If he could just get out of the cell, he knew the castle and all its hiding places, all its secrets; he felt sure he could get to the tunnel, get out. There had to be a way back through the waterfall. After all, Merry had done it.

He couldn't bear sitting still, so he got up and paced. He peered out of his bars but he couldn't see much. His cell was the farthest from the stairs, so all he could see were the empty cells opposite.

He paused when he heard the heavy step of someone descending the stairs. Any approach meant a chance of interrogation. Or worse. *Or* a chance of escape.

He stood ready, heart pounding, hands loose by his sides.

Aeron, the jailer and watchman, appeared, wheezing slightly. James flexed his fingers, readied himself. He wasn't stronger than the jailer, but he was nimbler and faster.

The man stopped before the cell, red-faced, furtive-looking. He was carrying a tankard.

"Here," he said roughly, passing it between the bars. "Ale, watered down. Kitchens think it's for me."

James nodded, took it. "Thank you!" His throat was so dry his words came out as a croak. He hadn't spoken for so long, his voice sounded odd. He'd only been in the dungeons overnight, had only been deprived of food and drink for perhaps fourteen hours, but it seemed a lot longer than that and he already felt weak. Not so weak that he didn't covertly study the man, note the ring of keys protruding from one of the pockets in his tunic.

"Don't sit right with me," said the jailer. "Starving you. Not as old as you look, are you?" he asked, squinting through the bars. "Not much more than a boy. I had a boy once. Died of the sweating sickness three years past. How many summers are you?"

"Sixteen," answered James. "Yesterday."

The jailer gave a snort. "Not the best way to mark it, banged up in the dungeons . . ."

James twisted his face in a wry smile. "Not really." He remembered with a flash of longing his birthdays past: nice dinner in his home, just a floor above but a world away . . . artful presents picked by his family, something fun and practical from Merry, who he was never allowed to see on his actual birthday, just the day after. Today. *If only . . .*

"Drink that," the man was saying. "I'll have something else for you shortly."

He returned fifteen minutes later with a steaming bowl. He pushed it under the door in the gap between the floor and the base of the iron bars.

James bent, picked it up. Some kind of gruel. "Thank you," he said, smiling. He ate it quickly, gratefully. He didn't care how it tasted. It was food and it was warm. He pushed the bowl back to the man. "Thank you," he said again. "It's Aeron, isn't it?"

"It is. And say nothing of it. Act groggy when they come for you, to question you next."

"When d'you think they will? What time is it now?"

"Midmorning. They're all busy with the king's tourney, so who knows? After that I reckon."

"And that's tomorrow?" asked James.

"So I hear." With a nervous glance behind him, Aeron took the evidence of his meal away.

James fell silent. Tomorrow Merry would come. He could only pray she would win the tourney—and then run.

Where was she? he wondered. Had she managed to sleep, knowing what was coming, what she would have to do, before an audience of earl, countess, and king?

God, he wished he could get out of here, for a million reasons, but to see Merry, to watch her compete, to help her . . .

James wondered about Longbowman Owen. Did he have any inkling, any sixth sense that someone would come to save him and his family, or was he lost in despair? It seemed the latter, for the man didn't speak. James had occasionally heard the low rumble of a word or two from the far end of the dungeons when the jailer gave him food and ale, but that was it.

"Don't give up hope," he called out now.

"Who's this offering me succor?" came the faint reply, contempt in the voice. "The fake Lord James? The thief?"

"So they say," replied James.

"Tomorrow the king will call on an Owen to come forward and honor our pledge," said Owen. "And I will not be there." He cursed bitterly in Welsh. "One day I shall avenge my family on the de Courcys. And God help them when I do."

James felt the hairs on the back of his neck stand up. This was not an idle threat, issued in the heat of the moment. This was the vow of a man who thought he was about to lose everything.

"An Owen will come forward," James said. "An Owen *will* stand for you."

There was an electric silence. Then a question: "Who are you?"

"A friend, strange as it may seem. And don't ask me more. Just wait and see."

"Someone will come forward? A *longbowman*?"

"No," answered James, voice full with pride. "A *longbow girl*."

There was a laugh of sheer disbelief. "Now that I *would* like to see" came the reply.

Just you wait, then, thought James, but he didn't answer. Time would answer for him.

He sat back on the bench once more and stared at the bars. When would his chance of escape come? He raked his fingers through his hair. He needed a weapon. An iron bar would be good, but he'd already yanked and pulled at the bars in the vain hope that one might come loose. Now he patrolled his cell, trailing his hand over the walls. He paused when his finger caught on a rough stone. He'd felt it give. He stopped, glanced around, then started to dig and scratch at the surrounding mortar, gouging away with his nails.

He didn't know how long it took him, he didn't care, time was all he had locked up in his cell, but finally he pried it loose. He pulled it from the wall and examined it. It was small, only about four inches long and two across, but it fit perfectly in his hand. It was smudged with blood from his skinned fingertips. He didn't notice. He felt exultant. Now he had a weapon and he felt the odds shift, just fractionally, maybe enough, in his favor. He pushed the stone down inside his waistband, hidden by the pleats of his doublet, and he waited for the next day to dawn.

Chapter Fifty-Four

Merry stood barefoot on the cold floor of the cottage, looking out at the valley of Nanteos. The sun rose, tinting the sky pink. There were only a few times in your life, she thought, when the stakes got really high. You could live an active life or a passive life, face competition of all sorts, whether you sought it or not, but to actually enter the arena . . . to compete for the highest of stakes . . . Whatever happened, she knew she would not be the same person when she walked out of it.

She picked up her glass eye and pushed it into place. The skin around it was unblemished, so unless someone came right up and peered at her, it looked as if she had two unmarred, functioning eyes. As a disguise, she hoped it would work. She saw no point in hiding her hair. Up close, no one would mistake her for a man. And her hair had been plaited and pinned up when she'd had her encounter with the countess.

She dressed quickly in her skins. Over them she pulled on the archer's clothes.

Mair came in with her pail of milk. She looked better than she had yesterday, but still her smile was tight. "Morning, Merry." Her voice was tremulous. "Did you get much sleep?"

"Morning, Mair. Went out like a light. Thanks to your potion." Merry put her hand on the healer's arm. "How are you?" There was a nasty bruise purpling her temple.

"Don't get to my age without suffering a few knocks," Mair replied, smiling. "I've a tough head. Come on, let's eat."

She poured some milk into the pan suspended over the fire, her long white hair streaming down her back.

"I've no—"

"Appetite," interrupted Mair. "I know. But you need all your strength today, so you *will* eat."

Merry sat down, resigned. Mair put a steaming bowl of stew in front of her.

"Let it cool while you drink this," she said, pouring out a stream of pale liquid from a jug on the table.

"What is it?" asked Merry, wrinkling her nose.

"An infusion of fennel to give you appetite, mugwort to ward off evil, sage to strengthen your nerves, and nettle seeds to give you energy. Sweetened with royal jelly, food for the queen."

"That covers all bases," said Merry with a smile. "Thank you, Mair."

She took the mug and sipped. Felt the warmth slide down her throat. There seemed to be something in it to give her courage too, for she felt better when she'd finished it.

She turned to the stew and spooned it up. The cottage was silent. No wind today, just the pale sun rising in a clear sky. Perfect conditions for arrows to fly straight and true to the target. Perfect conditions for the tourney.

Merry and Mair waited until they saw the crowds gathering across the valley. Great white pavilions had gone up, and there was the sound of hammering, as if arenas were being created. There also seemed to be a kind of raised area, like a dais, or a stage.

"Don't want to be there longer than you need. Not what anyone would call inconspicuous, are you?" Mair asked, nervously twisting her bonnet in her bony hands.

Merry was all too aware of the bounty on her head, of the risk of the countess recognizing her, but she hated to wait. Nerves fraying, adrenaline pumping, she felt cooped up in the cottage. She wanted to walk out of the door and let it begin. She knew Mair was right, but as the sun rose to what she thought was eleven o'clock, Merry could stand it no longer.

"We must go," she said. "I don't want to miss the king's challenge."

"The king'll probably be sleeping off last night's feast," said Mair with a pinched look. She paused, eyed Merry, looked out of her door again.

"But you're right. We don't want to miss it."

Merry took her bow and her arrow bag. She checked that all three strings were there, coiled safely. She slung the bag over her shoulder, took the bow in her left hand.

She picked up her waterproof backpack. If all went well, she'd be needing her headlamp for the swim home. And she had her catapult in there too. She hoped she wouldn't need it, but it was a weapon and it was portable and it gave her comfort.

"Can you keep this for me till after the tourney?" she asked Mair. "I need it for my journey back."

"Of course." Mair took it. "I'll hide it in my basket." She eyed the lime-green neon stripes. "It's a bit . . . outlandish."

Merry laughed, in spite of her nerves.

"When it's over we'll have to find each other quickly. I must leave straightaway."

"I'll find you," said the healer. "You just do what you must, then go," she added softly. "Back to *your* time. Back to safety."

Merry only prayed that she could.

Together they walked down the hill from Ty Gwyn.

"D'you think he's around, that man who attacked me?" asked Mair.

Merry wanted to lie, to give Mair peace of mind, to suggest that Parks was long gone, but that would do the healer no favors. She needed to remain vigilant. "I suspect Parks is watching the tourney," she replied. "It'd be too great a spectacle for him to want to miss it. He might be hiding in the forest, watching from a distance, but it wouldn't surprise me if he'd stolen more clothes to blend in. He'd be just another face in the crowd."

Mair frowned. "I'll tell everyone around that a stranger attacked me. After the tourney I'll organize a hunt," she said, her voice low with fury.

Merry glanced at Mair. She was loved in the community, had friends who would hunt for Parks. It made her feel easier.

They walked down to Nanteos Farm. Rhiannon, Angharad, and Gawain must have been watching and waiting, for they came straight out to join them. Angharad held out something in her palm.

"It's a four-leaf clover," she said. "For luck."

Merry felt tears burn her eye. She blinked and knuckled them away, then stooped and kissed Angharad's cheek. "Thank you, *cariad*. I'll keep it safe." She pushed it down into the deep pocket of her tunic.

"Spent hours looking this morning, she did," said Rhiannon. "Wouldn't give up till she found one."

Angharad smiled and Merry felt another surge of emotion. She seemed to go from being numb to being ambushed with emotions.

Soon they reached the earl's lands. The smell of wood smoke and cooking meat filled the air. The crowds grew thicker as they approached the tourney ground.

If Merry felt self-conscious, she did not show it. She walked with her head high, ignoring the stares of those they passed: the farmers, the men-at-arms, the women and the children. There were mutterings, but Merry supposed they thought she was carrying the bow for her father or for her husband. Why else would she have a bow? Merry smiled. Let them wait, let them see . . .

There were so many people, so many animals. Both she and Mair scanned the faces, checking for Parks, but they saw no sign of him. That gave Merry no comfort. She felt sure he'd be here, somewhere, watching. And waiting . . .

A commotion broke out ahead. The crowds parted to reveal a line of grooms leading high-stepping, overexcited destriers toward them. Huge, powerful horses, they were bred to carry an armored knight into battle. At a gallop, while wearing armor of their own. They were proud, fearsome-looking beasts with darting eyes and bunched muscles. Merry grasped Angharad's hand, pulled her well clear of the horses' snaking heads and stamping hooves.

It was to improve this breed that Henry VIII had ordered the destruction of the wild ponies he deemed undersized, thought Merry, with such fateful consequences for her ancestor, who had rushed to their defense. She remembered the pony hunt she'd seen . . . Longbowman Owen's protests, his doomed attempts to reason with the earl and king. His brutal silencing. She flicked a glance at the castle, where he languished in the dungeons just a few hundred yards away,

A pack of eight wolfhounds straining on leads dragged their handlers in the destriers' wake. Merry watched them pass, suppressing a shudder. It was no stretch of her imagination to picture these dogs chasing down and killing wolves.

Cheers and shouts erupted from a fenced-off arena where, in her time, the laurel bushes grew. Inside, raucous men in fine clothes were throwing an iron bar, competing to see who could lob it the farthest.

The five of them walked closer to the castle, weaving through the thickening crowds lining up by the food stalls that sheltered under the white pavilions. The Tudor version of fast food, thought Merry. Toffee apples, chicken legs, hot bread, and what smelled like mulled wine. Her stomach turned. She thought she was going to be sick. She walked away from the stalls, breathing deeply, willing her stomach under control. It seemed to work. Just.

And then Merry saw a group of powerful-looking men striding toward an arena marked off by ropes and poles. They were carrying unstrung bows. Some carried quivers of arrows that swung from loose belts. Most of them had arrow bags like hers.

Time to go. The crowds were gathering outside the arena. Rhiannon hugged her fiercely. Angharad stood on tiptoe and kissed Merry's cheek.

"Thank you," she said, eyes full of sweetness, "for all you have done for us. For all you will do."

Merry pulled the girl close, hugged her and Gawain too.

Mair stepped forward. "Good-bye, longbow girl. Be safe."

Merry hugged the old woman, breathed in her scent of herbs and wool.

Then she turned and she followed the archers. She gripped her bow, felt its power flood through her. She shut down her mind to all but the task ahead.

Shoot. Win. Escape.

Chapter Fifty-Five

Merry strode into the arena, grasping her longbow, her arrow bag slung over her back. She felt more alive than ever. There was more at stake than ever. Her life; the life and lands of those she loved. But she had one job, one focus. She could not think of what she might lose, just of what she needed to do. Of how she would do it. *Nock. Mark. Draw. Loose.* She'd trained for years. *This* was who she was.

She was aware of the wind blowing down from the mountains, carrying with it the scent of new-grown summer grass. She was aware of the voices rising in shock, in question, then falling away at a loud command. She was aware of a presence, huge and terrifying. The king in all his majesty.

Henry VIII sat on a carved, thronelike chair on a raised dais at the back of the arena. Merry looked up, eyed him full on. The small lips, pursed in judgment, the wide-set, piggy eyes, the square face padded by fat, the furs, velvets, and jewels.

Monarch, murderer, torturer, tyrant . . . the words ran through her head, but she kept her face impassive. She bowed low till her hair draped on the muddy grass. Then she straightened, whipped back her head so that her hair swung in an arc of gold.

"Who are you, girl?" thundered the king. "What do you do here with all the men?"

"I am Merry Owen, Your Majesty," she answered in a cool, clear voice that carried to the depths of the watching crowds. "I am the sister of Longbowman Owen, separated at childhood, raised by a family who could afford to keep me. I heard about Your Majesty's challenge and my brother's imprisonment. I have come to honor the pledge of my ancestors."

She felt the blood pounding in her veins.

"I am the longbow girl."

There was a roar. There were shouts and jeers. Then, as suddenly as they had started, the shouts stopped. The jeering men fell silent as King Henry stood, raised his hand high.

"Come here," he ordered Merry.

As she approached, she could see that on either side of the king sat the countess and an angular, angry-looking man who had to be the earl. Both glowered at her. The countess was scrutinizing her uncomfortably closely. But Merry felt sure the countess hadn't seen her hair, and now she had two eyes, not one.

Head high, Merry walked toward the king. She felt the fear she had desperately been trying to suppress bloom and grow inside her. She thought of Anne Boleyn, the wife he had recently beheaded. The brave, feisty, politically involved Anne, a woman who would have excelled in the twenty-first century with her motto of *Complain all you like, this is the way it's going to be*. She thought of Henry's current wife, resting in some palace as she prepared to give birth in the autumn. Dutiful, dull Jane Seymour . . . her motto—*Bound to serve and obey*—self-consciously differentiating herself as much as possible from her murdered predecessor.

Perhaps she wasn't that dull after all . . . *Displease the king and die a horrible death? Well, don't be Anne Boleyn. Be dull Jane. Do your job and get the hell out . . .*

Merry paused, just feet from the dais. She curtsied, then lowered her eyes, as she imagined Jane Seymour would.

"You can shoot a war bow?" boomed the king.

Merry glanced up. "I can, Your Majesty."

There was a hiss from the men-at-arms on the dais, from the earl, who got to his feet.

Another gaudily dressed, puppy-faced man jumped up. "You're not an archer!" he yelled, face red with outrage, grinning with the sport he thought he could make of her. "You're a *woman*!"

Something fused in Merry's head—the history lessons, her father's tales, her own refusal to be bullied. She raised her arm high, palm inward. She forked the first two fingers of her right hand in a V sign, directing it at the man.

The roars increased tenfold. Merry felt the blood sing in her heart. This was the sign with which the Anglo Welsh archers had taunted their French enemies from Crécy to Agincourt. *I have my two fingers; I curse you; I can draw a bow; prepare to die . . .* Crécy was two hundred years ago. But the gesture still meant *war*. Merry felt the heat of the crowd pumping back at her. She stood, head high, defiant. Finally, point made, she lowered her arm.

The king got to his feet, strode to the edge of the dais, turned to take in the whole crowd. He raised his arm again. The hissing and the jeering stopped. The puppy-faced man, murder in his eyes, stalked back to his seat. The earl eased back into his. The king looked at Merry, eyes creased with amusement now.

"So you are an archer, you say. Very poetically . . ."

Merry grinned back. "I am, Your Majesty." He looked massive, up there on the dais, enlarged by his splendid cape, the exuberant ruffles.

Carefully, Merry raised her hand, palm to him, fingers spaced. She wriggled her first two fingers, heavily callused from drawing the bow. She had never been more glad that she didn't use a glove or a tab on her right hand. Her skin told its own story.

The king's eyes widened. "*Why?* You would be a *warrior*? You would join my army? You would *kill*?"

Merry looked back at the king, and when she spoke, her words rang with truth.

"Not through choice, Your Majesty." She thought of Professor Parks. "But if I had to, I would. I am ready. All I ask is that Your Majesty give me the chance to show what I can do. And then abide by the results."

There was a low murmur of disbelief. "Impudent wench," Merry heard someone say.

The king looked at her speculatively. "Abide by the results?" he asked slowly, the smile leaching from his eyes. His huge, jowly face turned hard.

Merry felt her breath catch in her throat. She kept her gaze fixed on his, feeling that to look away, to show weakness to the bully would be fatal. She'd taken the confrontational Anne Boleyn route after all. For her, there'd never really been any other way.

"As I must, Your Majesty. As must the Owens. As must the generations to come. The longbowmen not yet born." She paused. "And the longbow girls."

The king gave a quick, instinctive smile and Merry felt her breath ease.

He glanced back at the earl, at his other men-at-arms; then he turned to the crowds. He raised his head, bellowed out so that they all might hear.

"Let the competition commence. One gold coin to the winner!" The king paused and it seemed that the earl, leaning forward, was suggesting something to him. The king smiled. "*Ten* gold coins to the winner!" There was a gasp from the competitors, and from the spectators. Ten gold coins was a fortune to most of them. Merry guessed that the earl wanted to make the men compete as ruthlessly as they could. To outcompete her . . . Something in the atmosphere in the arena changed, became gladiatorial. The men, seemingly friendly before, were eyeing each other narrowly. Merry felt another wave of fear.

"And if Merry Owen can draw a war bow, if she can loose her arrows with deadly aim," continued King Henry, "if she ranks with the best of these men here today, good enough to fight my wars and kill for me, then her family may keep their lands. Now and for as long as the Owens can fulfill the pledge of their ancestor."

Merry bowed low. She heard the roar of the crowd. It was time.

Chapter Fifty-Six

There were twenty men in the arena. They all turned to face Merry as she walked to the stake where they were gathered.

She saw many things in their eyes: outrage, mystification, disbelief, amusement, appraisal, and, from a few, pity. She kept her head up, swept her gaze over them all, face impassive. She hoped her glass eye would fool them. The less animated she was, the better. No good having one eye darting all over the place and the other dead. Plus, it suited her just fine. She wasn't there to engage with them. She was there to beat them.

She loosened her arrow bag, took out her string. The men watched her, eyebrows raised as she put her knee to her bow, flexed it, strung it. That in itself was a feat of strength that few other than trained archers could manage.

Ignoring their looks of surprise, she took out each arrow in turn from her arrow bag and eyed the flights, making sure each one was true. When she was satisfied, she looked up again. All the men were still watching her.

"I am ready," she said, in a voice loud enough to carry to the king.

There was a chorus of laughter from the crowd, then a low, mocking voice said:

"Ready now, is she?"

She turned to the speaker, the one man without a bow. The marshal, she guessed. She looked back at him and waited. Inside, her heart was beating wildly, but on the surface she was cool and controlled.

"Right then," said the man when he got no answer from Merry. "Here are the rules. With this"—he paused—"Merry Owen here, we have twenty-one competitors. We have ten targets set up, so we shall have three opening heats. The test is for skill and accuracy. "

Behind her back, Merry crossed her fingers tight, dared to feel a flurry of hope.

"The targets," continued the marshal, "are set eighty yards from the shooting line."

This news was met with shouts and jeers from the crowd.

"I know, I know, not the full distance by any measure but, believe it or not, we're short of space on this hillside today. Blame the knights and their destriers needing so much ground for the jousting! Blame the sloping Welsh hills!"

Merry felt a surge of elation. Eighty yards. She could *do* this.

"And as I said, accuracy is what His Majesty, King Henry, is seeking today."

That silenced the crowd.

"Each competitor must shoot three arrows. Judged by totaling their scores, the ten best men," continued the marshal with a dismissive glance at Merry, "will go into the next round, where we move the start point back ten yards. From those ten men, I shall select the winner. If no clear winner is discernible, we shall have a further round between the leading competitors, where we shall move the start point back another ten yards. All clear?"

There was murmured agreement from the men. Merry nodded, squared her shoulders, started up a rhythm of deep, slow breathing, working on getting her pulse to drop. A slower pulse aided accuracy. Not by much, but perhaps by enough to make all the difference.

"Right, are we all ready?" called the marshal.

"Yes," roared the men, drowning Merry's soft answer.

"Glory and His Majesty's gold to the winner!" bellowed the man, to roars from the spectators.

Merry glanced around, caught a glimpse in the crowd of the faces she sought—Mair, Rhiannon, Angharad and Gawain. Then she went into a kind of cocoon where the noise dimmed and her focus sharpened. She felt like she could see individual blades of grass, sense the direction of the wind from its feel on her skin, smell the lands over which it had blown.

The marshal stalked down the column of men, separating them. "Heat one," he announced, pointing to one group. "And heat two," he declared, pointing to the other. Like an afterthought, he turned to Merry. "You will be in heat three—alone."

Merry nodded, refused to acknowledge the implicit insult. It was fine. She'd have more time to watch, to sense the mood of the breeze, to adjust . . . let him think he was putting her off. Let them all underestimate her, until it was too late . . .

The contestants in heat one lined up. They stood with their backs to the king so there was no danger of a rogue arrow, or an assassin, felling His Majesty. The targets were round pieces of white-painted wood, with a central black circle and inside that a small white inner circle. They were attached to wooden stakes, just like the one she had practiced on.

Merry sized up her competitors. All the men were taller than her, most of them around six foot.

She guessed they were farmers or tradesmen, carpenters, blacksmiths and laborers. Some of them might have been full-time archers employed by a lord, perhaps by the earl himself. Either way, they would have been skilled archers. Henry VIII's royal edict commanded that all such men practiced weekly on their bows.

There was one man who stood out among the more humbly dressed competitors. A *gentleman* who wore elaborate clothes. That was unusual. Gentlemen or aristocrats preferred to be men-at-arms, swordsmen, or else to fight from the back of a destrier.

Not that the clothes had improved the gentleman's manners. The look he sent Merry was one of contempt. Merry looked away, but not before she'd registered the coldness, the flash of hatred, the barely contained violence. *Another Professor Parks.* Maybe he was an archer because he liked killing so much . . .

The marshal strode in front of all the men, ensuring they stood behind a white line, marked out on the grass with lime.

He moved off to the side, taking up position a few feet behind the bowmen.

"Ready your bows!" he cried.

The competitors stepped their bowhand foot forward.

"Nock!" called the marshal.

Arrows were slid into position. The men bent, readying themselves.

"Mark!"

All eyes were raised and focused on the distant targets.

"Draw!"

The archers pulled back their bowstrings, straightening as they did so.

"Loose!" yelled the marshal, and the arrows flew. They hissed softly, like deadly rain.

Merry watched them, eye flicking from archer to target. The commands came again in quick succession: "Nock, mark, draw, loose." Some competitors flaunted their skills at rapid shooting, but with only three arrows each, it was a showman's gesture and not very effective in most cases. Some competitors were slower and the marshal glowered at them. Merry wondered if he took away points for dithering.

The contestants were a mixed bag. Some were very good; most were average. In heat one, the clear winner was a small, wiry man just a bit taller than Merry. He hadn't spoken much, just got on with his business with an air of ruthless concentration. Some of the bigger, beefier men were powerful but not accurate, hitting only the outer edges of the target.

When all the arrows had been shot, the competitors stood back, some laughing and joking with each other, others gazing at the row of targets where the marshal prowled, scribbling on parchment with a quill pen.

He scowled at his jottings, eyed the targets again, then strode back to the competitors.

He picked out five men. There was cheering and shouting and back-slapping and dejection.

The losers trooped out of the arena. The next competitors

stepped forward. *Nock, mark, draw, loose.* The arrows flew. Merry's heart began to beat faster. This time, the winner was the *gentleman.* Five competitors were selected for the second round. Clearly, the marshal thought that Merry would never get that far. Time to upset his numbers.

"Heat three!" he called out. "Merry Owen."

Chapter Fifty-Seven

Merry stepped forward. She was dimly aware of applause, of cat-calls, of shouts, but nothing intruded above the roaring of blood in her ears.

She positioned herself behind the line, rolled her shoulders, and took a few deep breaths.

"We're all ready when you are," said the marshal, as if it were a great joke.

Merry selected an arrow, eyed her target. She felt a cool focus flood her veins.

"Ready your bow!" cried the marshal.

Merry took her stance, then, listening to the commands of the marshal, she nocked her arrow, bent from her waist, marked the target, drew back her bow, and loosed. The crowd had fallen silent. The only sound she could hear was the whisper of her bowstring and the hiss of her arrow. It seemed to take long seconds to fly home to its target. Merry saw it hit and lodge in the black ring, just left of the white center.

She chose another arrow, let fly. It lodged in the black ring again, just to the right of the white center. Then she took out her third arrow, aimed, loosed. Triangulation. Inner white! She was sure of it.

She turned, walked back from the line as the crowd, which had been stunned into silence, started to clap and shout. She didn't smile. Not yet. She just stood and waited. She was aware of the marshal staring at her, mouth hanging open, revealing stumps of discolored teeth. She just looked at the mountains rising behind the castle, tried to keep at bay the shouts and the noise and the attention. She saw a pair of red kites circling high, perhaps drawn by the archers, associating the war bows with carnage and corpses on which to feed.

"Well!" stated the marshal. His voice came out high-pitched. He cleared his throat and started again. "Well . . . it would appear that Merry Owen will go through to round two."

More noise from the crowd.

Merry walked forward to retrieve her arrows. She passed the marshal. He looked at her with sheer, unadulterated surprise.

"In round two," he declared as if for her benefit, "we move ten yards back, and each competitor will take it in turns so that we might better enjoy the spectacle. So we might better appreciate their skills."

The atmosphere became even more charged. The men glanced at each other, each thinking, it seemed to Merry, of the ten gold coins, of the fortune awaiting the winner. But for her, there was even more at stake than a purse of gold.

The ten other competitors all took their turns. The clear winner so far was the gentleman. He had two arrows in the black ring and one in the inner white.

Then it was Merry's turn. She walked forward. The crowd cheered. The men watched. Gone was the air of ridicule, amusement, or pity directed her way.

She waited till it fell quiet, then chose her first arrow. She nocked it, drew back her bow to its fullest extension. She needed all its power now to make the extra distance and to maintain accuracy. She felt and sensed the almost unbearable tension in the wood. *Please don't break*, she prayed silently. *Please give me just a few shots more.* She let out her breath, loosed the arrow. The bow held strong. The arrow flew to the target. Black circle.

Second arrow. She had to do better. No thinking, no worrying, just instinct and skill. She heard the ancient commands, in her head, in her body, and somewhere deep inside that must have been her soul. She pulled in a breath, released it smoothly as she loosed the arrow, as she watched it home in. Inner white! She felt the first flush of euphoria, pushed it down, selected her third and final arrow. She let it fly. Closed her eye, breathed, waited. The crowd roared. She opened her eye, looked at the target. Even from this distance she could see: dead center of the inner white.

Only then did she smile.

The marshal hurried up to the target, eyed the arrows, and smiled back.

"We have an outright winner," he declared. "With one first circle and two golds, Merry Owen wins!"

"Wait!" cried a voice.

All eyes flicked to the earl, rising to his feet beside the king.

Chapter Fifty-Eight

Merry's heart began to race again. Was he going to challenge her victory? Arrest her?

"With the blessing of our noble majesty, the King Henry, I would like to make the competition even more interesting," the earl declared.

Merry held her breath.

He raised his hand. In it was clasped a stave of wood. "All archers are familiar with splitting the wand."

Merry sucked in a breath. She'd heard of it. She'd never done it. Never tried.

The gentleman was calling back, "Indeed, my Lord."

"And you? Merry Owen?"

It felt to Merry that everything depended on this, that if she didn't win, the earl would manipulate events so that it was deemed that the pledge had not been honored, that the Owens' lands must be forfeited. *To him.* She felt a flare of pure, cold hate. She kept it from her face with great effort.

What could she say? *We don't do it in the twenty-first century?*

"Perhaps you could show us . . . My Lord," she added, as if as an afterthought.

There was a stunned silence, then a bark of laughter. Merry glanced down the dais. It was the king himself who laughed, and soon the crowd was laughing, but the earl remained steely faced.

"Very droll," he drawled when the laughter faded. "Marshal!" he yelled.

He handed over the stave of wood to the marshal, who scurried off to ram it into the ground beside the central target. Merry reckoned it was two inches across.

The blood roared again in her ears. But rage got in the way. She needed to find her calm. She sought out a single blade of grass, looked at it until she saw nothing else. Then she was aware of her name being called.

"Merry Owen!" the marshal was shouting. "Line up here, beside Bonneville."

Merry took her position beside the gentleman.

"You shall each shoot on my command. Bonneville, you first."

The gentleman nodded, glanced briefly at Merry with his cold eyes. Then he turned away, readied himself, drew his bow.

Merry heard the marshal's commands, saw the single arrow fly. The wand of wood stood intact.

She breathed again. Her turn.

She stepped forward, glad of her armor-piercing bodkin-tipped arrows. If she hit the wand dead center, the metal would split it with ease. *If . . .*

She reached back into her bag, selected an arrow. As always, she checked it.

She heard the commands, a distant echo of the words she said in her heart. She loosed her arrow.

And her luck ran out.

Chapter Fifty-Nine

There was a loud crack as Merry's bow broke in half. She felt the blow of the upper limb scything back against her temple, just above her ear, and then there was silence and nothingness as she lost consciousness and fell to the ground.

Her pulse beat once, twice, a third time; then her world exploded again as she came around. She found herself lying on the grass, the lower part of the broken bow still in her hands. She heard the crowd roaring. She opened her eye. She pushed herself up. Men were rushing up to her, talking at her. She pushed them away so she could see. She was dizzy, her vision clouded. She could feel blood running down her cheek. She walked on unsteady feet toward the other end of the arena, looking for the wand.

And then she saw it, lying on the grass. In two pieces. Like her bow.

She felt a wild surge of emotion: euphoria, relief, justice. She turned, sought out the earl. He was standing on the dais, his face rigid with rage.

The crowd fell silent as the king got to his feet. "Well," he declared. "Come forth, Merry Owen."

Merry brushed the blood from her cheek and walked toward the dais.

"I believe," said the king, "that this is yours." He took a purse from his pocket and threw it into the air. Merry's arm shot up and she caught it to more roars from the crowd and a smile from the king. She smiled back. Her head was thumping. She felt a sudden terror. She could feel the countess's eyes upon her. She wanted to get *away*.

"I think we have seen well enough the prowess of Merry Owen," said the king. "She is indeed a worthy longbow girl!" he announced to thunderous applause. He looked from the crowd back to Merry, his eyes solemn.

"Hear me!" he declaimed, chest thrust forward, head high. "I declare that the pledge given by the Owen family to the Black Prince has been honored this day." He beamed at Merry, beneficent, all-powerful, happy in his grace. "Your cottage and your lands remain in Owen hands for this generation. And if the generations to come produce longbowmen and women as fine as you, then your farm shall be yours forever."

Merry gave a huge smile. There was nothing the earl nor countess could do now. The king had given his word publicly. She bowed low, mouthed, *Thank you, Your Majesty* at the king. She saw the genuine appreciation in his eyes. She knew that once he had been a talented sportsman before a jousting fall from his horse damaged his leg and arguably his brain.

She risked a quick glance at the earl and countess. The earl's lips formed a bloodless line, so pursed in rage they were almost white. The countess looked furious, but more ominously, she looked curious. She tilted her pretty head side to side, eyeing Merry from different angles. She leaned across to her husband and said something. His eyes narrowed and he got up.

Time to go.

Chapter Sixty

>>>———————————→

Merry bowed again and rushed from the arena as fast as her wobbly legs would carry her. She was concussed. She knew that, could do nothing but keep moving. Applause rang in her ears. Several of the archers came forward to congratulate her, delaying her.

She struggled through the crowds, seeking Mair and Rhiannon and Gawain, and especially Angharad, the sister she had never had. She wanted to see her one more time even though her instincts were screaming at her to get away.

Suddenly she saw her nipping through the crowds. The girl leaped at her, almost knocking her over.

Merry caught her, grabbed on to her.

"Are you all right?" Angharad asked, eyes wide, looking with horror at the blood that dripped down Merry's face, making a dark trail down her tunic.

"I'm fine," replied Merry. "Just a cut."

Angharad burst into tears. "You did it! You did it!" she sobbed, and then Merry was crying and laughing with her. She pulled her close, thinking *This is the last time I'll see you, little girl*. Then Rhiannon was there, and Gawain, and standing by their side, beaming, almost bursting with pride, was Mair.

"You did it!" she declared, eyes shining.

Merry grinned back. "I did. Thanks to you. Thanks to Farmer Evans. Apologize for wrecking his bow."

Mair nodded. "I will. You were lucky. Nasty cut, but you were lucky."

"Don't I know it," replied Merry.

"You'll be going then . . . ," the healer continued.

Merry nodded. "Yes. I must. And this time I won't come back. I cannot do that to my own people again. I cannot risk it." Merry paused. The only thing she hadn't done was free Longbowman Owen, but she could see no way to do that.

Mair was handing her the backpack. "Here, take it; put my shawl over it and no one will see."

Merry slipped it on, tightened the straps so the pack lay smooth against her back; then she covered all trace of it with Mair's shawl.

"Thank you, Mair. For everything." She looked at her ancestors. "Be well. I'll pray for the release of your husband"—she turned to the children—"of your father."

They nodded gravely. Around them the noise of the tourney resumed as some new feat of physical prowess was performed.

"See to that cut, won't you," said Mair softly.

Merry nodded. "I will." Lightning had struck twice but she felt like she'd gotten away with it. It could have been her other eye.

With one last glance at her ancestors and Mair, Merry hurried off through the crowds. People ebbed and flowed around her, slowing her down. And then a hand reached out and grabbed her arm.

"Not so fast," said a voice.

Chapter Sixty-One

Inside the Black Castle, down in the dungeons, the jailer came running. His face was red with exertion and he couldn't keep his huge hands still.

"*Glyndŵr!*" he yelled, waving through the bars. "You're saved! An Owen came. The pledge was answered!"

James felt a surge of joy.

"And the most incredible thing!" continued the jailer, his voice rising ever higher. "A girl it was! A longbow *girl*!"

There was a curse of amazement, a laugh of disbelief, and a shout of triumph.

"Tell me. Tell me everything!" roared the longbowman.

In wonderfully exhaustive detail, Aeron the jailer told his tale, a tale he would repeat many times in the decades to come, but no retelling would ever compare with this first rendition to the man who thought he had lost everything.

In his cell, gripping the bars, peering out as far as he could see, James listened.

"*Duw,*" Longbowman Owen said at the end, after peppering Aeron with at least a dozen questions. "Who is she, this longbow girl?"

"That's what we all want to know, isn't it?" agreed Aeron.

Silent in his cell, James just smiled.

Chapter Sixty-Two

The hand gripped her arm and Merry gasped. Another hand closed around her other arm and she could feel the point of a dagger pressed against her side.

"Who the devil are you?" asked the voice.

Merry turned very carefully. A richly dressed, black-haired man with a viciously scarred face held the dagger to her ribs. Another man, her puppy-faced heckler, stood to the other side, smiling as if they were all best friends.

"Make a scene and I shall gut you. Do you understand?" the scarred man continued.

Merry looked into the hard eyes. If she tried to escape these two men, then she felt with utter certainty that the scarred man *would* kill her. For all his fancy clothes, he was very obviously a man of war.

She nodded.

"I'm going to remove my dagger from your ribs now and you are going to walk with me as if all is quite normal," continued Scarface. Merry could smell his rank breath as he bent down to whisper in her ear.

"Where are we going?" she asked.

"To the Black Castle."

"The countess would like to meet you," said the other man with a brief, mocking grin.

Through the crowds they walked. They were even stopped a few times by men and women wishing to congratulate the longbow girl. Merry forced a smile. She had saved her ancestors. Would the price be the gallows? She had to believe she could and would escape. *Fight clever*, said her father's voice. Her new voice.

As soon as they were inside the walls of the Black Castle, Merry's captors stopped grinning and ceased pretending to be charming escorts. They marched her to the servants' staircase. Down to the dungeons, to the deathly cold.

"Aeron!" bellowed Scarface as they descended the stairs. "Another one for you."

A huge man wearing leggings and a long tunic emerged. He looked like a blacksmith, thought Merry, with his big, scarred hands. His mouth dropped open.

"It's the longbow girl!" he exclaimed. "What are you doing with her? Why have you brought her here?" He looked from the men to Merry in disbelief.

"She's the one who stole Zephyr!" snapped Scarface. "She's a common thief. Lock her up with the other thief. The false *lord* who stole the ring. They're both for the hangman," he declared. "But the earl and countess want to have words with her first."

Merry's world spun. She could see the man called Aeron resisting the command, clearly knowing what was waiting for her, wanting in vain to protect her from it. Scarface took just one step toward him and Aeron quickly made up his mind.

He clamped his scarred hand around Merry's arm, gripping her like he would an unruly horse. Scarface gave Merry a lingering look.

"I'm sure we shall meet again very soon," he said, with the soft, hissing sibilance of a snake.

Merry held her head high, eyed the man till he turned and strode back up the stairs. *Never show fear.* She knew that lesson from her ponies. But inside she quivered with terror.

Merry would not submit to her fate. But for now, she didn't resist, knew she had to pick her time to fight. She allowed herself to be steered along but she looked around, trying to bank down her terror so she could think. She noted every detail: the short hunting bow and the quiver of arrows in an unlocked cell, the ax and the pile of wood in another cell. Weapons, opportunities. The jailer led her past the empty cells. Where was her ancestor, Longbowman Owen? And where was the false lord, the thief destined for the hangman?

The jailer paused before the end cell and extracted a bunch of keys from his tunic.

Merry's heart stopped. Behind the bars, staring at her with complete amazement, was James de Courcy.

Chapter Sixty-Three

Merry gave a violent start. James opened his mouth to speak, then quickly closed it again. The jailer, working a key in the lock, didn't notice either reaction.

"Stand back!" he ordered James, looking up. James took a few steps backward, eyeing Merry in silence.

"Friend for you!" said the man.

He gestured to Merry to go in with a gentle shove on the back.

Merry feared for a moment that he had felt her backpack, but he made no comment, just locked the cell door and pocketed the keys.

Merry and James stood frozen, listening to the man's departing footsteps. When the last echoes of his steps had died, they remained staring at each other, unsure what to say or do until with a strangled cry Merry rushed at James and then they were holding each other, gripping each other as emotions whirled through them.

Finally they drew apart. Merry looked at her feet, then forced herself to look up into James's eyes.

"You followed me."

He nodded. "I knew you were up to something. Something dangerous. I'd never seen you scared, Merry, but you were terrified. I sensed you didn't want my help 'cause you didn't want me mixed up in it."

"That worked well, didn't it?"

James laughed. "You should have known me better. I wasn't going to turn away and leave you to it."

"So I led you here. To the past."

"Not even in my wildest dreams did I imagine this." James's face turned somber. "I wondered if I would ever see you again. I didn't think it would be here . . . in our dungeons."

Merry looked back hard into his eyes. "They said you were a thief."

He nodded. "My signet ring, my mother's gift to me, turned out to have been stolen from this earl," he said, giving her a questioning look.

"It was me," she admitted.

"But how on earth did my mother get hold of it?"

"I planted it in the burial mound. Parks found it and sold it to some dealer, who sold it to your mother."

"Professor Parks? A thief?"

"He's a lot more than that. I'll get to him later," said Merry.

James rubbed his head as if it was all too much to process. "But the ring, why did you plant it?"

"I wanted him to authenticate it, then we'd sell it. We needed the money, and I wanted to get rid of it. I thought it was unlucky." She gave him a pained look. "I had no idea quite how unlucky. It's why you're here. It's all my doing."

James shook his head. "You didn't hold a gun to my head, Merry. I came of my own free will."

"But you had no idea what you were getting into. Maybe I should have told you everything after all."

"You should. You can start now."

Merry nodded. "I will. No secrets this time. And you can tell me everything that's happened to you. Come on, let's sit down, wrap ourselves in that blanket." She shivered. "It's freezing in here."

They sat on the narrow bench, huddling together for warmth, and began to tell each other everything.

She told him about how Parks had also traveled back, following her through the river, about how he'd attacked Mair, Seren's ancestor, who'd given her shelter. About how she'd chased and caught and shot him.

"Well done! You know what . . . I never trusted that man. There was always *something* about him, under the surface," declared James, outraged.

"Yeah, well, it's not under the surface anymore. It's right out there. I only hope Mair can get some of the villagers to hunt him down."

"Then what?"

Merry thought of the knowledge of a healer, the healing and the killing plants.

"Then they'll deal with him." She raked her hands over her face, gazed at James with a kind of bleak despair. "God, what a mess!" She jumped up, gazed down at him. "You turned sixteen two days ago! You were meant to sign with Manchester United!" She turned away. "What have I done?"

James got up, grabbed her arm, pulled her back to face him. His eyes blazed at her. "You did what you came back to do, Merry! You saved your ancestors. The jailer rushed back and told me all about it."

Merry nodded and her face brightened for a moment. "I did that at least."

"What's with the glass eye?" asked James.

"Disguise," said Merry, voice laced with regret. "Not that it seems to have worked. The countess recognized me as a horse thief."

She told him about nearly being caught, wrestling with the countess, fleeing on the Arab stallion.

She reached out, touched his face just below the vicious cut that disfigured his cheek. "What's with the cut?"

"The earl. He's fond of ornate rings," said James, eyes darkening.

Merry studied him. She could see in him the same new ruthlessness that ran through her, the same wiping away of the remnants of childhood and innocence and belief that things would always turn out all right.

"You've got a new wound too. Still bleeding," added James.

Merry frowned, touched her fingers to her cheek. The blood was still flowing, but more slowly now. "Bow broke." She felt a whirl of dizziness as her concussion made itself felt again. "They *will* hang us as thieves, don't think they won't because we're young. That makes no difference," she said, face hard. "What we need to do is figure out a way to escape."

She got up, went to the bars, gripped them, and tried to peer down the line of cells.

"Is my ancestor down here? Longbowman Owen?"

Before James could speak, another voice answered from the other end of the dungeons.

"Yes, I am, longbow girl."

Chapter Sixty-Four

"And who are you, apart from being my family's savior?" the voice continued.

Merry gave a quick, sharp laugh. "That is a long story, Longbowman."

"Well, that's all right then, longbow girl. Time is all we have in here."

Merry didn't answer. How could she start? How much could she tell him?

"You can start by telling me exactly who you are," said Owen, as if reading her thoughts. "And exactly what you mean by *saving the ancestors*." His voice hardened. "And you, fake Lord James, can tell me what you mean by *our* dungeons."

Merry and James just stared at each other. They hadn't realized their voices would carry so perfectly.

"Come on. I'm growing old here," said the man with a mix of humor and impatience. "Let's give you an easy question, then. How old are you, longbow girl?"

"Fifteen," replied Merry.

"Ha! Well, you aren't my long-lost sister then!" declared Owen. "She's twenty-three."

Merry fell silent again.

"All right, let's get to how a fifteen-year-old girl is the best long-bowman"—he paused—"*longbow girl*, in the county."

"I've practiced since I was five," answered Merry simply.

"*Why?* Are there no men in your family? No sons?"

Gawain, she thought. Would she ever see him again? A piercing, strangling emotion clenched her stomach.

"It fell to me," she said. "My father was, *is*, the longbowman. There wasn't a baby boy to take over, not until last year. So I was trained. He trained me."

"Who is he?" asked Longbowman Owen.

Merry sucked in a breath. "His name," she said, "is Caradoc Owen."

"Another Owen! Where's he from? I've not heard of him."

James and Merry stared at each other. James's look was clear and honest and Merry saw the way forward in his eyes. No more lies. No more evasions.

"He's from Nanteos Farm," she said slowly. "The Nanteos Farm that lies in the shadow of the Black Castle."

There was a silence, then Owen spoke. "Well now, longbow girl. You know that's impossible, don't you?"

"No more impossible than a longbow girl winning the tourney."

There was a quick laugh. "You got me there. So. Explain the next impossible."

"Time," said Merry simply. "James and I, we're not from your time. I am related to you. That's what we meant by saving the ances-tors. You and Rhiannon and Angharad and Gawain *are* my ancestors. I am your blood." Her voice came out lower than usual, rich with emotion. "I am your descendant. James is the descendant of the earl and countess holding us all prisoner. These *are* his dungeons, but nearly five hundred years from now. We're from the future and we've come back to your time."

The air seemed to quiver with unasked questions. Pacing, caged footsteps were the only sounds. Finally there was a curse of amazement.

"My mind cannot comprehend it. But it makes sense," Owen declared. "*That's* how you knew about the longbow girl coming, Lord James." His voice was full of wonder. "*That's* how you knew what was going to happen! You're *not* an oracle!"

James laughed. "No, I'm not. There's a book, a lost tale of the *Mabinogion*, that tells of an angel warrior with hair of gold, coming to save the land of families old . . ."

"A book," marveled Owen. "Telling you a tale that hadn't yet happened in my time . . ."

"Telling my fate nearly a thousand years before I was even born," said Merry.

"Merry came back to save you," concluded James.

They couldn't see the far cell where Owen stood, clutching the bars. He was a longbowman, a warrior, but he could not hold back his tears. He gazed at the dungeon walls, seeing in his head his family, safe in their home.

Merry and James stood next to each other, looking in his direction, smiling despite everything.

"My debt to you can never be paid," the man said at last.

"It's paid," said Merry. "I'm alive. At least for the moment."

"Well, it would seem that you are. Merry Owen and Lord James de Courcy." He enunciated their names slowly, as if amazed to say them in the same breath. "The closest of friends, by the sound of it . . ."

"We are," said James. "And I trust I'm not your sworn enemy?"

Merry turned to James, raised her eyebrow.

There was the sound of rueful laughter. "Ah, yes, I did vow to destroy the next de Courcy I clapped eyes on . . . I suppose that's one vow I'll have to break."

Merry reached out in the damp cell, took James's hand. The look in his eyes was full of so many things that could not be said. Not here. Not now. There was another silence, punctuated by the slow, percussive drip of water dropping from the ceiling, pooling on the rock floor.

"So tell me," said Longbowman Owen finally. "How in the name of heaven did you travel back in time? And how are you planning to get home again?"

Footsteps sounded on the stairs. No one spoke. Merry and James moved apart and waited.

Two men appeared. The jailer unlocked the cell door. Then, with a sweep of velvets and lace, a reek of lavender and a glower of outraged self-importance, the Earl and the Countess de Courcy stepped forward.

The countess stalked up to Merry and examined her closely.

"I was right!" she exclaimed, eyes narrowing in fury. "It *is* you!"

"The longbow girl," observed the earl, frowning.

"Longbow girl and thief!" cried the countess. "*This* is the one-eyed pirate who stole Zephyr!"

"But she has two eyes," said the earl, stepping closer.

"Let's see!" shouted the countess. "Brioc, Cranog, hold her arms."

Merry knew what was coming. The two men approached her. She struggled but they were stronger and they held her with both hands, fingers digging into her arms.

"Let her go!" shouted James.

Scarface took one hand off Merry and tried to backhand James in the face. James blocked the blow with his forearm. The man-at-arms let go of Merry and turned, pulling a dagger from his waistband.

"Like to defend your little friend?" he asked, with a snarl.

James stood his ground, rage flooding him. But he knew that Brioc wouldn't hesitate to use the dagger, would probably enjoy it, so he kept his fists by his sides and managed to say nothing.

Merry stopped struggling. She did not want to provoke Scarface in any way, but the urge to ram her hands out and send the countess flying from her cell was almost overwhelming. *Pick your battles*, said the voice in her head. Her breath came harsh and ragged and she fought to control herself as the countess reached out her finger and poked her in the eye. The glass eye. To get better leverage, the countess grabbed her head with one hand and probed and poked with the fingers of her other hand, and seconds later Merry's false eye popped from its socket and bounced onto the rock floor. It rolled to a corner under the bench.

"Ha!" shrieked the countess, releasing Merry. "A fake eye! It's her all right. The one-eyed horse thief!" She turned to her husband, triumphant. "I *thought* she looked familiar!" She looked at her own hands in distaste. They were smeared with Merry's blood.

"Urgh! Disgusting. We've seen enough. She's guilty and will hang!" she declared, before striding from the cell.

The earl followed her, speaking to the jailer on his way out.

"Keep her locked up. No food or drink for either of them." He turned back to Merry and James. "I'll have a little talk with you both in a day or two. That's if you can still talk by then . . . ," he added, with a meaningful glance at Brioc.

The man-at-arms gave a quick, grim smile. The countess nodded in approval.

"Have word sent to the hangman," the earl said to Aeron. "He can come and dispatch two little birds with his one noose." He paused. "Maybe even three . . ."

Chapter Sixty-Five

"I'm sorry, longbow girl," called out Longbowman Owen when they were alone again.

Merry nodded. She could hardly speak. She was trembling with rage, shock, and a deep feeling of violation. "Thank you," she managed to say.

"They'll pay for that," said her ancestor. "One way or another." His words drifted through the dungeons like a dark promise.

Merry paced around the cell. Back and forth like a caged animal. James watched. Understood too well. He said nothing, just stood in the darkness out of her way.

Finally Merry stopped pacing and gripped the bars, looking out. Then she turned back to James.

"You okay?" James asked. He'd never seen her without her eye patch but he looked at her now unflinchingly. Merry let him look. There was nothing to hide anymore.

"I'm all right," she answered. "I honestly don't know how I managed to control myself when that woman was gouging at me." She blew out a long breath and rubbed her arms as if to clean something dirty off them. "What about you? Looked like you had a hard time reining yourself in too."

James nodded, his face grim. "I could see where it would end up.

We couldn't fight them. We were outnumbered. They had rapiers and daggers. We had our bare hands."

Merry shook her head. "That's not quite true."

She pulled up her tunic, took her knife from the leg strap, held it up so that the faint light glittered on the cold metal.

James raised his eyebrows. "Not bad."

He reached inside his doublet and pulled out his sharp little stone. He clenched it in his palm so that the sharp end protruded like a knuckle-duster.

"Handy," said Merry.

She pulled off her shawl and backpack, took out her catapult and stones.

"Useful," said James.

"Best present you ever gave me," replied Merry. She stashed the catapult inside the skins she wore under the archer's woolen leggings. The stones she zipped into the tiny pocket at the back of the waistband.

She put her backpack and shawl back on, making sure the pack was concealed.

"They will hang us, but God knows what Scarface is planning on doing to us in the meantime. We've got to escape, and soon," said Merry grimly.

"I've got an idea," replied James.

Merry listened carefully.

"I like it," she said at last. "But it's risky and we'll only have one chance. We've got to get it right."

Side by side in their cell, Merry and James waited. No one came. They were left alone. They could not tell Longbowman Owen of their plan in case Aeron was near, in case anyone overheard.

Despite their nerves, their fear, they were dozing when, hours later, they finally heard footsteps. They jumped up, stamping to bring some circulation back to their feet.

James pushed his face against the bars, trying to see. "Aeron, the jailer. With food," he whispered.

Merry had already taken out her catapult and stones, moved into position. She could feel her heart again, thudding in her chest. *Calm*, she told herself, *keep calm*. But the guard moved away to the other end of the corridor. Spoke to Longbowman Owen. Their voices were subdued, as if neither of them wanted to be overheard, but then Longbowman Owen raised his voice in anger.

"You have to do something," they heard him say.

"They'll have my head if I do!" the jailer hissed back. "And it'll change nothing. They'll never get away. You and I both know the truth, evil as it is. They're dead already. So'll you be if you're not lucky."

Merry and James just looked at each other, eyes full of so many conflicting emotions, almost vibrating with tension.

But the jailer didn't come to them. His echoing footsteps just faded away.

"Maybe he'll come back with food for us," whispered Merry, blowing on her hands to warm them up.

"Maybe," echoed James.

But the minutes slipped by and it became obvious that the jailer wasn't coming back.

Colder, hungrier, thirstier, and ever more frightened, Merry and James waited in the darkness of the cell. Exhausted, they lay down on the narrow bench, holding each other tight, for warmth, for comfort. Finally, they fell into a nightmare-filled sleep.

Chapter Sixty-Six

Footsteps woke Merry again. She had no way of knowing, but it *felt* like dawn. She sat up, whispered to James.

"Quick! Wake up. Someone's coming!"

James sprang up, pushed his hair from his face.

Merry was freezing, her fingers numb. She rubbed her hands together, desperately trying to get the blood moving. She pulled the catapult from her skins and palmed a couple of stones from her pocket. She kept her hands hidden behind her back.

The jailer appeared, sleepy-looking himself, with a tray and two bowls of what looked like gruel.

"Morning," he said gruffly. "Starving you don't sit right with me. Just can't do it. You being the longbow girl and all," he added.

Merry and James glanced at each other. They felt bad for the man, for his act of kindness. For what they were about to do. But survival had rules of its own.

"Thank you," said James. "That's really very nice of you. We're both grateful." He wanted to keep the man's attention on him. "What have we got, then? It smells delicious. Gruel?"

Aeron nodded. He bent down, pushed two steaming bowls under the bars. James moved out of range as Merry took her catapult from behind her back and fired. She hadn't time to aim, just firing from instinct with a shaking hand. The stone shot through the bars and smashed into the wall opposite.

Startled, the jailer straightened, looked around with a curse. Merry was already reloading. Desperate now, she fired off a second shot. This one hit the man square on the temple. He crumpled and began to fall.

James stuck his arms through the bars and grabbed him, holding him firmly against the cell. The man was obviously heavy and James struggled to hold him up. Merry reached inside the jailer's tunic pocket. She grabbed the keys, pulled them out. James's arms began to shake with the effort.

"Keep him there," urged Merry, moving to the lock, trying the keys. "Have to be sure it's the right set of keys. He could have more."

She tried one key, then another, then another, without luck. Heart pounding, she tried the last one. The lock sprang open. With a great sigh James released their captor and let him slump.

Merry pushed open the door, moved out with James. Together they pulled the man into the cell. They threw the blanket over him and locked him in.

"Let's go!" whispered Merry.

They ran to the empty cells containing the ax and the hunting bow and arrows—the watchman's tools. Merry still felt light-headed from lack of food and water but the concussion seemed to have eased. She grabbed the bow and arrows as James took the ax. Then they hurried to the end of the dungeons, to her ancestor.

Merry took him in close up: tall, powerfully built, with fair hair and beard, and intelligent blue eyes. Another version of her father. She felt a spasm of longing.

"Hello, longbow girl," said Owen. His gaze was sharp with curiosity.

Merry could see the emotion in his eyes and a kind of amazed recognition as he studied her. He opened his mouth to form a question; then the sound of distant footsteps echoed down the stairs.

Merry fumbled with the keys, trying them in the lock.

"Get ready to run," she whispered.

"I was planning on it!" Owen grabbed a blanket and what looked like a kind of animal-skin water container from his bench as Merry struggled with the lock.

"C'mon! Open," she pleaded. Two keys later, it did. Longbowman Owen grabbed the handle, turned it, and pushed free.

The three of them ran to the tunnel door. It was locked. Merry tried the set of keys again, getting desperate as the sound of footsteps drew nearer. The first key failed. Next to her, James and Owen stood, legs braced, facing whatever threat was coming down the stairs.

The second key turned the lock.

Almost whimpering with relief, Merry pushed open the door, which creaked horribly. The three of them rushed through. Merry locked the door behind them.

Fumbling in the darkness, she reached into her backpack, yanked out her headlamp, switched it on. Her ancestor stepped back from the light, blinking in shock. He moved his hand toward it in speculation but froze at the cries coming from the other side of the thick oak door. He flicked his head, eyes grim. *Time to go.*

Chapter Sixty-Seven

>>>>———————→

Merry, James, and Owen raced down the tunnel in the shaking light of the headlamp. They emerged, breathing hard, into the slanting rain of a gray dawn.

Owen turned to Merry and James. "I thank you both." He smiled at Merry. "You're every inch an Owen, longbow girl."

Merry looked at him, at the so-familiar features. On impulse, she grabbed him, felt his own arms come around her, pulling her tight. Merry felt tears roll down her cheek. She pulled away, knuckled them from her eye.

"Where will you go?" she asked.

"I'll hide until I get this travesty cleared up," Owen replied, a hardness darkening his gaze. "Look after each other," he said, slapping his powerful hand on James's arm. "Hang on to your weapons. You've a long way to go!"

James nodded. "We will. Good luck." He grabbed Merry's hand. "Come on."

Merry gazed at her ancestor for one more moment as he powered up the hill toward the wildness of the Beacons; then she and James turned and ran.

Soon they made the cover of the Black Wood.

"They're bound to try to track us with dogs," said Merry. "We'll never outrun them. Our only hope is to head down to the stream, cross it, hope they'll lose our trail, then head up to Sarn Helen."

"Good plan."

After five minutes, they found the stream, jumped in, waded along it, then exited on the far bank. They ran alongside it in single file on the narrow track.

Suddenly the far-off baying of hounds echoed through the trees. Exchanging a quick, silent look of fear, they hurried on. Running with the ax and the bow and arrows slowed them down, but they knew they had no choice. Five minutes later, they heard the hounds again, but they seemed to be farther away, maybe seeking their trail in the wrong direction.

"We have to head uphill soon," panted Merry. "We *have* to risk recrossing the stream."

James nodded. "Let's hope the hounds are too far away to pick us up." They forded the stream and found another track through the wood, leading up the side of the valley, toward where Sarn Helen cut across the high plain.

They ran in silence, the sound of their breathing loud in their ears. At last, each daring to hope they might have gotten away, they emerged from the wood, onto the plain. They ran from the shelter of one copse of trees to another. They had maybe half a mile to go to get to the thick forest that hid the waterfall when they heard the wolfhounds again. Much nearer.

Then a pair of hounds burst from a thicket two hundred yards behind them.

"We have to stand and fight," rasped Merry. "We'll never make it."

They slid to a stop, side by side, blowing hard. Turned to face the two wolfhounds, a hundred and fifty yards away now and closing fast.

Merry nocked an arrow. Life or death. Her heart pounded as the dogs closed, baying for blood.

She sucked in a breath, waited. The dogs were fifty yards away. Accurate range of thirty yards with this little bow, just time for one shot.

"I'll get the one on the right," she said to James, not taking her eye from the beast.

"Got that," he replied, moving sideways.

The hounds charged toward them, all snarling teeth and flying saliva. Merry took aim. At twenty yards she loosed her arrow.

She was aware of a great squeal; then the wolfhound was cartwheeling through the air, the arrow embedded in its chest.

Beside her, James jumped in the air. "Here! Over here! Come and get me!" he roared. The second hound was nearly upon them. Then, at the last moment, James stepped sideways, braced himself, and swung the ax at the dog, knocking it off its feet. It gave a chilling howl, rolled, got up, then, as James raised the ax again, it took a stumbling step and collapsed, a mass of muscle and bone and teeth.

They exchanged a glance mingling horror and relief, then they started running again. They sprinted for the forest, desperate for cover. Human hunters would be following, they both knew. Merry kept glancing over her shoulder, and moments later, she saw four horsemen emerge over the brow of the hill, galloping across the plain toward them.

James saw them too. They didn't look back again. The trees were in sight, just three hundred yards away. But the horsemen were closing. They could hear the pounding hooves.

"Faster." Merry sobbed out the word as they ran, legs burning. Though she was fleet, James was faster, but he kept back with her. At last they were into the trees, just a hundred yards ahead of the huntsmen.

They heard the shouts of fury, of frustration. The men would have to dismount to follow them. The forest here was too dense to ride through. They ran on, branches whipping their faces, brambles raking their skin as they pushed through the undergrowth. Behind them they could hear the men swearing and shouting and hacking at the branches with their swords.

They found a track, narrow but passable, and picked up speed. They were young and they were fit but they hadn't eaten or drunk for over twelve hours. Adrenaline gave them strength, but how long could it last?

And then, out of the bushes stepped Anthony Parks.

Chapter Sixty-Eight

Merry and James stopped running. Behind were the hunters. In front Merry's murderous enemy.

Merry nocked an arrow.

"Get out of here, Parks, or I *will* shoot you."

The man gave a mocking smile. "Oh, I think we've established that you haven't the stomach to kill," he replied.

And then it was Merry's turn to smile. "Maybe not, Parks, but I can stop you."

Parks just laughed and began walking toward them as if her words meant nothing. In her side vision, Merry saw James lift the ax.

"Oh, please, Lord James. Put down your toy," jeered Parks. "You don't have it in you either!"

Merry thought of Mair, of Angharad and Gawain and their mother, with no one to protect them from this man.

Mark. Draw. Loose.

With a sickening thud the arrow embedded itself into Parks's thigh. He fell to the ground, screaming in pain and rage. It was enough to stop him—for now and perhaps forever.

But there were answering calls from the hunters, closing on them.

Merry and James glanced around. They could see the outlines of the men, weaving through the forest, just fifty yards away. Merry grabbed her remaining arrows and together she and James ran past Parks, who writhed on the path, screaming curses after her.

The deer track widened and they sped up, but so did their hunters.

They could hear the heavy footfalls, the snapping branches, the cries of pursuit. And then came the sound of baying. More wolf-hounds. Rapidly closing.

Desperate now, muscles on fire, Merry and James ran on uphill. Then the forest began to slope away to the left and they saw the flash of silver that was the stream.

They plunged through the thornbushes, heedless of the cuts and blood. There was a great thundering of hooves and Merry thought the huntsmen were upon them. She and James turned to face them, James with his ax at the ready, Merry with her bow.

But instead, careening out of the forest, came the Arab stallion. He must have made his home here in the forest.

Gasping with relief, they turned and jumped into the stream, splashing through the water, wading toward the waterfall.

"It's easier this way," panted Merry. "The current takes you forward. Just swim down and keep your head below the rock ceiling."

James nodded. There was no time for more talking.

The shouts and the drumming hoofbeats got nearer. A wolf-hound shot from the trees, pursuing the stallion. Another one appeared and changed direction, heading for them, baying hideously.

Merry grabbed James's hand, looked into his eyes. They blazed back at her, full of life, full of fire. She allowed herself just a moment more to look at him; then she released his hand.

They dropped their weapons.

"See you on the other side."

Chapter Sixty-Nine

Air, light, soft rain falling. No wolfhounds. No huntsmen. Just birds fluttering and squawking as Merry and James stepped from the water.

They bent over, arms braced on their legs, sucking in air till their breathing slowed to normal. Then they straightened, looked at each other. They saw every detail of faces they had known for almost all of their lives. Every freckle, every cut, every scratch.

"D'you smell it?" asked Merry.

"What?" asked James.

"Petrol fumes. The faintest whiff." Merry smiled, stepped toward James, pulled him into a hug. "We're home," she said, her breath warm on his neck. "We made it!"

James pulled back from her, looked at her face, so full of life and of something else, some new kind of light. Then he drew her to him and he kissed her. Not on her cheek; on her lips.

Merry hesitated, just for a moment. All the fears, all the *what ifs*, everything else was irrelevant. Nothing else mattered save the here and the now. Save this time. *Their* time. She kissed James back as the water flowed around them.

There was a sudden wild thrashing behind them. They pulled apart, wheeled around, ready to face whatever had followed them from the sixteenth century.

But all that came out from under the waterfall was the Arab stallion.

Merry gave a laugh of delight. She held out her palm. "Come on, boy. You're safe now. Here. With us."

James put his arm around Merry's shoulder.

"Looks like you might not have to sell your mare after all . . . ," he said.

Chapter Seventy

The police ordered everyone to convene at the Black Castle. There was more room there. The de Courcys were pleased by that; it gave them an element of control over the proceedings, or so they believed. The castle was their fortress. And they needed it. Their unblinking self-confidence had been shaken. There were things they could not control. There were miracles their money could not buy.

Auberon de Courcy stood before a roaring fire, eyeing the assembled throng. Anne de Courcy sat with James on a small green sofa. She had her son's hand clamped in hers like she'd never let go. She kept flicking him glances as if she didn't quite believe he was there. James smiled back at her, squeezed her hand. He looked exhausted and cold but strangely tranquil in the way that those who have overcome appalling danger sometimes can be. His sister, Lady Alicia, sat beside the fire, glancing nervously from her father to her brother.

Caradoc and Elinor Owen sat on a plush plum-colored velvet sofa flanking Merry. They looked worn out, ecstatic, relieved, and fiercely protective.

Gawain snuggled in Merry's arms, warming her. He beamed up at his sister and gazed around the big room in wide-eyed curiosity.

Merry felt deliriously exhausted and relieved. The ruthlessness that she had drawn on, that had gushed up inside her when needed, was hidden back down deep inside.

Mrs. Baskerville, still wearing her apron and a look of stubborn determination, hovered by the door, trying to make herself invisible. Nothing was going to keep her out of the room.

Seren Morgan sat in a tub chair, glancing from Merry to James with her quiet scrutiny. The local policeman, PC Griffiths, stood, feet planted, arms folded behind his back, off to the left of the Earl de Courcy. He was flanked by the two senior detectives who had been responsible for the major manhunt to find Merry Owen and James de Courcy: Detective Inspector Williams and Detective Constable Evans.

"So, let me get this straight," began DI Williams nasally. "Having spoken to you both separately, what I'm to gather from each of your stories is the following: Merry Owen and Lord James ran away four nights ago. You slept rough in the mountains, because you both like living rough so much." At this the detective raised his eyebrow and scanned the opulent drawing room, all velvets, brocades, Persian rugs, and oil paintings . . .

"Then, on the fifth day, you decide you've tortured your families enough and you come back. Seren Morgan, out for a drive, finds you riding back along the road on a black Arab stallion with a fleece top as a halter, both of you in filthy costumes, looking fit to drop, covered in cuts and scratches like you've been in a brawl." Williams raised his arms in a shrug of disbelief.

Merry and James just nodded.

"But back to first things. Your disappearance," continued the detective, eyes flicking between them.

They said nothing. It was the countess who spoke.

"Why?" she asked in a desolate voice. She gave James's hand a shake, as if to liberate the truth. "Why?"

James looked deeply uncomfortable. Twelve people turned to him. Even Gawain was riveted.

Finally, he uttered a kind of strangled sound. "I can't say. Just can't say."

"Can't. Or won't?" asked Williams. "You need to answer for the heartache you've caused. Not to mention the manpower used searching for you."

"It's not like that!" shouted Merry. "Don't blame him."

"No!" agreed the countess in a voice of ice. "Don't blame my son!" She pointed at Merry. "Blame her! She's a bad influence on my son. Always was!"

Elinor Owen jumped to her feet. "How dare you! Don't you *dare* judge my daughter!"

"Quiet! Please. Stop it!" Now James de Courcy was on his feet.

Gawain looked from participant to participant with goggling eyes. This was huge fun, the grown-ups shouting.

"You don't know what you're talking about," James told his mother.

The countess's mouth dropped open. She moved to say something but the earl clamped his hand on her arm and gave her a warning look.

"Merry and I ran away to have an adventure. Simple as that. Nothing else went on."

"And it's going to stay that way!" declared the countess, wriggling out of her husband's grip. "As from now, you two shall never meet!"

"Well, that'll keep them happily to their homes, won't it?" observed Seren.

The countess turned on her. "So what would you do, then?"

"I would let them be free. Let them follow their destiny," she declared.

The earl raised his eyebrows almost to his receding hairline. "What the devil does that mean?" he asked crisply.

But Seren just smiled. She *saw* the images in her mind as time scrolled forward: the portrait hanging in the hall: the blond beauty, part witch, part horse whisperer, part longbow girl; the one-eyed countess . . . In this very drawing room, she *saw* James and Merry, in their sixties, just as much in love as ever, chatting animatedly with their five children.

The images swirled and disappeared. She looked at the young James and Merry. She wondered if they had any inkling. She'd seen the love in their eyes when she found them riding back along the road, but she wasn't sure either of them acknowledged it. She supposed that for them, living in the moment was going to be just fine.

Chapter Seventy-One

The police declared the case of the missing teenagers closed. Merry and James had returned to their parents, scratched, cold, starving, clearly lying about something or other but none the worse for wear. No crime seemed to have been committed.

Neither Merry nor James spoke of Parks. He'd probably have died back in the sixteenth century, they thought. Without antibiotics, it would have been very unlikely that his arrow wound would have healed. Mair would not have tended him. Enough damage had been done. Some secrets needed to be kept.

The burial mound was covered over by a large tarpaulin while Merry and her parents debated what to do. Merry thought that the chieftain should be left at peace, but there was pressure from Dr. Philipps and the museum to continue the excavation.

Merry hid her talismans: the gold coins given to her by King Henry VIII and, her favorite, the four-leaf clover. She pressed it to preserve it. Sometimes she would take it out and hold it on the palm of her hand and that day would come flooding back: the young girl with the blond hair and the blue eyes handing it to her with a shy smile and wishing her luck.

James signed with Manchester United. His parents, in a radical change of approach, born of their terror that they had lost their son forever, did a deal with him. He had to take his exams in a few weeks' time; then he could leave school and play soccer full-time. For as long as he wanted to. For as long as he was able. The Black Castle and his inheritance would wait for him.

In the wilds of the Owens' five hundred acres, the herd of Welsh Mountain ponies and the Arab stallion ran free. His stud fees brought in a healthy income. And Merry Owen and James de Courcy . . . they too knew the meaning of freedom and what it meant to be alive.

The book stayed in the Museum of Wales. It didn't take Dr. Philipps long to raise the sixty thousand pounds that secured the future of Nanteos Farm for the Owens.

Merry went to look at the book from time to time. She thought there was nothing more for her in it, that after all that had happened, it had relinquished her.

But deep inside the Brecon Beacons, the River of Time rolled on.

Acknowledgments

Longbow Girl began in my own childhood. My father brought me up in the same way as he raised my older brothers. I was expected to do just what they could and did and for that I am profoundly grateful.

When I was eight, my father gave longbows to me and my brother Kenneth for Christmas. I had never had anything quite so wonderful! Kenneth and I would go off for hours shooting at tin cans with some success and, in the case of my brother, the high wires of the electricity pylons with, I am now extremely happy to say, zero success. I loved the satisfaction that came with honing my aim, with being able to shoot a tin can cleanly from the top of a wall a decent distance away.

Some years later, my parents brought more magic into my life—they gave me a Welsh Mountain Section B pony called Ceulan Jacintha. She was an eleven-month-old weanling, and effectively became my child. Every evening after school I looked after her, and when she was old enough to ride, I trained her. And then the wild Welsh hills that were our home became our playground. We would ride out for hours, and for full days on the weekends and school holidays. Girl and pony with incredible freedom . . .

Quite often, my father or my mother would come with me when I went to look after Jacintha, especially when it was pitch-dark when the nights drew in in the seemingly endless winters. My father and I would walk to the farm where we kept Jacintha, but my mother and I preferred to cycle. We only had one bike, so we both squeezed on. The way back was all downhill. Perched on the bike, we would career down the hills, roaring with laughter.

All these are such happy memories. To plunge back into this world of my childhood has been such an exhilarating and joyful experience for me.

I have so many people to thank for these experiences, first my father, the late Professor Glyn Davies, and my mother, Grethe Davies. And my brother Kenneth, for all those hours on our longbows, chatting away, shooting more than the breeze. And of course my pony, Jacintha, for taking me to worlds both physical and mental that I could never have reached on my own or on foot.

You are all my inspirations and the gifts you have given me are as powerful today as they ever were.

And now we jump many years forward in time, to the writing of *Longbow Girl*.

And here I have my husband, Rupert, and our three children, Hugh, Tom, and Lara, to thank. Rupert has read aloud probably ten different drafts of this novel to our children over a four-year period. The children have listened loyally and interestedly and have given me excellent if sometimes painful input. My husband has also risked wifely wrath by daring to tell me when things weren't working on the page. He has lived patiently and supportively with my *Longbow Girl* obsession for a very long time! My debt to Rupert and our children is profound.

My brother Roy is a fluent Welsh speaker and writer with an encyclopedic command of all things Welsh, and his knowledge, suggestions, and enthusiasm have been a great help.

Marc Grady of the Longbow Emporium not only made the most beautiful longbow for me, but has also cast his eye over the longbow scenes and shared with me many fascinating bits of longbow esoterica.

Dr. Wynne Davies, breeder extraordinaire of Welsh Mountain Section B ponies, many, many years ago sold us the wonderful Ceulan Jacintha and more recently sat with me and recalled so many lovely memories as well as discussed the fascinating history of the Welsh Mountain pony and how they were hunted centuries past by King Henry VIII.

Thank you all.

When it came to bringing *Longbow Girl* to the world, I have my fabulous agents at AGI Vigliano Associates to thank: the wonderful Matt Carlini, who has now moved on to other things; and the ever-smiling Thomas Flannery; and the guru himself, David Vigliano, who are due special thanks for their faith and commitment.

I believe, as I suspect all Chicken House authors do, that in finding a home with Chicken House, I have hit the jackpot. I could not conjure a more wonderful publisher. From the charismatic, visionary, and wildly creative Barry Cunningham, to the clear-eyed mastermind Rachel Hickman, to the superefficient and incredibly helpful head of publicity, Jasmine Bartlett, and to my beyond-wonderful editor, Rachel Leyshon, *she who sees what can be*, and what others miss. Rachel read the manuscript when it was quite far from what appears here now, but she saw enough in it to love and had sufficient faith in me to run with the amazing guidance she has given me, and for that I give her my very profoundest thanks.

Also, huge thanks to Elinor Bagenal for wizarding foreign rights, and Kesia Lupo for fielding panicked calls re: the finer points of copy editing. You all are an amazing team!

In the United States, I am lucky enough to be published by the amazing powerhouse that is Scholastic. And here I would like to give deepest thanks for her faith and commitment to the fabulous Emellia Zamani. Looking forward very much to seeing you in New York again!

You have all enabled me to live with this book, which is very much written from the heart, and which I love and must now hand over to *you*, my reader. I thank you for picking it up. I hope that you love it too.

Linda Davies

Suffolk, England, May 2015